ETERNAL GLORY

LINDA FAUSNET

For Mark, Jake, and all the other reckless teenagers we've lost along the way. You are forever loved and missed. May you rest in peace until your mothers get there.

My books contain steamy sex, bad words, and human beings of all sorts, include gay people. If you're not a fan of those things, you may want to stop reading now. If you're cool with that stuff, come take my hand and join me on this journey...

This book is a work of fiction. References to real people, events, establishments, organizations, or locales are intended only to provide a sense of authenticity and are used fictitiously. All other characters, and all incidents and dialogue, are drawn from the author's imagination and are not to be construed as real.

Published by Wannabe Pride 2021

Editing by Linda Hill

Cover Design by Chuck DeKett

FIRST EDITION.

Library of Congress Control Number: 2021905634

ISBN: 978-1-944043-57-5

❀ Created with Vellum

1

Kendrick wrapped up her strange Sunday afternoon shift at Milligan's Wine and Cheese Shop, reflecting on the day's events. For the most part it was boring as usual—either the same customers buying the same stuff or tourists wandering around, looking but barely buying anything. Then there had been that one lady who gave off a decidedly powerful vibe that Kendrick had picked up on.

Namely, she had reeked of death.

As an avid ghost hunter, Kendrick frequently sensed the presence of spirits around her, particularly here in Colonial Williamsburg. But despite the odd, deathly feeling the woman had exuded, she was most certainly alive. She had touched things and made a purchase just like any other customer. It was so bizarre.

Though Kendrick was rather tired and had planned to go home and do absolutely nothing after work, she changed her mind after the strange encounter. Ghost hunting was one of the few things she had any interest in; she figured it was time she paid another visit to one of her regular ghostly haunts. Yorktown Battlefield.

"You headed out?" Sallie asked after Kendrick finished balancing out her cash drawer. Sallie was a pretty girl, with her short black hair and piercing blue eyes. She also had a ton of tattoos, only a few of which Kendrick had actually seen. Sallie was pleasant enough to work with, but she didn't really know her all that well, even though they worked together several times a week.

"Yep."

"Okay, have a good one," she said.

"You too."

Kendrick headed out to her car. Thankfully, she'd left her thermal imaging camera in the trunk. She had more elaborate ghost-hunting equipment at home, but the camera would do for now.

Yorktown Battlefield was a terrific place to ghost hunt. It was mostly just field and trees, with no need for much security. Unlike many famous battlegrounds, there weren't a lot of monuments to protect. With no fencing around the area, it was easy for Kendrick to roam the fields, though technically it wasn't permitted after dark.

Clutching her electric lantern, she trudged onto the battlefield. Sometimes she could explore for hours and not get anything. But after walking for only a few minutes, she froze.

There's a presence here.

Though Kendrick had never actually seen a ghost, she had seen round, glowing orbs on her photographs, had felt cold spots when she walked through allegedly haunted houses and battlefields, and had even heard disembodied voices. Plenty of times, like now, she simply felt an unseen presence close by. Though anybody could be an amateur ghost hunter with the right equipment, she considered herself lucky to have the natural ability to sense spirits.

A cold shiver rippled through her. Was it a ghost passing nearby or just the crisp November air? Kendrick gazed around at the dark field, lit only by the small lantern she set on the ground by her feet. The Yorktown Battlefield stretched for miles; she had explored all of it. The area included Yorktown National Cemetery, George Washington's headquarters, and Surrender Field where she stood now. Surrender Field was where the final battle of the Revolutionary War had been waged.

She held up her thermal imaging camera. The small screen showed a clear blue spot confirming the air temperature change that frequently signaled there was an otherworldly spirit nearby. The cold spot was directly in front of her.

"You're right there aren't you?" she asked, her muscles tight, her senses on edge. She wasn't afraid, though. Just excited. It was rare to feel a presence this strong.

To her disappointment, the cold spot on her camera suddenly vanished. She had found that many spirits were skittish. As if they didn't want to be acknowledged.

Kendrick gasped and whirled around when the silence of the battlefield was suddenly broken by a deep male voice coming from right behind her.

"You know, you don't need all the fancy equipment to see a ghost. All you gotta do is ask," said a full-bodied yet slightly transparent apparition.

Eyes wide, she stared at the spirit as it went from transparent to fully formed. If she hadn't seen the man fade into view, she might never have known he was a ghost.

She had always dreamed of this, and now she could hardly believe her eyes. He was clearly the spirit of a Revolutionary soldier, in a tricorn hat, black boots, tan breeches and a long blue jacket.

Kendrick stared into the man's dark brown eyes, too stunned to speak.

He smiled, and there was such gentleness to his face. "Are you afraid of me?"

When she found her voice, she spoke with confidence. "No. I'm just surprised."

The man grinned at her, amusement dancing in his eyes. Glancing around at the dark battlefield, he said, "You're trespassing."

"I sure am."

A dead guy. I am standing in the middle of a battlefield at night talking to a dead guy.

Though she wasn't scared, she did feel a bit dizzy and disoriented. This was all so *surreal.*

"Park closes at dusk," the deceased soldier informed her.

"You gonna rat on me?"

The man laughed, making her jump. His expression softened into that gentle look again. He seemed concerned about scaring her.

"No. I won't tell anyone. Do you come out here ghost hunting a lot?"

His question reminded her of the cliched *Do you come here often?* pickup line. Kendrick nearly laughed at the absurdity of it.

"Yeah. I do. Had to take yesterday off because of Halloween," she said, rolling her eyes. "Amateurs all over the place."

The soldier laughed land nodded. "Tell me about it."

"Security's tighter in October, too," Kendrick said, and he nodded again. Halloween was pretty much the only time she saw guards around.

"What's your name?" he asked.

"Kendrick Banner. And you?"

"Silas Murphy."

Such an old-fashioned name. Hearing it made her realize how long he must have been around.

"You're really a soldier?"

"I was," he said quietly. "That was a long time ago."

"Incredible." Kendrick shook her head in wonder.

"You should consider yourself lucky. I don't usually appear like this. Normally, I just touch ghost hunters and let them feel the cold for a second. Enough to give them a cool story to tell, but not enough to scare them too much."

"Then why did you show yourself to me?" Her eyes swept over his military clothing as she continued to grasp the notion that she was speaking to a soldier who had fallen in battle.

"I dunno. You seemed so determined to have a ghost encounter. That, and you're the prettiest ghost hunter I've ever seen."

Kendrick met his gaze and smiled. For the first time, she saw him as a man and not as a ghost. "Thanks."

"Why are you so interested in ghosts?"

"I have my reasons," she said more sharply than she'd intended.

"Oh. Sorry." He held up his hands in defense.

"It's okay." Kendrick did have a deeply personal reason for searching for ghosts, and she was sick of defending herself to friends and family about it. She'd stopped talking to others about her hobby long ago, which was why she always hunted alone.

Staring at Silas, she thought of a million questions she wanted to ask. Who was he, what was death like, what did he do all day, and why was he still here? However, after snapping at him when he asked an innocent question, it felt unfair to grill him about anything.

Silas smiled at her. "You must have a lot of questions."

"You have no idea," she said. "Is it ... I mean, do you mind if I ask you stuff?"

"I don't mind at all. You can ask me anything you want."

"Anything?"

"Sure," he said with a shrug. Kendrick marveled at his lifelike movements.

"How did you die?" she asked bluntly, both because she wanted to know and to see if he'd meant it when he'd said she could ask anything.

"I died October 14th, 1781," he said as if discussing the weather. "I'd been locked in combat with a bunch of redcoats for what felt like hours. Hard to say for sure how long it was. Time on the battlefield can seem to slow down or speed up, depending on what's happening. I almost had 'em. I swear. Killed one of 'em. I managed to hold off three more, but then in the end, *blam!*"

Kendrick jumped at his description of that final death shot.

He chuckled. "Sorry. One of them Brits—I'm not even sure which one—managed to shoot me square in the chest. And that was it."

"How old were you?"

"Twenty-six."

"That's so young."

Silas shrugged. "Been a long time since I've felt twenty-six. I'm well over two hundred now."

"You look good for your age."

He laughed. "Thanks."

"So what ... you've just been hanging around the battlefield since your death? How have you not gone completely mad by now?"

The notion of drifting around the battlefield all alone for hundreds of years was mind-boggling.

"I'm not always here at the battlefield. I can travel a distance of fifteen miles or so in any direction, from what I can tell. Probably why I haven't seen you here before, because I tend to wander. That, and I can vanish if I want. Vanishing means I can kinda go unconscious for a while. It's a lot like sleep. Some spirits choose to vanish for a really long time. I'm talking hundreds of years or so."

"Why do they do that?" Kendrick asked, fascinated by this information.

"They get tired of existing, I guess. Tired of being alone. Sometimes they get to feeling pretty hopeless about their situation. There's always a reason a ghost gets stuck here on Earth. Most spirits know why they're still trapped here. Either they don't want to face it or don't know how to fix whatever's wrong with them. And then some of them don't know why they haven't crossed over."

"Do you know why you're still here?"

"Yes," Silas said. Sadness clouded his expression.

"Will you tell me?"

He considered her question for a moment, then nodded.

"Here, why don't you sit down?" Silas gestured at the ground. "Doesn't make any difference to me since I can't feel anything, but I want you to be comfortable."

Kendrick took a seat on the ground, pulling the electric lantern close so she could see. Silas sat down across from her. Sitting here on the dark battlefield, speaking to a Revolutionary soldier, made her feel like she had walked backward in time. She'd always had a vivid imagination, and she loved stories. Being here was like stepping into the pages of a book. Her stomach quivered with excitement, and she felt as if she could talk to this fascinating man all night.

"I'm still trapped here on Earth because in life I was really stupid and selfish."

Kendrick was surprised to hear that. Silas seemed so kind and gentle. At least for the few minutes she had known the guy.

"I became a soldier for all the wrong reasons. I'm from Massachusetts originally, and people got pretty fired up about the revolution over there. I don't know how much history you know about the war. You've heard of the Boston Massacre?"

She winced, feeling dumb. "Yeah. I've heard of it. I learned about it in school, but I have to admit I don't remember exactly what it was."

"That's okay," Silas said with a warm smile. "Happened way back in 1770. A bunch of British troops shot at a bunch of colonists and killed five of 'em. People weren't happy with the Brits before, so things really got crazy after that. Have you heard of the Boston Tea Party?"

"Yes. That I do remember. Colonists were mad that the British were taxing their tea, so they dumped a bunch of tea into the Boston Harbor."

"Very good, Kendrick," Silas said with a rather sexy grin. A shiver of delight went up her spine when she heard him speak her name. The sensation took her by surprise.

"It's funny. When I was a kid, we took a trip to Boston," she said. "We went on this boat ride through the Boston Harbor. They had these boxes of tea strapped to a rope, and we got to take turns throwing tea into the harbor."

"Are you serious?" Silas asked, eyes wide.

"Yeah."

"That is hilarious!" he said, chuckling with delight.

Kendrick laughed. "It was pretty cool."

Silas shook his head in wonder before continuing with his story. "So as you can imagine, there was lots of anti-British sentiment throughout all the American colonies, but it was really bad up in Massachusetts. That's pretty much where the American Revolution got started. Everybody wanted to join up and get the Brits, ya know? Our freedom! Our rights! Kill the tyrants, and all that."

He rolled his eyes, acting as if American independence from the British was no big thing.

"So what, you don't think Americans should be free?"

"No, I don't mean that. Of course they should. It's just, back then, I didn't *care*. I guess I should have, but I really didn't give a damn. But I sure acted like I did. I joined the fight because I wanted to be a hero, Kendrick."

"That's not a bad thing, is it?"

"Maybe I'm not explaining it right. I didn't want to *be* a hero. I wanted to be *thought of* as one. Plenty of soldiers joined the fight because they believed deeply in the cause of freedom and independence. They sacrificed their comfortable home life for the life of a soldier because they believed it was the right thing to do. Me? I tore my family apart because I wanted everyone to think I was brave," he said bitterly.

"What do you mean you tore your family apart?" Kendrick's body tensed. Those words hit home.

"I had a family back home that needed me. My parents, my sisters, my brother. We had a farm in Berkshire County, Massachusetts. But they all supported me. They believed in the cause too, and they knew it was something I just had to do." Another bitter laugh escaped his throat. "They thought of me as a hero, all right. Maybe that brought them comfort when they shipped my sorry, dead carcass back home."

Kendrick's throat tightened as she listened to his tale.

His poor family.

"Just think, I made it almost all the way through the stinkin' war. Joined up in '75. Made it all the way to the very last battle." Silas glanced around at the dark battlefield. "Then I croaked here in Yorktown. Another day or so and the war would have been over."

"What was it like? Fighting in a war?"

"Kinda hard to explain. Only way you can really understand it is to go through it. Sometimes I miss having my brothers around. I don't mean blood relations. I'm talking 'bout other soldiers. They know what it was like."

"Are there others still around like you?" Kendrick asked. For all she knew, dead soldiers were floating all around her right now, even though she didn't sense anyone else present.

"Not too many anymore," Silas said, his dark brown eyes filled with sorrow. "There were a bunch of men around after the war, but over the years many of them crossed over. Also, some spirits keep to themselves. During the war, I was lucky to have my childhood best friend with me the whole time. Levi."

Silas smiled as he spoke his friend's name.

"We fought side by side up until the very end. He was with me when I died."

"I'm glad you didn't have to die alone," she said quietly.

"Yeah. So to answer your question, war is basically long periods of real boring time occasionally interrupted by a fight now and again. Believe me, I spent lots more time walking and marching and sleeping in strange towns than I did in actual battle. We soldiers were either real hot or real cold all the time. We were never comfortable. Thing I remember most was we never had enough victuals."

"Victuals?"

"You know, bellytimber! Eatables," Silas said, his eyes dancing with amusement. "That's old-fashioned talk for food."

"Oh, I see," Kendrick said with a laugh.

"There was never enough food is what I'm saying. And when we did get stuff to eat, it was usually awful. We'd get disgusting beef that was burned on the outside and raw on the inside. Sometimes we'd get corned beef and hard bread, and half the time the bread was full of worms."

"That's horrible. And it was like that the whole time you were a soldier? From what, 1775 to 1781?"

"Yep, pretty much." Silas grimaced and added, "That's why I'm so damned scrawny. Not all built up like the guys you're probably used to."

Even in death, he was self-conscious about his weight. It was so odd. And she hadn't thought of him as scrawny. Just tall and lean.

"So when we weren't starving or sleeping on the cold, wet ground, we fought."

"How could you have enough energy to fight?"

"Well, there's nothin' like having a loaded musket pointed at your head to perk you up."

Kendrick laughed at his comment and the snarky way he'd said it. Then she felt bad for laughing, but he chuckled right along with her.

"What was battle like?"

"Could be bad, that's for sure." Silas fell silent for a moment.

"You don't have to talk about it if you don't want to."

"I don't mind," he said. "Been a long time since I've had anybody to talk to about it."

"What's the worst thing you've ever seen in battle?" Kendrick asked, then immediately regretted it. She recalled a presentation about drunk driving in high school given by a medic. The man had told the students never to ask that question. Most EMTs had seen some awful, tragic things, and they may not want to talk about it.

"That's easy. I once saw a man get split right in half by a cannon ball," Silas told her.

He got quiet after that.

"I'm sorry, Silas. I didn't mean to upset you."

"It's all right. Truly." Gazing into her eyes, he asked, "Now will you tell me?"

"Tell you what?"

"Since I spilled my guts about my life ... and death, will you tell me why you're so obsessed with ghosts? You said you had your reasons."

Kendrick nearly said *absolutely not*. The words were on the tip of her tongue, yet she didn't speak them. Something deep in her heart told her it was okay to confide in this relative stranger.

"I had a twin brother," she began softly.

Silas's expression softened into a tender look of sheer compassion.

"How old was he when he died?"

"We were sixteen."

He nodded. "I'm so sorry, Kendrick."

"Thank you," she said, looking into his eyes. She didn't simply hear his words of compassion. She felt them.

"It was a car accident. He and his friends were driving recklessly, acting stupid."

Silas leaned in to listen but kept silent, giving her time to gather her thoughts.

"I just ... I have to believe there's something more when you die. That he's not really gone. He can't be just ... *gone*," she said, her voice quivering.

"That must have been hard. To lose him suddenly like that. And when you were so young."

Kendrick nodded, still feeling the warmth of his compassion.

"I know something like that changes everything. Everything you believe and how you see things and even the kind of person you are."

"Yes," she whispered. "I'm glad you get that. Nobody else does. People think I should get over it. It was nine years ago, but I'm not the same. I'll never be the same. That's not how it works."

"No, it sure isn't. You don't get over it. You get through it and somehow you keep going. I always thought of grief as like walking through fire. You come out burned in every way possible. You survive, but you're never the same. The burns and scars fade a bit over time but they're still there."

Kendrick's eyes filled with tears. She cried for her brother, but even more, she wept with relief that someone had finally *heard* her.

"Are you all right?" he asked tenderly.

She nodded, wiping her eyes. "I've never heard anyone describe grief so beautifully before. Who did you lose?"

"What do you mean?"

"Only someone who is bereaved can understand it the way you do."

He fell silent for a long time. A soft breeze rustled through the dead leaves. Finally, he spoke.

"Everyone. Everyone I've ever known and loved is dead."

"My God," she said. "I can't even imagine. That's so much worse than what I've been through."

"It's not a contest, Kendrick. And I'm not trying to minimize your pain. I'm just, you know, telling the truth."

"I know. And I appreciate it. Believe me, nobody else

wants to talk about this kind of thing. Everybody knows in theory that death can happen at any time, but they don't get it. You don't really understand until it happens to you. My friends just want to drink and party and have fun, and nobody wants to talk about anything real. I'm not allowed to talk about the heavy stuff on my mind."

"That's the thing about death. When you lose somebody, it ages you. You're still young and beautiful, Kendrick, but I can see it in your eyes. You aged a million years the day your brother died. You're every bit as battle-weary as I am."

"Yes," she said, gazing into his eyes. "Thank you for understanding what nobody else does."

"Tell me about the heavy stuff on your mind. The stuff you're not allowed to talk about with your friends."

"You don't want to know."

He held her gaze. "Try me."

"I want to talk about the way my dead brother looked when he was lying in his casket," she said bluntly with a harsh edge to her voice.

Silas smiled gently. "You think you can scare me with talk like that? I've seen my *own* dead body."

"Did you really?"

He shrugged. "Of course."

"Wow," she said, shaking her head.

"What was your brother's name?"

"Kurt."

"Tell me what Kurt looked like when he was laid out. And tell me how it made you feel."

Kendrick was suddenly overwhelmed with various swirling emotions, but the strongest was still relief. Silas didn't think she was crazy for needing to talk about something so terrible.

"He looked ... lifeless. Almost unrecognizable. They'd

fixed him up pretty well after the accident. He looked like himself ... but not like himself," she said, her words spilling out quickly as a flood of memories filled her mind and heart. "It was as if somebody turned off the light switch on his life. At first, I was just completely numb. In shock. Then I saw that familiar scar on his cheek. Right here," she said, pointing to just under her eye. "I gave him that scar. Well, sort of. When we were little and chasing each other around, he fell and hit his head on the corner of a table. He needed stitches. We both got ice cream that day, I remember. After the hospital."

Her words came quickly as a flood of memories filled her mind and heart.

"That day of his viewing, it all became real to me when I saw that scar on his cheek. I knew that soon enough they'd close the casket, and I would never see it again. That's when I lost it. Oh God, I tried to be strong for my parents, but ... but ..."

Tears poured down her face as she spoke. She was dimly aware of Silas quietly saying, "You were only sixteen, Kendrick."

"I don't remember a lot after that. I might have passed out. I'm not even sure." Kendrick laughed bitterly. "Believe it or not, my friends don't want to hear me talk about that."

"It's hard for them to hear because then they have to face the fact that terrible things happen. They have to know that people can die at any time and with no warning. But if it's hard for them to even think about, they should stop and think about what it feels like for you to go through it."

"Exactly! And I've definitely learned that grief can be very different for people. My mother, for example, would never want to talk about stuff like this."

Silas nodded. "Yeah, I get that, too. I think if you want to help a grieving person, follow their lead. If they want to talk, for God's sake let them talk and put aside your own fears. But don't ask personal questions they may not want to answer."

"Yes!" Kendrick said. Where had this amazing, insightful man been all of her life?

Dead. That's where he'd been. God, what a weird day this had turned out to be.

"Kendrick, I want you to know ... In my experience, I've seen that the dead person is almost always allowed to remain behind for their funeral. Seems to be true whether they cross over after or if they're left behind like me. I was there, in Massachusetts, for my own memorial services before I had to come back here. On that awful day when you buried your brother, I'm pretty sure he was there by your side to help you through it."

"I did feel his presence. I really did. I just thought I—"

"It was real, Kendrick. I'm sure of it. He was there."

"Thank you, Silas. I can't tell you how grateful I am to you for sitting here and talking with me like this. All this time I've never been able to get this stuff off my chest."

"I'm glad to be able to help in any little way I can. And I enjoy talking with you. Gets pretty lonely here sometimes. This is the longest I've ever spent talking to a living person since I died. Either people are scared, or I have to keep my distance so they don't find out I'm dead. I can talk to people, but usually not for too long.

"That does sound lonely."

"Must be gettin' pretty late. And cold, too, for that matter. You better get on to your home. Do you have a family? Are you married? Or ...."

"No, I live by myself."

"Me too." He grinned. "Except for the 'live' part."

"I would love to talk with you again."

"Sure. I'll give you a call," he said with a wink.

She laughed uncomfortably, worried his joke might have been a brushoff. Maybe he just wanted to be left alone.

"Kendrick, I would love to see you again. Any time, any place. You're the one with a life, so you tell me."

"Tomorrow night. Same place?" she asked.

"I'll be here," he said with a smile.

2

Her mind reeling, Kendrick walked back to her car in the dark. She put the electric lantern and camera in the trunk, in a daze, too preoccupied to feel the chill of the November night. She had no idea what time it was or how long she had spent talking to Silas. The entire evening had been utterly surreal. Silas being dead wasn't even the craziest thing. For her, the most unbelievable part of the whole night was finding someone she connected with so deeply. Not even those closest to her would talk about Kurt. But Silas had listened to her most painful thoughts and feelings with compassion, and most importantly, understanding.

Kendrick *had* aged a million years that terrible night when the police came knocking on her door to deliver the news about her brother. Silas was more than two hundred years old, so no wonder she felt connected to him. Talk about an old soul.

She drove home on autopilot and walked up the stairs to her second-floor apartment, still trying to grasp everything that had happened. After all these years of ghost hunting, today she had finally found proof that there was life after death.

Which meant that Kurt Banner still existed somewhere, in some dimension or other.

It was mind-blowing.

Fumbling with her keys, Kendrick finally stumbled into her barely decorated apartment. She'd never cared to do much with the place. Besides, the one-bedroom unit was really only supposed to be temporary until she got money together to buy a house. She wasn't particularly excited about owning her own home, it just made the most sense financially. Though she didn't have any art or other decorations up on her walls, she did have several framed photographs of family.

Kendrick's eyes locked onto a picture of her beloved twin brother from a carnival they had attended when they were about eight years old, their faces a messy blue from eating blueberry snow cones. She seized the framed picture from the wall and held it close to her chest, nearly breaking the glass.

Maybe she really would see him again.

Tears trickled down her face as some of the deep heartache that had wrapped itself around her since the day Kurt died finally began to ease.

But then a frightening thought occurred to her. What if Kurt hadn't crossed over? What if he was out there in the dark, wandering all alone as Silas had been for the last two centuries?

There was really no way to know, was there? Kendrick had visited the crash site many times over the years. She'd gone to add flowers to his roadside memorial, even though the idea of Kurt wanting flowers was laughable. Still, she'd felt compelled to let passing motorists know that a beautiful life had ended on that very spot. She had even visited the roadside late at night, just so she could stand there and weep, to release all the pent-up emotions she'd had to hide during the week. But she had never felt a ghostly presence.

Even so, there was that artist lady in the store today who had given off an otherworldly vibe. Kendrick wondered if she could trust her supernatural-detecting abilities at all. Although, she'd been spot on when sensing the ghostly presence of the soldier man she had befriended tonight.

Sweet Silas.

Just thinking of his gentle, handsome face made her smile. She hoped he wasn't too lonely out there on the battlefield. Talking with him had made her feel so much better, and she fervently hoped being with her had brought him comfort as well.

The things Kendrick was passionate about could be counted on one hand, but she felt her heart skip a beat when she thought about meeting up with Silas again tomorrow night. Everything about this man brought her peace and comfort. She believed she could talk to him about absolutely anything with no fear of judgment. And he made her feel *normal* again. Like maybe she wasn't crazy to still be grieving. And that maybe everybody else was wrong to tell her she should "get over it" and "move on."

Shakily, she hung the picture of herself and Kurt back up on the wall.

Even if her darling brother was a ghost somewhere, he wasn't permanently *gone*. And that would have to be enough for her.

After everything that had happened tonight, she figured she would be too wound up to sleep, but exhaustion suddenly hit her. Kendrick glanced at the pile of library books on her coffee table. One of her few pleasures in life was getting caught up in mysteries and thrillers. They grabbed her attention and helped her turn off her obsessive thoughts for a while. She'd been totally absorbed in the book she was currently reading and was eager to finish, to find out who had committed the crime, but that would have to wait. Not only was she overly tired, but she was too caught up in today's extraordinary events to concentrate on a work of fiction.

For once, real life was far more interesting.

AFTER WANDERING the battlefield through the night, Silas headed to Colonial Williamsburg before first light. He'd always considered himself lucky that he could travel as far as the historical district, which attracted lots of tourists. It was great for people-watching and made him feel less lonely. Eternally clad in his Revolutionary War uniform, he could easily blend right in. Living people took him for a reenactor, and he loved talking to the tourists. As long as he took care not to let people get close enough to touch him, they were none the wiser.

Silas walked the quiet streets of Williamsburg as the sky gradually brightened. A deep, unfamiliar sense of calm filled him, and he knew he had Kendrick to thank. He smiled to himself, picturing her pretty blue eyes and light strawberry-blond hair that fell just below her shoulders. Her hair looked so soft, and he longed to be able to touch it.

Speaking with her had been lovely. By God, she had been through so much. He truly understood her grief, and he could only hope that letting her talk openly about it had brought her some measure of comfort. He had certainly felt comforted in speaking with her. For the first time in centuries, he had felt normal. Kendrick had treated him like a man and not simply the ghost of one. So often, he'd been driven to despair by the crushing loneliness of being dead. Now he had somebody to talk to.

Not just somebody.

Silas had never been this attracted to any woman during his long existence, and he'd seen an awful lot of ladies over the centuries. Kendrick was beautiful, but it was so much more than that. Talking about real things with her had been so refreshing. Everyone thought he was pretending to be a soldier. They couldn't possibly know what he had been through, the things he had seen. Kendrick didn't simply know. She understood. He could see it in her eyes.

Lost in thought, Silas strolled down Duke of Gloucester Street, the busiest thoroughfare of the whole tourist spot. At least it would be, later in the day. Right now, things were quiet, peaceful. He walked past Chowning's Tavern, the courthouse, and Market Square, which was the open area shopping space where people could buy old-fashioned toys, soaps, and other souvenirs. The historic buildings wouldn't be open to the public until 9am, so he had the run of the place. Still, he remained invisible so as not to attract the attention of any early morning joggers.

How he wished he could smell the crisp fall air and feel the breeze on his face. During the day, he often saw the smoke rising from the fire pits where meat was cooked, but he couldn't smell the wood burning or the smoky beef.

He gazed up at the tall, lush trees with leaves of orange, red, yellow, and brown. Nature was an inspiring thing to be sure. He had lost a lot when he'd died: his sense of touch and smell and taste. He'd learned to be grateful for what he still had. His eyes that allowed him to see the beauty all around him and enabled him to greet the faces of tourists with a smile. His ears that let him hear the birds and the sounds of children's laughter. His voice that allowed him to speak to others and maintain some kind of human contact, even if he had to constantly keep people at a safe distance from his fragile physical form.

But he didn't have to take such care with Kendrick. She knew what he was, and she was not afraid. A ripple of excitement went through him when he thought about seeing her again tonight. How long it had been since he'd had anything to look forward to! His days were pretty much the same, but now things seemed new and exciting. *Anticipation*. Silas had truly forgotten what that felt like.

Another emotion made its way through his ghostly body as he thought about Kendrick.

Guilt.

He had lied to her.

She had bared her soul about things that were deeply personal, and he owed her the truth about his own life. Silas decided to be forthright with her when he saw her tonight.

He just hoped she wouldn't be angry when he confessed.

3

———

Kendrick showed up not too long after dark. Silas hoped she wouldn't get in trouble for sneaking onto the battlefield at night. Then again, she'd done it who knew how many times before with all her ghost hunting. He figured he could always do something "ghostly" to frighten off any security guards, if need be.

Silas couldn't hide his smile when he saw her walking toward him with her pretty hair blowing in the breeze. She looked so lovely in the glow of the electric lantern, and he hoped to be able to see her in the bright light of day someday.

Unless she got angry with him for lying and refused to see him again. The thought was too painful to imagine. He'd only known her a day, but the idea of being without her was devastating. He would be lonelier than ever before if she abandoned him.

Silas was determined not to let his fear stop him from being honest with her. Kendrick had spoken to him about the worst, most painful days of her life, and it was wrong not to be completely honest with her.

She smiled, holding up her lantern. "You're here, aren't you?"

Silas had forgotten to become visible for her and yet she sensed his presence.

How fascinating.

He faded into sight slowly so as not to startle her. "Sorry about that. It wasn't deliberate. I'm not used to having visitors, I suppose."

"You didn't forget that I was coming, did you?" Kendrick looked somewhat self-conscious, like she was afraid she was bothering him.

"Of course I didn't. Do you know how long it's been since I've had a meeting scheduled on my calendar?" he asked, eyes wide.

She laughed, seeming more at ease.

Even after a full day of thinking about seeing her again, he was unsure how to start the conversation. Lucky for him, she took the lead. Kendrick sat down, and he took a seat not far away from her.

"So what did you do all day?"

"Went over to Colonial Williamsburg."

"Really? You can do that?" she asked, looking astonished.

"Sure. Like I told you, I can travel several miles from here, where I died. I love going to the tourist district. So many people around all the time. Gives me somethin' to do, watching them tour around and all that."

"I work there," she said with a smile.

"You do? How is that possible?"

"What do you mean? Why wouldn't it be possible?"

"I just mean, I thought I knew every inch of that place. I would have remembered seeing a beautiful woman like you."

"Thanks," she said.

He stared at her, trying to figure out where she might work. Perhaps he had seen her in costume. The women frequently wore bonnets that covered their hair, and maybe he just hadn't seen her face. Or perhaps she was a new employee.

"I work weekend day shifts and some evenings over at Milligan's Wine and Cheese Shop."

"Oh, I see. Over in the modern shopping area."

"Right."

"I've been there of course, but I spend more time in the historical district."

"That's just a part-time job, so it makes sense you probably wouldn't have seen me. So you just wander around invisible all the time and nobody knows you're there?"

"I'm not always invisible. I like to talk to people sometimes, just gotta be real careful so they don't get close enough to touch me. Other times I do wander around invisible so I can watch people without worrying about getting too close. Every once in a while, somebody senses when I'm there, even when they can't see me. You know, people like you who are more attuned to the supernatural."

She nodded.

"But even those people can't sense me if I'm in with a crowd of people. I kinda blend in, I guess. It's only if I'm the only one around that certain people can feel me there."

"Yes, that makes sense. That's how I am. When things are really still and quiet, I can sometimes feel a presence when I'm supposedly all alone. Except yesterday ... It was so weird. I was in Milligan's, and I got the strongest feeling that there was a ghost nearby. There was a customer in the store, a *living* one. When I walked closer to her, the feeling got stronger."

"That is strange," Silas said.

"Yeah, I was beginning to question my supernatural-sensing abilities. I was never totally sure to begin with. I often sense there are spirits nearby, and my thermal imaging camera usually confirms it. Still, I was never totally sure. Until I met you, that is."

Silas could see the relief in her eyes. He was glad his mere presence, and the proof of life after death it offered, comforted her.

"What do you do when you're not working part time?" Silas asked.

"I work full time."

"But you said you only work part time."

"I work part time at the wine and cheese shop. You asked what I do when I'm not working part time. I have a full-time day job as well. I'm an accountant."

"You're a what?" he blurted out, making her laugh.

"Why does that shock you?" Kendrick asked, eyes filled with amusement.

"Because you're so pretty!"

Kendrick laughed again. The glow of the lantern softly lighted her face, making her look especially lovely. The breeze blew, rustling the leaves on the trees and whipping her hair around slightly. "What does that have to do with being an accountant?"

"I don't know. You just don't look like an accountant."

"What, I should be a skinny, balding man with glasses?"

"Exactly. At least that's what they look like on television."

"You've seen television?" she asked.

"Girl, I was around for the invention of television. Happened more than a hundred fifty years after I died, but I remember it. I've seen television on in people's houses, in bars, the hotels around here, stuff like that."

"I see," she said. "And I guess you're right. I don't look like the stereotypical accountant. I've always been good with numbers, so I majored in accounting in college. Then I got certified." She shrugged. "I work for a small law firm now, but I'm sure I can make more money when I eventually move to a bigger company."

"Do you like accounting?"

Kendrick furrowed her brow at the question, almost as if she had never thought about it.

"I don't know. It comes naturally to me, so it's not all that hard. It's a good stable way to earn a living."

"That would be a no."

"I didn't say that."

"Hey, accounting doesn't sound all that fascinating to me, but if that's what you like, that's great. But you don't like it."

"I don't dislike it," she said.

It made him sad to think of her spending all day in a job she didn't seem to have much interest in.

"Do you like working at Milligan's better than the accounting job?"

She shrugged again. "I guess so."

Not a lot of excitement there either, he noted.

"Why do you work so much?" Silas asked with concern.

She smiled softly, seeming touched by his question. "I'm saving up to buy a house. My parents are moving soon. They're buying a house in Newport News, Virginia. Right now I'm just renting an apartment temporarily. Then I'm gonna move in with them for a short while so I can save money for a down payment on my own house."

"Sounds like you've got it all worked out," he said. She sounded no more excited about owning a home than she did about her jobs. "How long have you lived in your apartment?"

"Five years."

He chuckled. "Temporary, huh?"

"What's your point?" she asked, an edge in her voice. It probably sounded like he was judging her life choices. A niggling sensation of guilt prickled him as he realized he was doing just that. And he had no right to do such a thing.

"It must be hard to work so much all the time," he said quietly.

"Keeps my mind off things." She no longer sounded angry. Just tired.

"How far away is Newport News from here?"

"Only about a half hour drive from here."

By car, it was nothing. For him, it was an impossible distance to travel.

"I know we just met, but I'm already sad about the idea of you leaving. Is that strange?"

"It might be strange, but I feel the same way."

"You do?"

"Yes," she said. "Talking with you last night helped me so much. I didn't realize how much I still needed to say about Kurt, even after all these years. Nobody wanted to hear about it after the accident, and they sure as hell don't want to hear me talk about it now. Thank you for listening, Silas. It meant so much to me."

Her pretty eyes were filled with deep gratitude. Silas had spent most of his existence feeling entirely useless, and it lifted his spirits to be able to help somebody. Especially if that somebody was her.

The time had come. This was the perfect opening for him to tell her the truth. He glanced off into the darkness and then back at her.

"There's something I need to tell you, Kendrick."

"Okay," she said, looking a tad suspicious at his serious tone.

"I kind of ... Well, I lied to you last night."

"What, you're not really dead?"

"No," he said with a weak smile. "I'm dead. But I lied to you about how I died. I did die on the battlefield here, but not in the way I said I did."

"Then how did you die?" she asked.

"I told you I got killed after being locked in battle with a bunch of redcoats, but the truth is a lot more boring." Shrugging sheepishly, he said, "I got sick."

Kendrick nodded. She didn't seem angry. Instead, she seemed concerned.

"I'd been sick for a while by the time my regiment got here to Yorktown. Yellow fever. It's not like I was strong and brave and fell in battle. I was really sick and, as the fight was raging around me, I pretty much just crawled under a tree and passed away."

He lowered his eyes, feeling utterly humiliated. Already second-guessing his choice to tell the truth, he wished he'd stayed with the fictional war story.

"I'm sorry you had to die like that," Kendrick said without a trace of anger.

When he lifted his gaze to meet hers, he knew he'd done the right thing by fessing up. He'd felt deeply connected to her since the moment they'd met, and keeping secrets from her would have been wrong.

"Why did you lie?" she asked.

"I swear, if I'd known I would see you again, I never would have done it. Fact is, if you'd asked me toward the end of our talk last night, I wouldn't have fibbed. But we talked about how I died as soon as we met. And you were ... are ... a beautiful woman, Kendrick. And when a beautiful woman asks a man about battle, he wants to tell a tale about how brave and tough he was."

"Well, I still think you were a strong and brave soldier, Silas. You served our country for more than five years, and you made it to the very last battle before you breathed your last breath. For what it's worth, I'm proud of you."

For what it's worth.

Kendrick said the words like they didn't mean anything. They meant *everything*.

"Thank you," he said. "I need to tell you … There's something else I lied about."

This time, she furrowed her brow. He supposed one lie might be all right with her, but another? That indicated a pattern.

"My childhood friend. Levi."

She nodded.

"He didn't make it all the way to Yorktown like I said he did. He was my best friend, that was certainly true. As close as a blood relation to be sure. We did fight side by side, but not for long. I lost him pretty early on in the war."

"Oh, Silas," Kendrick said, her voice filled with sorrow.

"That man I mentioned I saw got split in half?"

Kendrick gasped.

"Yep," he said grimly. "That was him."

"I'm so sorry," she whispered.

"I lied about that because … Well, I guess I like telling that story the way I wish it had been and not the way it really was."

"I understand."

Gazing into her eyes, Silas could see that she did.

"You asked me who I'd lost in my life that made me know grief. It was Levi. I've lost a lot of people since then, but he was the first one. We grew up together and we truly were like brothers. I haven't spoken about him in more than two hundred years."

"I'm honored that you shared your story with me. But wait ... If your friend got killed early on, does that mean you were all alone when you died? You had told me he was with you."

"Yeah, I was alone. There wasn't anybody with me when I passed."

Kendrick let out a deep sigh.

"Is there anything else I need to know?"

"No. Well, there's plenty more I can tell you. But I swear to you, Kendrick. That was all the lies I told you, and all the lies I'll ever tell you. You told me so much personal stuff once we really got to talking last night, and you deserve total honesty from me. And that's what you'll get."

"Good," she said with a gentle smile.

"Thanks for not being angry."

"Thanks for thinking I'm pretty enough to lie to," she said with a laugh.

Kendrick zipped up the hoodie she was wearing and hugged her arms around herself.

"You're cold, aren't you?"

"Just a little."

"You know, there's no reason you got to come out here to the battlefield late at night to talk to me. I can easily meet you somewhere during the day. The historical district works fine. Outside of there, I look like a nut dressed like this. In Colonial Williamsburg, this outfit works."

"Yeah, I guess it does."

"We can meet up tomorrow in the daylight. You don't need to stay out here and freeze all night."

Though his heart sank at the idea of her leaving early tonight, her comfort was far more important.

"Are you trying to get rid of me?"

"No. I don't want you to leave," he said. "But I don't want you freezing either."

Kendrick smiled at him. "I'm fine. We can meet in the daytime tomorrow, but I'm good for a while out here tonight. November in Virginia isn't too bad. Besides, I hate the idea of you being out here by yourself all night."

"You get used to it," Silas said wearily. "You got to. Or you can just vanish if you get tired of being lonely."

"I still don't really understand why you've been stuck here after all this time," she said, gazing into his eyes with sympathy and concern. It had been a long time since anyone worried about him. By God, it felt good to be cared for.

"I told you. Because I was selfish in life."

"Who isn't at one time or another? Nobody's perfect. I still don't get what you did that was so bad to sentence you to eternal suffering, wandering the Earth lost and alone."

"When you put it like that ..." he said with a laugh.

"Be honest with me, Silas. Is there something else you're not telling me? Something you did in life that you regret?"

"Oh, there's lots of stuff in life I regret. But no, it's not like there's one thing; some dark secret I'm not telling you. I *would* tell you, Kendrick."

She nodded, and Silas got the feeling she trusted him. Good. He was trustworthy, having no intention of ever lying to her again.

"You, more than anybody else, should understand why I deserve to stay here and suffer."

"What do you mean?"

"The way you felt when your brother died," he said

softly. He didn't want to stir up bad memories, but he wanted her to understand. "When you got the horrible news that he'd been killed. And all the grief you've endured every day since. I did that to my family. I had sisters and a brother. My father. My moth—"

His voice cracked when he pictured his beloved mother's horrific grief. He'd witnessed his own funeral. His father had had to help his mother remain standing. The woman had been utterly destroyed, just as Kendrick had been at her brother's wake.

"Silas, you died of yellow fever. That wasn't your fault," she told him gently but firmly.

"I never should have joined the war effort. But no, I just couldn't let anybody think I was yellow." He scoffed loudly at the irony. "Yellow. I didn't give a good goddamn about the cause. I fought for years. I *survived* for years. I didn't have to re-enlist. So why did I? Why, Kendrick? Why did I do that?"

She watched and listened intently to his tale, but of course she had no answers for him. There *were* no answers.

"I got letters from my family all the time. They told me how proud they were of me. Told me how much they missed me. How they couldn't wait until I came home."

"They're still waiting for you to come home, Silas."

Silas glanced up at the dark sky and then back at her.

"Do you think this kind of suffering is what they want for you?" Kendrick said, her voice shaking. Then she began to cry.

"Oh, Kendrick. I'm so sorry. I didn't mean to upset you."

He felt terrible for making her cry, but he wasn't entirely sure of the cause of her tears.

"I'm scared," she said.

"Of what, my sweet?" The term of endearment had just

slipped out, but he didn't regret it. He did think of her as his precious sweetheart.

"I'm scared that Kurt is a ghost somewhere. I'm scared that he's lost and alone in the dark of night. And I can't get to him. I can't help him," she managed to say as she sobbed harder.

Silas ached to pull her into his arms and let her cry on his shoulder. Instead, he was powerless to ease her suffering.

She pulled a tissue from her pocket and wiped her eyes. She spoke again once she had calmed down a little.

"There are times when I'm angry with my brother for being careless with his life. He and his friends were driving recklessly. That's what the cops said. And that's why he died. It makes me mad to think about it sometimes, but *my God*. I would *never* want him stuck like this as punishment. Do you really think that's what your family ... your *mother* ... wants for you?"

Silas gazed at her tear-stained face, more worried about her trauma than his own.

"It's not like I haven't thought about that, Kendrick. But it's not that simple to just get past everything that happened. If it was, I'd have done it long ago. I know from the experiences of other spirits who have crossed over that being trapped here is mostly self-inflicted."

Kendrick soaked in his every word.

"I'm here because I feel terrible about what happened. What I did and how it affected my family. And I don't know how to get past it."

"I'll help you," she said, her voice stronger and full of determination.

"I don't want you fussing over me, Kendrick. Last thing I want to do is burden you."

"You're not a burden, my sweet," she said with a smile.

For a moment, he feared she was mocking him by using the phrase "my sweet." He quickly realized she wasn't. She would never mock him.

"If there is any way I can help you heal and cross over, then I'm going to do it."

He was about to argue again but thought better of it. She seemed so determined. That, and the truth was he needed help. He had gotten nowhere on his own for centuries. And he was tired of existing like this.

And he was going to lose Kendrick.

All too soon, she would move away. To be trapped here alone, without her, would be like dying all over again.

Maybe she really could help him cross over and finally be at peace.

The weariness in her eyes broke his heart.

"You need to go home. Rest, get warmed up. We'll meet again soon, all right?"

"Tomorrow," she said firmly. "We'll meet tomorrow."

"Yes, Ma'am," he said with a grin.

"I get done work at 3pm at Milligan's. Can you meet me around there?"

"I'll do my best to fit you into my busy schedule," he told her.

Silas decided he would vanish for the night once Kendrick left. The sooner tomorrow afternoon came, the better.

"It's a date," she said.

4

Kendrick stepped out of Milligan's Wine and Cheese Shop at a few minutes after 3pm and found Silas walking toward her. Her heartbeat quickened; he was even more handsome in the light of day. He had longish hair under his tricorn hat and a slight stubble on his chin. A few tourists looked at him, interested and without a trace of fear. He certainly did blend in seamlessly here.

"Hello," he said with a smile as he approached her.

"Hi there."

Sallie, wiping down the outdoor tables, stopped to look curiously at Kendrick with Silas.

"I knew it. You're even more beautiful in the daylight."

"I was just thinking the same about you, but substitute the word 'handsome' for 'beautiful.'" Even as she spoke, she realized it was more than a matter of Silas being good looking. Now she knew him—his heart and his tender compassion—and that made him sexier in her eyes. She found him intensely attractive as a person. Was it possible they had only met the day before yesterday?

Sallie finished wiping down the tables, and then she surveyed Silas.

"Soldier," she said with a grin and a salute.

"Ma'am," he replied with a wink. Sallie laughed and then went inside.

"Want to go for a stroll through the historical district?" Kendrick asked. The district began just one block away from the shop. "Or are you tired of doing that by now?"

"Wouldn't matter if I was tired of it. There's not much else I can do," Silas said. "But I would love to walk with you."

Kendrick began walking, and he fell in step beside her. "It's been a while since I've wandered through here."

"Probably because you work so much," he said. She noted a hint of concern in his voice. "Do you ever go out with friends?"

"Not really. Once in a while if it's somebody's birthday or something, I might go out for a drink, but that's about it."

They walked a short distance down Duke of Gloucester Street and turned left so they could stroll down the Palace Green. A large grassy area, it was a popular spot for tourists to sit and rest or to let little kids run around.

"The leaves are so gorgeous this time of year," Silas said, gazing up at the treetops.

Kendrick glanced up too. "It amazes me that you still find trees interesting after all this time. I can't imagine how many autumns you've experienced."

"A lot to be sure."

Not only had he seen innumerable seasons come and go, for the last two hundred-plus years he'd been stuck here within a fifteen-mile radius. And somehow, he still enjoyed seeing the trees. Though it was admirable, it was hard for Kendrick to understand.

"Too bad there's so many people around," she said. "Have to be careful what we talk about."

"I don't know. I kinda like when there's lots of people around."

How easy it was for her to forget how lonely Silas must be. At the moment, there were no tourists close enough to hear what they were saying. They kept their voices down just in case.

"I really miss being alive," he said, a deep sadness in his voice.

"Do you want to cross over? Are you scared?"

"No, I'm not scared. Not sure why, but I'm not. I've seen what it's like to cross over."

"You have? What do you mean you've seen it?"

"Other people. I've seen others make it to the other side. Kendrick, it's so beautiful. You can tell by the look on their face that they're going somewhere incredible. Somewhere beyond our understanding. They're welcomed home by loved ones. The ones I saw, they cried out the names of the people that came to greet them."

"Amazing," Kendrick whispered.

"Kendrick, I hope with all my heart that your brother made it. If he's not still a ghost somewhere, I promise you he's happy. He's all right, you know?"

"God, I hope so."

"I know, my sweet."

A sense of calm settled over her. It wasn't just his words of comfort. It was the way he said them. He sounded so different than all those well-meaning yet empty assertions from people telling her that he's in a better place now, or everything happens for a reason. Silas never said things like that to her because he knew firsthand how she felt.

"Do you want to cross over? Are you ready?"

Silas shrugged, which surprised her. Why wouldn't he want to go to this wonderful place he'd glimpsed several times before?

"I guess so. I sure as hell don't want to be like this anymore. Crossing over is the only way out. Nothing I can do about that."

Kendrick wanted to ask him more questions, but she forced herself to keep silent while they walked. She got the impression he needed to talk right now. And he needed to be heard.

"What I hate most is feeling utterly helpless. I feel like I wasted my life being selfish, worrying more about what people thought of me than anything else. It's like ... I get it now, if you know what I mean. Helping people, being kind —that's what's most important in life. Knowing that now doesn't do me any good, though."

She nodded with sympathy, hearing the frustration in his voice.

"I can't help anyone. I can't touch anything. I can't—"

"You're helping me," she said. "You're the first person to help me realize I'm not crazy to still be grieving. That it's okay to feel the way I feel."

"That's the first good thing I've been able to do for anyone in a long time," he said. Some of the frustration in his tone eased.

"You have a good attitude, that's for sure. I wish I could believe you about the meaning of life."

"You don't believe me?"

"I guess I'm not sure I agree with you. Helping people is nice and all, but I can't help but feel like what's the point? What's the point of doing anything if you're just gonna wind up dead in the end?"

"It makes me sad that you feel that way, Kendrick."

"I can't help it," she said defensively.

"I'm not judging you," he said in a gentle voice. "I'm just telling you how I feel."

"Fair enough."

They continued walking until they reached the end of the street, which dead-ended at the Governor's Palace. The large brick building with lots of windows was the most recognizable place in Colonial Williamsburg. Featured on countless postcards, calendars, and posters in every gift shop, it was a popular place for tourists to pose for photographs. Kendrick and Silas stood off to the side of the historic building and away from the crowds.

Kendrick chuckled. "They say this place is haunted."

"It is," Silas said casually.

She gasped. "Oh my gosh, you must know lots of ghosts that haunt Colonial Williamsburg! I've taken the ghost tour a bunch of times, so I've probably heard most of the stories about hauntings."

He grinned at her. "Ghosts are the only thing I've seen you get excited about so far."

"Lucky for you."

"Indeed," Silas said flirtatiously. "People like to think the Governor's Palace is haunted by the governor, but it's not. It's just one of the servants. William. He likes to slam doors, make the lights flicker. And he loves to set off the fire alarm."

"Nice," she said with a laugh.

"There's a few people that like to cause trouble over at the King's Arms Tavern. Touching the tourists and freakin' them out."

"Do you ever do that?"

"Oh, no. Well, I never try to scare anybody on purpose, but some people on the ghost tours are really hoping to have a ghost encounter, so sometimes I'll give them one. I'll turn visible real quick and then disappear. Maybe I'll walk through them so they feel a cold sensation, tap them on the shoulder. Things like that. But only with people who seem to want it."

"Are there any soldiers that haunt the historical district?"

"Some. And not just Revolutionary soldiers. Some Civil War battles were fought nearby, and I got to know some of those men before they eventually crossed over. I even ... Well, I was there when some of the soldiers were killed in battle. I knew what it was like to die alone, and I didn't want them going through that. I stayed with some of the men as they died on the battlefield." He laughed gently. "They were understandably confused, me being dressed like this. I told them I was an angel. I didn't want them to be afraid."

"That's lovely, Silas. That you did that for them."

There was no one with Kurt when he died, as far as Kendrick knew. The other teenagers in the car survived, but they were incapacitated when the paramedics arrived. The most she could hope for was that he died instantly.

"There are other spirits around here that I've talked to. You ever hear of the Weeping Woman?"

"Yes! I have," Kendrick said.

"Her name is Rebekah. Talked to her a bunch of times over the years, but I haven't seen her in quite some time."

"Do you think she crossed over?"

"I hope so. I really do."

"It must be really hard to have your friends just disappear like that."

"It is," Silas said. "Many times, spirits do have some warning that it's almost their time. They know when they've finally figured out how to fix whatever their problems are. Not always, but sometimes you get a chance to say goodbye.

Other times, they just go away. You never see them again, and that's the only way you know they've probably crossed over."

The anguish in his voice broke her heart, and she wished there was something she could do or say to ease his pain.

"Of course, there are lots of ghosts who keep to themselves. There's one lady that usually makes herself known by grabbing tourists by the ankles."

"Oh, I've heard of her! They say she was a slave at the Peyton Randolph House."

"Right. Never actually seen her myself. Haven't heard of any attacks recently, so maybe she's gone, too. I hope so. God knows she must have been through enough in life," Silas said, shaking his head.

Kendrick was quiet for a moment.

"What are you thinking about?" he asked.

"I was thinking that I hope all the people you loved, all the souls you've met along the way ... I hope they're all waiting in Heaven to welcome you home."

Silas smiled at her, making her feel warm all over. She knew the sorrow he carried in his heart was always with him, yet he still managed to smile. She wondered how he did it.

"Silas, you are such a good man."

He shrugged his shoulders. It was clear he didn't believe her. Silas had done a lot of good over the years. Kendrick couldn't help wondering what she had really done with her life. Could she say that anybody was better off because of her?

"You've helped so many people over the years. You've been a good friend to other spirits, and the way you comforted those soldiers as they lay dying was an incredible act of kindness. Even simple things like giving the tourists a thrill and a cool ghost story to tell all their friends. You *are* a good man. I don't understand why you're so hard on yourself."

"I've killed people, Kendrick."

His words came as a shock to her. She took a moment to process them and realized she shouldn't be surprised. He'd been a soldier for years before he died. "Only in battle, right?"

"Of course."

"Is that why you're still here? You feel bad about having to kill others?"

"That's part of it, of course. That, and the whole abandoning my family thing."

That anguished look was back.

"In a way, meeting you made it worse."

"What? Why?"

He smiled at her with a look so tender that it eased her anxiety instantly.

"Being with you is wonderful, Kendrick. I haven't had a true friend in a long, long time. Spirits around here, they're more like acquaintances. We have the shared experience of the loneliness of being dead, but we don't often sit and talk about ourselves. Mostly, I think we're lost in our own pain. I will never be anything but happy that I met you."

Kendrick nodded, still trying to understand how being with her had worsened his suffering.

"You've suffered unimaginable grief, and it's colored every aspect of your existence. Your life is forever divided between *before* and *after*."

"Yes," she whispered. Once again. Silas cut right to the heart of the matter in a way no one else could. There was the time before that fateful night, January 10th, and the time after when nothing was ever the same.

"Because of my pride and hubris, my father, my mother, my two sisters and my brother all endured that kind of suffering. There was before October 14th, 1781 and after. And each of the men that I killed in battle, they all had families who knew that kind of grief. I think often of the ripple effect that kind of thing has over the course of time."

His voice took on a faraway tone. As if he were contemplating out loud rather than talking to her.

"I cannot help but think that the world would have been a much better place if I had never been born."

"Oh, Silas, how can you say that?" Kendrick asked sorrowfully. She hated that he felt that way about himself.

He simply gazed sadly off into the distance.

"I've only known you a short time, and I already know in my heart. You are a good person. Caring and compassionate. Does it help at all to know that?"

Silas turned to look at her. "I think you're wrong about me. But yes. It helps to hear that."

Kendrick smiled. "Well, that's a good start."

At least she had some idea of what they were dealing with. Silas seemed to be trapped on Earth because he didn't feel worthy of crossing over.

Her job was to work to change that.

5

———

Silas had gotten together with Kendrick several nights that week after she was done working at her day job, but it was getting colder and darker with each passing night. He suggested they meet up when it would be warmer at mid-day on Saturday in the historical district. Silas worried she might be getting bored with just walking around all the time, so he told her to bring her lunch and they could sit together outside while she ate.

As he strolled down Duke of Gloucester Street, Silas made eye contact with tourists and smiled at them. The visitors enjoyed seeing all the men and women in colonial dress, and they seemed to take particular interest in the men wearing military uniforms.

"Ma'am," he said with a grin, appearing to touch his hat in deference to a young woman, without actually touching it. The woman smiled.

"Good afternoon," she said as she continued on her way.

Silas caught sight of Kendrick sitting under a tree on the front lawn of the Capitol where they'd agreed to meet. He was struck by how lonely she looked, sitting there by herself. Unlike him, she didn't watch the crowds or look at the trees. She simply sat and waited.

Her face brightened when she saw him approach, which he took as a high compliment. It seemed to take a lot to get her attention, and yet somehow, he had. How lucky he was to have her as a friend.

"Hi there, gorgeous," he said, taking a seat next to her under the tree. He wondered if the ground was cold and damp. He wouldn't have cared if it was. He'd have been grateful just to feel anything.

"Hey, handsome," she said.

"Watcha got there?" Silas gestured at her lunch.

"Just a sandwich."

"Is it good?"

"It's okay. Got it at Milligan's, so I get an employee discount."

"How practical of you," he said dryly.

"And what is that supposed to mean?" she asked with amusement.

"You could choose to eat anything you want, and you go with that sorry-ass sandwich," Silas said, shaking his head.

"What would you eat if you could?"

"Oh man. You have no idea how much I've thought about that over the years."

"Really? Do you miss food a lot?"

"So much. I can't smell food anymore, and I'm never hungry. It's not like I need food anymore, but I miss it. For me, it was one of the great pleasures of life. I told you how I never got enough food when I was a soldier. You don't forget something like that. I remember what it felt like to be hungry—literally starving—but I can hardly remember what it feels like to be full. All that time, during the war, I dreamed about going back home and eating all my favorite foods. Never got the chance."

"That's really sad," Kendrick said. Glancing at her sandwich, she looked slightly guilty.

"Steak, to answer your question. If I could have anything I wanted, I would eat the thickest, juiciest steak you ever did see," he said enthusiastically. "I would also love to try some of that Virginia ham everybody's talking about around these parts. I'd also wanna check out the Welsh rarebit they got over at Chowning's Tavern."

"You've put some thought into this, haven't you?"

"I surely have. You don't think much about food, do you?"

"Not really. I don't know how to cook much, either. Just kinda eat whatever. Frozen meals, stovetop macaroni and cheese, that kinda thing. It's just me at home, so there's no point in making a big meal just for one."

"You don't think you're worth the trouble?"

Kendrick shrugged. "Never really thought of it that way. But yeah, I guess that's how I feel."

"I think you're worth the trouble."

"Thanks, Silas."

She took a bite of her sandwich while Silas watched the tourists. A little boy of about five years old or so spotted Silas and waved at him. Silas saluted him in return, which got a huge smile out of the kid. The child started to walk toward the tree where he sat with Kendrick, but his mother gently pulled him back.

"No, honey. Let's not bother the man while he's taking a break."

"No bother at all, ma'am!" Silas called out while gesturing for the lad to come toward him. "After all, a soldier never rests."

The boy shyly walked over with his mother just behind him.

"How are you today, my fine fellow?"

Silas was pleased to see not only the child's smile, but Kendrick's as well.

"I'm good," the boy said shyly.

"You know what he needs, Mother?" Silas said with a wink. "One of those noisy tin whistles from the gift shop."

The woman laughed. "Oh my. I don't know about that."

"Tell me, my good lad. What do you like best about your trip to Williamsburg?"

"The ice cream!"

Silas laughed heartily. "A man after my own heart! Oh yes, indeed. The food here is quite terrific. Do you know what my favorite dessert is?"

The boy shook his head.

"Pumpkin pie! I would eat a whole pie myself, I would." He leaned in closer to the child, but not too close. "You, uh, wouldn't happen to have any, now would you? In your pockets, perhaps?"

The kid laughed and shook his head.

"Ah, well. Next time perhaps."

"Okay now, let's be on our way," the boy's mother said. "Thanks," she said to Silas with an appreciative smile. She also waved to Kendrick, who nodded and smiled back.

"Do you do that a lot?" Kendrick asked after they had walked away. "Talk to the tourists?"

"Yeah. I do."

"You're really good with kids," she said admiringly.

Silas had learned long ago that being kind to children was an excellent way to attract female attention. That wasn't why he'd done it, of course. Impressing Kendrick was just a bonus.

"I like talking with tourists, especially the little guys. It might be a small thing, but talking to that boy made him smile. Who knows? He might remember talking to a 'pretend soldier' years from now when he recalls this childhood trip. I hope so. I hope it's a happy memory for him. And see his mom?"

Kendrick glanced off into the distance where the mother was still smiling.

"She looks happy. She might go smile at somebody else, and that good feeling will get passed around."

"What's your point?" Kendrick asked.

"The point is I might have made a tiny difference in the world today."

She shrugged, and he found himself feeling a bit irritated. Kendrick was free to speak to anybody at any time. And yet, she didn't go out of her way to talk to anybody.

"Is this the part where you say what's the point of doing anything if you're just gonna wind up dead anyway?" he asked.

Kendrick sighed, but she didn't argue. That said it all.

"I try to talk to people whenever I can. If I have a chance to brighten somebody's day, I'll take it every time. I have to be really careful, though. Gotta keep my distance. Can you imagine if that little guy had gotten close enough to touch me? My God, he'd have been terrorized when his hand went through me."

"Has that ever happened?"

"Yes," he said sadly. "But not with a child, thank God. I hate scaring people. At least the ones who aren't actively ghost hunting. That kind of memory probably stays with a person for a lifetime, too. Being frightened by a ghoulish dead guy."

"You're not a ghoul, Silas. You're a dear, kind man with a

heart of gold," she said softly. "You would have made a wonderful father. I'm sorry you never got the chance."

"Thanks," he said, feeling a heaviness in his heart.

"Did you want to have children?"

Silas nodded. "What about you? Wait, never mind. I know the answer. What's the point of having children, right?"

Kendrick nodded sadly.

The niggling annoyance grew stronger. Kendrick had the *ability* to have children, but she wouldn't. Some women didn't want to bear children, which was fine. It was the right choice for some. But with Kendrick, it was just another opportunity to squander for no apparent reason.

"What would you normally be doing right now if you weren't here?" he asked.

"Not much. Just hanging out at home, I guess."

Kendrick had the freedom to go anywhere, eat anything, be with friends and family, and yet she chose to do absolutely nothing. It made him angry. He genuinely liked Kendrick, and he had tremendous sympathy for the hardships she'd endured. He didn't want to be angry with her, but he couldn't help the way he felt.

For once, Silas found he wanted to be alone. He didn't have the mental energy to pretend he wasn't upset with her.

He managed to fake his enthusiasm after Kendrick finished her lunch. They went for a walk, and as usual, Silas admired the trees, the grass, and the sunlight. He did so out loud, only to be met with Kendrick's typical, cynical shrugs.

From the moment they'd met, they'd spoken openly about things they were feeling. At least they'd been open after Silas had quit telling stupid fibs. He wondered if perhaps he should be honest now and tell her what was on his mind.

Namely, that he was angry and annoyed with her.

"You're not as chatty as usual today. Is everything all right?" she asked.

"Sure. I'm fine."

Best to hold his tongue. Silas desperately needed a friend, and he didn't want to start an argument. Besides, it was entirely possible he was judging her too harshly. Though he did understand her grief, he couldn't possibly know what was going through her mind and heart.

After they'd strolled around a while, Kendrick said, "I guess I better get going. I have to get some groceries on my way home."

"All right," he said.

"I have to work until 3pm tomorrow. Do you want to meet at the battlefield? We'd still have several hours before sunset."

"Sounds good," he told her.

Silas hoped he would calm down by then. Perhaps he would feel differently about the situation tomorrow.

6

Silas felt differently the next day, all right. He felt worse. He'd spent the whole night stewing over the issue of how Kendrick chose to throw away her life.

He knew he was likely being unreasonable. Part of it was jealousy, pure and simple. He was trapped in an ethereal prison of his own making, and Kendrick was not to blame for that. Yet he couldn't help envying her for having a physical body and opportunities to do so many things in life. Deep down, he pitied her, and he tried to focus on that. Having empathy for her might keep him from saying something in anger that he might regret. So many years had passed since Levi's sudden, violent death. Though he still grieved for his friend, time had certainly eased his pain. Even though it had been nine years since her twin brother died, Kendrick's grief was still raw. He did remember how that felt. The mental and physical exhaustion of grief weighed heavily on the soul. Simply getting up in the morning was hard. Life certainly had felt meaningless when Levi died, and that was how Kendrick was feeling now.

Silas did feel sad for her, living what seemed to him to

be an empty life devoid of fun and pleasure. It was clear she had succumbed to hopelessness after suffering such a devastating loss at such a tender age. Focusing on that helped him to quell his fury, but only temporarily. Then he would remember that he, too, had suffered horrific losses and still did his best to find the good in life wherever he could.

Despite being fairly worked up by the time Kendrick arrived, he was relieved to find his anger soften when he saw her walking toward him. She appeared as such a lonely figure, reddish hair blowing in the breeze, those blue eyes filled with familiar sorrow.

He felt like an ass.

Who the hell did he think he was, expecting her to live her life the way *he* saw fit?

My poor darling Kendrick.

And now he was being presumptuous. In no way could he consider Kendrick *his.*

"Hello, Kendrick."

"Hey," she said with a smile. With a brief glance around the battlefield, she said, "This place looks different in the daytime. Can't remember the last time I was here when the sun was up."

"Let's walk by the water. It's so pretty there."

"Okay," she said, falling into step when he started walking.

The edge of the Yorktown Battlefield bordered the York River, and Silas had always found the water calming. He hoped it would help him get into a more peaceful mood. He'd really gotten himself worked up into quite a fury overnight, and there was still a risk of lashing out at Kendrick.

Silas gazed out at the river as they approached. The

sunlight across the ripples was lovely to behold. Watching the water, hearing the small waves lapping against the rocky shore, and seeing the occasional boat pass by were all daily reminders to Silas to be grateful for his eyes that could still see the world, even as it went on without him.

"I love this spot so much," he said. "It's just so beautiful."

He sat in the grass at the edge of the water, and Kendrick sat down beside him.

"Yeah. I guess so."

And that was all it took to make his mood turn sour once again.

"Nothing much impresses you, does it?" he snapped.

"What is that supposed to mean?" she responded in a clipped tone that matched his own.

"You don't want to know," he said, still fighting to keep his peace.

"Yes. I do want to know. I wanna know why you're so snippy with me now, and why you were so pissed off yesterday."

So she had noticed. He figured he'd best just tell her the truth. Silas clearly couldn't hide his feelings, and he had promised to always be forthright with her.

"Fine. You want to know why I'm 'pissed off,' as you say? I'm mad at you because you never seem to appreciate a damn thing in life when you have so much. You have no idea how maddening it is to have to exist like this!" Silas shook out his lifeless, utterly useless arms. "I can't *do* anything. I can't touch anything. I can't eat or drink, or smell the autumn air. I haven't felt the comfort of physical, human contact in more than two centuries. I may be trapped like this forever for all I know. And I still appreciate things more than you ever do!"

Kendrick's mouth went rigid, her eyes blazing as he raged at her.

"You have food and warmth and comfort. You could have goals in life and work every day to accomplish them. You don't have to work at crappy, boring jobs, but you do anyway. I wouldn't even be bored at those jobs if I were you! Well okay, maybe the accounting one is boring, but not the customer service one. You can talk to people all day long and not be afraid to get too close for fear they will end up screaming and running away from you."

Kendrick jumped to her feet, ready to storm away from him. But he wasn't done. He wasn't about to let her off that easily. He stood up too and got near her face.

"Kendrick, you have a roof over your head, and you've got money toward buying a house of your own soon. I slept on the cold, wet ground for *years,* dreaming of being at home in my nice warm bed. You have food, shelter, a life, a future. What the hell else do you want?"

"*I want my brother back!*" she roared.

"That's not fair," he said firmly.

"Why the hell not?"

"Because Levi and my whole goddamn family are just as dead as Kurt is. I want them back, too. I want my body back. I want my life back. But that's not going to happen, is it? I've lost almost *everything*, Kendrick," Silas said, his voice shaky with emotion. "Yet I still manage to get through with more gratitude than you. I'm thankful for what little I do have. My eyes and my hearing and my memories. And *you*. I'm grateful for you. I'm not alive anymore, and I wish like hell I was. You have a life, but you're not living. You. Are. Wasting. It."

Silas's eyes burned into hers. Tears rolled down Kendrick's face. Seeing her cry nearly broke him. Though he meant what he'd said, he hadn't intended for it to come out as such a vicious attack on this darling girl who was already wracked with raw pain. Silas was angry about his own torturous situation, much more so than he'd even realized, but that was hardly Kendrick's fault. In his own warped way, he'd wanted to help her. To snap her out of her grief-filled haze and help her rediscover the joy in life. No matter his intentions, shouting in her face was a terrible thing to do.

Her jaw tense, Kendrick's eyes flashed with hurt and anger and betrayal. She stayed silent for quite some time. Silas wracked his brain to find the right words to apologize for his cruel outburst.

At last she spoke, so softly, he could barely hear her. "Fair enough."

Slowly, she sank down into the grass. Silas sat down beside her. Covering her face with her hands, Kendrick wept openly. He cursed his useless, ghostly body that wouldn't allow him to take her in his arms.

Wiping her eyes, she took a deep breath and slowly let it out.

Turning to face him, she said, "If *anyone* else said something like that to me, I'd probably never speak to them again. People who haven't suffered loss have no place telling other people how to grieve. But you know what I've been through. And I think you might be right."

His heart ached to see her in such pain. He felt bad that he had been the cause of it. Silas spoke gently to her. "I'm so sorry I yelled at you, Kendrick. I didn't mean to be so harsh. You don't deserve that. I don't blame you for saying you wanted your brother back. I would give anything if I could make that happen for you."

"I know you would. And don't be too sorry. I think I

needed a swift kick in the ass like that. Believe me, I usually don't take too kindly to people telling me to just get over it and move on with my life."

"I didn't say that," he said carefully.

"I know you didn't." Kendrick smiled sadly. "People who are bereaved don't often say that to others who grieve because they know it doesn't work that way. I guess I know I've been going through the motions in life. I'm just not sure how to change."

"Kendrick, I hope you know I'm not just jealous of you for being able to do the things I can't. Another reason I said all this to you is I want you to be happy. I want you to find the joy and humor and pleasure in life. It breaks my heart to think you're just killin' time until you can see your brother again."

"Do you think I will see him again?"

"Yes," Silas said without hesitation. "But you most likely have a long time until then. I want you to make the most of it."

She sighed deeply, looking emotionally wrung out.

"Being twins, you must have been very close with Kurt," he said. After launching into an angry tirade against her, Silas wanted to remind her how much he cared.

"We did everything together," she said in a faraway voice. "At least, when we were little kids. Then as we got older, we had our own friends, our own interests. But we were still close. He was still my best friend. And I lost him because he acted stupid and reckless one time too many." Her body trembled and her eyes filled with tears. "It's like ... like I don't even have the words to describe how much I miss him. Feels like a part of me is just ... gone."

"You don't need words to explain. Not with me."

Kendrick looked deeply into his eyes and nodded.

"I want to do better, Silas. I really do. Sometimes I just don't have the strength. And I still feel like I don't understand the point of living."

"You know what? I don't think we're supposed to know the point. Not while we're on Earth, anyway."

Kendrick gazed out at the water as if really noticing it for the first time.

"I'm on your side, you know. Always," he said.

"I know. And I'm glad you were honest with me." She laughed. "Besides, you're kinda sexy when you get all fired up."

Silas grinned at her, rather enjoying the way she looked at him.

"So I'm just supposed to go out and start doing things? You took away the only hobby I had, you know."

"I did?"

"Yeah. No more ghost hunting."

Silas laughed. "I never thought of that."

"I got the proof of life after death that I needed. Being with you is a lot better than using a thermal imaging camera and hoping to feel a cold spot. In fact, I feel rather warm when I'm with you."

Though there was amusement in her tone, Silas got the impression she meant what she'd said.

"I wish I could touch you, Kendrick."

"Me too. Since that's not possible, we'll just sit here and make the most of what we have," she told him.

Her simple words meant so much to him. She was already trying to be more open to life, more grateful. Silas hoped that kind of attitude would make her happier.

They sat and watched the water for a while. Silas listened to the birds, the sound of the wind through the trees, and the rippling water. He wondered if Kendrick had begun to notice those little things, too.

After a while he broke the silence. "I know it's hard. I know you're hurting. The loss you've suffered, it's always gonna be with you. But that pain shouldn't be the only thing you let yourself feel. There's so much more to life. You'll have good days when it doesn't hurt so much, and then there'll be a memory that shoves you down that dark hole of grief. But then you have to work to find the light. Never stop searching for the light."

Kendrick turned to Silas and said, "Really? You're telling *me* to go toward the light?"

Silas burst out laughing. "Fair enough, Kendrick. Fair enough."

She smiled at him, then turned back to the water.

"It is beautiful here," she said, watching the rays of sunlight on the river.

"Yes, it surely is."

7

I am grateful that I'm tired because it means I have a job.

The eight-hour workday at Silver Law Firm had been so long and boring, it had felt like twelve hours, but Kendrick still chose to be grateful. She flopped down on her couch and closed her eyes. Though mental affirmations like *I'm grateful to be tired* felt a bit silly, she was determined to change her attitude for Silas's sake. She hadn't realized how negative her thoughts had become over the years until he had called her out on it.

She smiled just thinking of him. His demeanor was usually so calm, wizened old soul that he was. How strange to see him get all worked up like that. She couldn't blame him for getting frustrated with her. She'd been dealt an unfair hand in life when she'd lost her brother, but Silas was right—she tended to forget everything she did have going for her. Despite the effort it would take, she'd give it a shot. Being with him always put her in a better mood. The last thing she wanted was to bring him down with all her negativity; he had enough to deal with already.

Her heart felt heavy when she pictured Silas alone on

the battlefield. Most of the time, he had nobody to talk to. He would never again feel the warmth of a hug or even a handshake from a fellow human being. How she would have loved to be able to touch him.

As she rested on her couch, she felt her body relax. Her mind drifted to especially pleasant thoughts of Silas. She fantasized about what it would feel like to kiss him. Feeling a delicious quiver of excitement in her stomach, Kendrick realized how long it had been since she'd been attracted to any man. Though she'd been on a few dates, set up by her friends in the last year, there hadn't been any sparks. Of the two steady boyfriends in her past, she'd never felt a connection like the one she'd instantly had with Silas. Once she'd overcome the initial shock of speaking to a dead man, being with him had felt like coming home. She was amazed at how much they had shared with each other the night they'd met. After knowing him for a matter of minutes, she'd told him things she'd never told another living soul, because she'd instinctively known he would understand. And that was why she hadn't stayed angry when he told her she was wasting her life. Silas knew what he was talking about. And he knew *her*.

Kendrick envisioned an increasingly detailed fantasy of kissing Silas. For once, she allowed her imagination to run wild. She shoved aside the reality that physical touch was impossible, picturing exactly how he might kiss her. He would gaze at her lovingly with those gentle brown eyes as he tenderly stroked her hair. He'd press his lips to hers in a sweet kiss that would quickly become deeper and more passionate. A soft moan escaped her lips. The fantasy was so vivid, she could almost feel it. The pleasant, tingling sensation between her legs took her by surprise. Silas had awakened a sexual desire she hadn't felt in ages.

I really was just going through the motions in life before I met him.

Kendrick couldn't remember the last time she'd even thought about having sex, much less desired it. Vividly imagining Silas changed that. Her fantasy rapidly progressed from his lips on hers to his hands reaching under her blouse and massaging her breasts. Soon, they were naked, making passionate love by the picturesque York River. She moaned again and slid her hand between her legs to indulge in a private pleasure she hadn't enjoyed in a long time.

The sharp sensation of bliss reminded her of how long it had been since she'd experienced sexual relief. She imagined Silas pleasuring her, pounding in and out of her as she cried out in ecstasy. Panting now and already near release, she said, *"Don't stop,"* as if Silas was in control of her body. She might have felt stupid and embarrassed for getting so caught up in her fantasy, but the intensity of her orgasm was *so goddamned good*, she felt nothing but sheer sexual delight.

She drew in a deep breath and let it out, her entire body calm and relaxed. Opening her eyes, she smiled with the knowledge that Silas would probably be proud of her for this. For allowing herself, at last, to indulge in the pleasures of life. That, and he'd certainly be proud to know he was the star of her sexual fantasy. Not that she would ever be brave enough to tell him about this little escapade.

Kendrick's stomach grumbled. On autopilot, she got up from the couch to heat up a frozen dinner. After taking a few steps toward her tiny kitchen, she stopped. *What would Silas do?* He would eat something he was in the mood for rather than grabbing whatever was easiest.

Sushi. I haven't had sushi in ages.

There was a restaurant nearby that would deliver sushi.

Less than forty-five minutes later, Kendrick sat at her kitchen table, savoring a delicious meal while reading the latest book in her favorite thriller series. Somehow, she'd gotten three books behind in the "Killer" series. Thoroughly absorbed in the book, *Killer in Midtown*, she read for almost two hours before realizing she'd better get some sleep.

After brushing her teeth and washing her face, Kendrick settled into bed. She reflected on her lovely evening; simple, but wonderful all the same. A delightful orgasm with Silas's help, a good dinner, and a great book. All of those options were available to her all the time, yet she never indulged in them. Her life consisted of work and sleep and not much else. Closing her eyes, she allowed herself to luxuriate in the warmth of her cozy blanket and the comfort of her soft pillow.

Silas had to sleep on the cold, wet ground for years. And at this very moment, there are homeless people suffering in the same way.

She said a silent prayer for those less fortunate than her and drifted off to sleep feeling grateful for everything she had.

"YOU'RE IN A GOOD MOOD," Sallie said, noting Kendrick's new demeanor.

Kendrick was already tired from her full day of work at the law firm when she started her later shift at Milligan's. But Sallie was right. She was in a good mood anyway. Silas had stopped by the shop to visit with her for a few minutes when she'd first arrived. Seeing his handsome face had renewed her energy. He hadn't stayed long, but they'd agreed to meet the next evening at the battlefield.

"Yeah, I guess so," she said as she stocked the imported cheese in the refrigerated display case.

"This peppy attitude wouldn't have anything to do with that hot reenactor guy you were talking to, now would it?" Sallie teased.

Kendrick laughed. "God, I could feel your eyes burning into me the whole time I was outside talking with him."

Silas had approached her on the street to say hello but didn't enter the store with her. It had been crowded, and there was too much of a risk that someone would accidentally touch him. He'd said he didn't want to incite a panic at her work and get her fired.

Getting fired wouldn't be good, but she was considering cutting back her hours so she could spend a little more time with him. That, and working two jobs was wearing her out. After almost a year, it was getting to be a bit much.

"Funny how soldiers always look sexy, even fake soldiers in those goofy tricorn hats," Sallie observed.

"Yup," Kendrick said.

He's a real soldier. And damn right, he's sexy.

"So, dish. What's his name?"

"Silas Murphy."

"Is that his, like, stage name? Phony soldier name?"

"Nope. That's his real name."

"Oh," Sallie said, looking apologetic.

"Sounds so old fashioned, doesn't it? *Silas*," she said, loving the sound of his name. She was thrilled to finally be able to talk to somebody about the man she had the hots for. Kendrick was surprised to find she didn't feel like an idiot for having feelings for a ghost. But then, Silas was all man as far as she was concerned.

"What's the deal with you two?" Sallie asked.

"I don't know. Just friends I guess."

"But you'd like to be more than friends," she said with a sly grin.

"Can I help you with anything?" Kendrick said randomly to a nearby customer. Sallie giggled and Kendrick suppressed a smile.

"Nope, I'm good. Thanks!" The man smiled, and she noted his smile remained for a bit as he shopped. Silas would approve. Being kind to people was so easy, and she couldn't help thinking of all the opportunities she'd squandered in the past. Times when she could have smiled and brightened someone's day but hadn't. It was never too late, she supposed.

"Hey, good to see you," Kendrick said, happily greeting one of her favorite customers who had stepped up to the counter to check out. Though the woman came into the shop almost every week, she always paid with her company credit card, so Kendrick didn't know her name. Kendrick just thought of her as Sweet Lady, since she was always so nice. She was quite pretty, with vibrant blue eyes and light brown hair. "How's it going?"

"Great, and you?" she asked.

"Doing good." Kendrick surveyed Sweet Lady's usual order and noted something was missing. "What, no brie today? We should have some. I just restocked."

"Nope, no brie for me, as much as I love it." Her face lit up in a beautiful smile. "It's just that I've heard you're not supposed to eat soft cheeses like that when you're pregnant."

"Oh my gosh, are you expecting?"

"Yes," Sweet Lady said, blue eyes shining with joy.

"That's so exciting! Congratulations. Is this your first?"

"Yes, the first for me. My husband has a daughter from a previous relationship."

"That's so great."

"Thank you. 'Til next time," she said with a friendly wave.

Kendrick watched her walk out of the shop. Though she was still grateful for everything she had, she felt a sense of loss. Moments ago, Sallie had been teasing Kendrick about her intentions with Silas, hinting around at a possible future with him. But there was no such thing as a future with him. She couldn't help feeling jealous of Sweet Lady, who was carrying her husband's baby. Silas had wanted to be a father, but it was impossible for Kendrick to give him a child.

Possible or not, wasn't it strange to even think about having a child with a man she had met a few short weeks ago? It should have felt weird, but it didn't. Kendrick had connected with Silas so quickly and on such a deep level that the idea of spending her life with him wasn't strange at all. It felt right. As if it was meant to be.

Kurt had been the only other person she'd felt that deeply connected to. And he was dead. And so was Silas.

It was like some kind of cruel, cosmic joke.

Another customer entered the shop, and Kendrick forced herself to smile.

Because of Silas, I am choosing gratitude and not self-pity.

It was the right thing to do. But that didn't mean it would always be easy.

8

The sun was just beginning to set on the battlefield, which was how Silas knew to expect Kendrick soon. He caught sight of her familiar stride in the distance, her reddish hair whipping around in the wind. Despite his lack of a body, it truly felt as if his heartbeat raced when he saw her. He smiled broadly as he watched her approach.

"Hey," she said, returning his smile. The simple, one-word greeting was enough to fill him with elation. Being with her was the highlight of his existence. Clutching her electric lantern, she said, "Let's go sit by the river while it's still light enough to see the water."

"Good idea," he said.

"Crazy to think how I'd never paid much attention to the river until you pointed out how pretty it is. You're an amazing person, Silas."

He shook his head.

"I mean it. Ever since you yelled at me, I've taken a hard look at my life. So I'm trying to be better. It's still hard to find the energy to care about stuff, you know? But I want you to know I'm making the effort."

A small sense of pride bloomed in his ghostly heart to think he had been able to influence Kendrick that way.

"And you've inspired me to try to be nicer to people," she continued. "It's not like I was mean before, but I find I'm trying to do better. To smile at customers. Like one of my favorite customers told me she's expecting a baby. And I'm so happy and excited for her."

Silas gazed lovingly at Kendrick, watching her blue eyes light up as she spoke. Grief had understandably hardened her, but it hadn't taken everything from her.

"I guess it's not so hard to find the good things in life if you try." She favored him with a smile that warmed his phantom heart.

He was surprised at the intensity of emotions this woman brought out in him. Existing the way he did, it was hard to feel anything, sometimes.

"When I'm not at work, or not with you, I usually don't do much. I'm trying to be better about that, too. Not spend so much time just hanging around doing nothing. Like, there's this book series that I love. The "Killer" series by Carolyn Penne. I'm way behind on reading them, and I got a bunch of books out from the library, that I've been putting off reading. Why? I have no idea. But I finally sat down and started reading, and I'd forgotten how awesome they are. She's my favorite author. Everything she writes is such a page-turner."

Kendrick's pace got faster as she talked, and Silas's grin grew wider as he stepped up his stride to keep up.

"Oh, I wish you could read, Silas,"

"Hey," he said. "I can read. We did have the printed word back in the 1700s, you know."

She laughed. "I didn't mean it that way. You can't hold a book is all. I wish you could read one of her books, especially the first one in the series, so we could talk about it. The first book, *Killer in Queens,* has this unbelievable twist ending. It would be cool to have somebody to talk to about it."

"You sound so much happier, Kendrick. I love that."

"Thank you. For everything. I do feel a little better already, though I know it won't always be easy. There will still be dark days. Especially in January on Kurt's death anniversary and on our birthday. And those nasty surprises when something really stupid and random triggers a memory and shoves me back down the hole of grief, like you talked about. But I know I'll always get back out of the hole. I'll have lots of light days. And maybe I'll have a little more control over those light days than I thought. Thank you, Silas. For all of that."

"I don't know what to say." His emotion overcame him.

Kendrick laughed softly. "You don't have to say anything."

Silas watched Kendrick as they walked across the battlefield. She was focused on the sunset over the river, the orange light landing softly on her sweet face. He saw such strength in her eyes, filled with wonder at the beauty of nature but also with the pain of having experienced the fragility of life. By God, how he admired her.

Then she stopped short. Grabbing her chest, she let out a cry like a wounded animal.

"Kendrick!" Silas said, alarmed at the agony in her expression. "What's wrong?"

"I—I don't know. But it hurts. Oh God, it *hurts,*" she said before collapsing to the ground. She rolled onto her back, moaning, still clutching her chest near her heart.

Silas dropped to his ghostly knees beside her. Kendrick was deathly pale, her eyes wide with horror and pain.

"My sweet, what is it? What happened?"

Trembling, she rubbed the area above her ribcage. "I—I don't. I can't ..." Her breath came in rasps as she struggled to speak. "I don't know what's happening to me. I—I'm too young for a ... for a ... heart attack. Right?" Her piercing blue eyes pleaded with him to reassure her.

"Yes, you're young, but ... it is possible," Silas said, wracking his brain for any rational explanation for what was happening to her. Yet, he knew that sometimes there was no explanation, no rhyme nor reason. He'd seen enough death to know it could strike at any time, with no warning.

"I'm s—scared," she said, her voiced filled with pain and fear.

"I know, my sweet. I know." Silas glanced across the vast, deserted battlefield. As a spirit, he could travel miles in a few seconds. He could go and get help from someone who was alive and not utterly useless like he was. Still, the idea of leaving Kendrick alone and petrified tore his heart in two.

This decision could be a matter of life and death. There was no time to waste.

Kendrick let out a shriek of agony. The sound echoed across the field.

"Darling, darling," he cried. He stroked her cheek with his hand, and the cold sensation made her jump. *"Goddamn this useless body!"* he roared, startling her further. "Kendrick, I can't bear to leave you, but I must go for help."

She nodded weakly.

Staring at her as she lay on the ground, he was suddenly struck by flashbacks of battle. The terror and agony in her eyes, it was all so familiar. That primal fear of death and indescribable suffering. Kendrick's face held the same desperate look he'd seen in war countless times. On the faces of his brothers who'd died in battle during the Revolutionary War and that Civil War soldier he'd stayed with as the poor man had breathed his last.

And then, Silas understood what was happening to her.

"Kendrick! Does it feel as if you've been shot?"

"Y—yes," she answered weakly. "It does. I—I mean, not that I know what that feels like. But it is a sharp pain right here." She placed her hand near her heart without touching the area.

"Listen to me," he said firmly, looking her in the eye. "I think I know what's going on. And if I'm right, you're gonna be just fine."

Hope blossomed in her eyes. She hung on his every word.

"I've heard of this happening to others, but I wasn't sure if it was true. I've never seen it myself. Kendrick, I think you're feeling the phantom pain of a fallen soldier's last moments."

"What?" she asked hoarsely.

"Oh, my sweetheart," he said, stroking her face again. This time, she didn't flinch. "It's because you're so attuned to the supernatural. The way you always know when a ghost is present. I've heard that if you're very sensitive and you have the bad luck to stand on a battlefield at the exact time of day when a soldier was fatally wounded, you can ... you might ... feel their death."

Kendrick gasped, seized with terror again.

"But you won't die. I promise. The pain is real, Kendrick. I know it is. But it will pass. Just as the pain stopped when the soldier died, so it will stop with you. But you'll live because you haven't really been pierced with a bullet. Do you understand?"

"Yes," she whispered. "But how long ..."

"I don't know," Silas said mournfully.

Some men lingered for hours.

Kendrick moaned again, writhing in agony.

"I wish I knew how to stop this," Silas said, fighting the urge to yell with fury again. He needed to stay in control for her sake. "Maybe if we can get you away from this spot. God, if only I could carry you!"

She managed to turn over and crawl for a few seconds, but she collapsed onto her back again.

"I can't. I can't." Kendrick began to sob, and Silas could do nothing but bear witness to her pain. It was a torture far worse than any physical affliction he could have been forced to endure.

"It will be all right," he said in a soothing voice. "It won't be long now."

Her sobs eased a bit as she clearly believed his lie. In truth, he had no idea how long this might last, but he'd had to give her hope. She was getting weaker by the moment, her cries fading into whimpers of torment.

"I'm sorry, Kendrick. I'm so sorry," Silas said as he knelt by her side. "I should have known. I should have realized this could happen, with being on the battlefield so much."

"Not ... your ... fault."

Silas smiled weakly. Leave it to Kendrick to try to make him feel better at a time like this.

"I feel like I'm going to die, Silas. I really do." She began to weep harder again. "D—do you think my brother suffered like this?"

"No," he said firmly. Once again, he had no idea what happened with Kurt. He had no way of knowing how bad the accident was. But he couldn't bear Kendrick's anguish. "I bet it happened so fast, he didn't even kn ow what hit him. I think he was in the car one moment and in the arms of the angels the next."

Kendrick nodded, tears still spilling, but she seemed comforted by his words. Then she closed her eyes for a moment and grew still. It frightened him.

Suddenly, her eyes flew open. He watched closely, seeing the pain fade from her face.

"Is it over?" he ventured hopefully.

"Yes. Yes. It doesn't hurt anymore." Kendrick drew in a deep breath and let it out.

"Oh, thank God," Silas cried.

She closed her eyes again, and he watched her chest move up and down as she breathed. "Silas," she said softly. "Touch my cheek again."

Gazing down at her, he gently placed his hand on her cheek. "Isn't that cold?"

"Yes. But I like it because it's you. Feels good to me."

After a moment, she opened her eyes again. "I need to get away from this spot."

Kendrick struggled to her feet, and Silas stayed by her side. "I wish I could help you."

"I'm all right, Silas."

Darkness had begun to fall, so she turned on her electric lantern to light the way. She began to walk on shaky legs, and Silas fell into step beside her.

"Are you sure you're okay?" he asked.

"I think so. Feel very weak, though."

"Are you parked far away?"

"Kind of. I never park at the Yorktown Battlefield Visitor Center because it's nowhere near where we usually meet."

"Oh."

Tourists could go on a self-guided tour of the battlefield by car, and Silas knew from park maps that Stop D was probably the closest to where he and Kendrick usually met. Most likely, she was parked around there somewhere.

"We can't meet on the battlefield anymore," Silas said. "It's too dangerous."

Kendrick shuddered. "God, that was so bizarre. I had no idea a thing like that could happen."

"I feel terrible. I did know. At least, I'd heard of such a thing. Never knew if it was really possible. Until now. Kendrick, I'm so sorry." He heard the anger and weariness in his own voice. It was his own damned fault that she had suffered so horribly, and he'd been powerless to save her as she endured the agony of battle wounds.

"Silas, this was not your fault. And other than being super tired, I'm okay. I really am. In a weird way, it was kind of ... cool."

"What?" he asked so loudly it made her laugh.

"I know it sounds crazy, but it's kind of fascinating that I could feel what happened to somebody so long ago. I guess it's the price of being attuned to the supernatural."

"I guess."

"I do wonder about the soldier, though," she said softly. "Makes me sad to think he suffered like that. I hope he didn't die alone."

"I hope so too."

At last, they made it to where her car was parked on the street. Kendrick unlocked the door and sank down into the driver's seat. She left the door open so she could speak to him.

"I don't remember ever being this tired in my entire life."

"Are you gonna be all right to drive? Not that there's any damn thing I could do about it if you're not," he grumbled.

"I'll be just fine. My apartment isn't too far away, and after a good night's sleep, I'll be good as new."

A car drove down the street, so Silas moved away and Kendrick closed the door. Once it was safe, Silas went to her window and she opened it.

"Gets dark so early now," he said mournfully. "And it's cold. Maybe we should …" He trailed off, not wanting to say they should stop meeting up. That was the last thing he wanted.

"Maybe we should just meet during the day," Kendrick said with a smile.

"Okay, yes. Would have to be only on the weekends, though. Since you work all week. But then you also work some weekends at Milligan's, so …"

"I could run over to the historical district on my lunch hour when I'm working at the law firm. We can meet over near the courthouse and Market Square, since you love to people-watch so much."

"Sounds wonderful. I'm sorry it's so difficult being with me."

"You're worth it."

"Even now?" he asked. Kendrick looked utterly exhausted.

"Yes," she said softly.

"Go home and rest. Be safe."

She nodded and then rolled up her window. Silas stood in the street, watching her drive away.

9

———————

When Kendrick arrived in Colonial Williamsburg on her lunch break, she found Silas sitting under a tree across the street from the courthouse. He stood up and smiled as he watched her approach.

"You look great, Kendrick. Really great. Got your color back in your face." He sounded relieved.

"Had a good night's sleep, and I feel perfectly fine."

"You look perfectly fine," he said, eying her up and down. She wore a black, knee-length skirt and under her jacket, a delicate blue blouse that brought out her eyes. Kendrick had been acutely aware this would be the first time he'd seen her in her day-job work clothes, and she'd wanted to look her best.

"Thanks," she said, laying down a small towel she'd brought to sit on.

"We can move to a bench if you want. Hate to have you sitting on the ground like this."

"I'm fine here," she said.

"What's on the menu today?" Silas asked, peering at her lunch bag.

She laughed. That man was obsessed with food.

"It's an Italian meat and cheese sandwich from my favorite sub shop near work."

"Looks delicious!"

"I always feel so mean. Eating in front of you like this."

"You know I'm never hungry anymore. And I love watching you enjoy yourself."

"Thanks," she said. "So how are *you* doing?"

"Same old," he said, looking over at the shoppers milling about the outdoor market a few yards from where they sat.

"I feel like all we ever do is talk about my problems, and I really want to help you with yours. I promised you I was gonna help you cross over."

"Good luck," he said miserably. "I've been here so long, I can't help but feel hopeless about the whole thing. In two hundred-plus years I haven't figured anything out. What makes you think it'll change now?"

"Because now you have me," she said before taking a bite out of her sandwich.

"How is it?" he asked, eying her food.

Though it still felt wrong to talk about how delicious her food was while he could never eat anything, she was starting to learn that Silas really wanted to know. Like he was living vicariously through her.

"Great. It's got mayonnaise on it, plus balsamic vinegar, which makes it kinda tangy. Just the way I like it."

"Nice," he said with a smile.

"Now quit changing the subject."

"You caught me," he said, throwing his hands up.

"So, is it just guilt over becoming a soldier that's kept you here all this time? Sure, maybe you joined the war effort for the wrong reasons, but you served honorably. You fought for your country and endured so much hardship. I feel like you've already done your penance in life."

Silas didn't say anything as he watched her eat potato chips.

"They taste salty and crunchy, Silas," she said dryly.

He chuckled.

"You feel terrible about some of the things you did in life," she said. "I get that. But you can't do anything to change the past, and there's not much you can do to atone for it. Not existing the way you do now."

"What's your point?"

"My point is there's no sense in you just hanging around here if you aren't able to change anything."

"You make it sound like it's my fault I'm stuck here," he said defensively. Kendrick didn't back down. He'd called her out on her bullshit before, and now it was her turn. Not as an act of vengeance, though. She was trying to help him.

"It seems to be strong emotions that keep a spirit trapped on Earth. Something from their past they won't let go of. I think that's what you're doing. Wallowing in self-pity instead of dealing with the problem and literally moving on."

Kendrick eyed him carefully, a bit worried he might storm off in a huff. It was no fun being confronted with your own shortcomings. She knew that firsthand.

Silas watched the shoppers at Market Square and kept silent for a few minutes.

"You know I'm right, don't you?" she asked at last.

"Yeah. I think so. But I still don't know what to do about it."

"The problem is that you feel bad about your family and the grief that they endured in life," Kendrick said, thinking out loud. "And you feel bad about the soldiers you had to kill in battle, and about their loved ones."

"Had to kill is being generous," he said bitterly.

"Did you kill them for sport?" Kendrick asked, eyes flashing. She hated when Silas was too hard on himself, and she wanted to snap him out of that habit.

"Of course not!"

"It was war, Silas. You did what you had to do to survive. I will never tell you I know how you feel because I don't. I don't know what it feels like to take another human life because I've never been in a situation where I had to make that decision."

"I stupidly put myself in that position."

"You fought honorably," she reminded him again.

Silas shook his head and looked away.

"Okay, Silas," Kendrick began sternly. "You were a horrible person. You left your family behind so you could go prove to the world what a hotshot you were, and in the process, you witnessed your best friend's death and you killed a bunch of people."

He turned back to her, eyes wide. But he was listening.

"What's done is done. The question is, what are you going to do about it?"

"Nothing I can do. You said that yourself."

Kendrick took the last bite of her sandwich and gathered up her trash and stuffed it into a plastic bag. After taking a sip of her diet soda, she turned to focus her full attention on him.

"For the record, my dear, I do not think you're a horrible person. Not then and not now. But what I think doesn't really matter. The only thing that matters is how you feel about yourself, because it's your self-loathing that's keeping you here."

Silas nodded. At least that last part was something they could agree on.

"Have you ever tried talking to your family? Like, through meditation or just flat out trying to speak to them?"

He shook his head.

"I think that might help. Talk to them, Silas. You have that battlefield all to yourself a lot of the time. Tell them how you feel. That you're sorry you made mistakes in life, and if you had it to do over again, you would make different choices. Say you're sorry for the pain you caused them. And then do the same for the soldiers you had to kill and for their families. One thing is for sure, you have absolutely nothing to lose by doing that."

"You make a good point, Kendrick," he said with a smile. Not only was he not angry with her, but she saw a gleam of hope in his eye.

"Do you believe in reincarnation?" she asked.

"Not sure. You?"

"I'm certainly open to the possibility. There are so many things about life and death and the universe that we just don't know. Strange to think we might have lived other lifetimes. Maybe we knew each other in different lifetimes, Silas."

"I like that idea."

"I keep thinking about how fast we connected when we first met. Talking to you felt so easy right away. I don't know. Maybe our souls recognized each other." Kendrick laughed self-consciously. "I know that sounds stupid."

"Kendrick," he said, "that doesn't sound stupid at all."

He gazed at her in a way that let her know he understood what she was saying. And that maybe he felt the same way.

Glancing at the time on her cell phone, she sighed. "I'm gonna have to head back to work soon."

"You don't like your job, do you?"

"It's not that I don't *like* it. The people are nice, and it's stable work. Pays well. I really can't complain."

"What would you do for a living if you could do anything you wanted?"

"I would be a thriller author," she blurted out without thinking. She'd never said those words out loud before.

"Is that so?" Silas looked impressed.

"Oh, I have no idea if I would even be any good," she said with a dismissive wave.

"Not until you try, you won't."

Kendrick shrugged. "I just think it would be fun to write thrillers."

"Then do it."

"Just like that," she said. "Because it's that easy."

"I never said it would be easy. But I agree it would be fun. You could write in your free time if you didn't work so much."

"It's such a competitive business. Would be really hard to make it as a thriller author."

"I'm not saying you should quit your job and live on the streets while you write. You do it on the side. If it didn't work out, you won't have lost anything. But you know what you wouldn't have?"

"What?"

"Regret. You'll never have to wonder *What if*. On the day you die, I doubt you'd think *I shouldn't have written those novels*, even if they didn't become a big success. But you might regret not trying."

She smiled at him. "Here you are again, worrying about me when you should be focusing on your own issues."

"I worry about taking up all your time and keeping you from doing other things."

"There's nowhere I'd rather be than with you, Silas."

"Well, I do enjoy hearing you say that. Meet again tomorrow?"

"I'd love to."

KENDRICK MET up with Silas every day during her lunch break for the next week. Fortunately, the weather had held up and it didn't rain. She looked forward to their talks and always felt refreshed afterward, ready to take on the rest of her workday. Sometimes Silas met up with her on North England Street and walked with her toward their usual spot at Market Square rather than just meeting there.

She watched with amusement as he spied her walking and hurried over to her. His enthusiasm at seeing her made her tingle all over. Nobody had ever looked at her the way he did, and she liked to think it was more than just his loneliness. It wasn't as if he had a lot of people he could talk to, and yet he had a way of making her feel he would still have chosen her out of a crowd.

"No food today?" he said by way of greeting.

"Nope, sorry. We had a breakfast meeting at work, and I'm still full."

"What did you have?" he asked eagerly as they walked toward Market Square.

She laughed. "They had breakfast sandwiches, coffee, and orange juice. I had a bacon, egg, and cheese croissant."

"Sounds divine."

"It was. They also had fruit, and bagels with cream cheese. I've been snacking all morning."

"That's my girl," he said proudly.

How she adored his zest for life. She'd been thinking of him the whole time she'd enjoyed her food this morning, knowing he would approve.

Silas grinned at her, then turned away, giving Kendrick the distinct impression something was on his mind.

"So, I went and did something really dumb," he began, sounding nervous.

"What could you possibly have done?"

"I went and fell in love with this incredible woman."

Kendrick held her breath. She stumbled a bit but quickly recovered.

"She's really beautiful," he said fondly. "Got this kinda reddish-blondish hair. The prettiest blue eyes you've ever seen in your life. She can be a little bitter sometimes, but she's got amazing strength and a sweet, loving heart. Her initials are K.B. ..."

"Silas."

He stopped walking and turned to look at her. "I'm in love with you, Kendrick. Is that stupid?"

"Of course not. I think I've been in denial about how I feel about you. But I love you too," she grumbled.

"Gee, thanks," he said with a frown.

Kendrick gazed into his sweet brown eyes. "I do love you, Silas," she said softly. "I love you very much. But you know how I am. I don't want to love anybody because it's too risky. Since I lost Kurt, I've lived in fear of people dying. My parents, my friends. It's not a risk with you, Silas. It's a certainty. I'll lose you because you're already—"

Her eyes filled with tears, and Silas tenderly touched her cheek. "Oh, my sweet. Please don't cry. Here, let's go some-where private."

Kendrick followed Silas across the street where they sat

under a large tree across from the Peyton Randolph House. Once they were settled, he looked into her eyes.

"I love you so much, Kendrick. My God, when you collapsed on the battlefield ... I've never felt so helpless. That's when I knew I was in love. When I thought I was gonna lose you," he said in a voice choked with emotion.

"Why did we have to meet like this? When it's impossible for us to be together? I feel like we're soulmates. What's the point of meeting a man as wonderful as you if I can't ever—" Kendrick put her head in her hands and began to weep. She hadn't realized until this moment how much she had repressed her feelings for Silas. The fate of their love had been sealed before they had even met. She was going to lose him, and she knew all too well what that kind of grief did to a person.

I'm not strong enough to go through that again.

Wiping her eyes, she took a few deep, steadying breaths. She turned to find Silas staring at her with an expression of sheer torment.

"Kendrick, I'm so sorry."

"It's not your fault you're dead, Silas." She barked out a bitter laugh. "No way I'll ever get married now. I'll never love anybody the way I love you."

"Don't say that, my sweet. You're so young. You have plenty of time—"

"I don't want *time.* I want *you.*"

"I feel the same way," he said mournfully. "I've been around a long time, and I've never known anybody as wonderful as you. It doesn't make any sense to me, either. Why we should meet when there's no hope for a happy ending. Then again, some days it feels like nothing makes sense."

Silas had always been the one with all the answers. The

one who told her to keep the faith, to look on the bright side. Now he sounded utterly bereft of hope.

His expression softened. "Maybe we were supposed to meet so we can help each other."

Kendrick laughed. "I should have known you'd figure out a way to try to turn this into a positive." She sighed wearily. "Maybe you're right. Losing you is going to be awful, Silas. But somehow, even now, I can't bring myself to be sorry we met. And if being with me helps you to finally go to your eternal reward, it will all have been worth it."

Upon reflection, she realized how much she had truly meant those words. Somehow, she would find the strength to go on after Silas was gone. And any suffering and grief she'd have to endure would be worth it if it helped him find peace.

"You know how it goes, Kendrick. There's no guarantees in life, no matter what. Even if I was alive and we could be together like a normal couple, there's no way of knowing how much time we would have. But we do have now, my sweet."

Gazing into his eyes, she said, "I love when you call me that."

Silas touched her cheek with his icy hand. "We'll just have to talk and laugh and love for as long as we can. And even when I'm gone, I won't really be *gone*. Our love won't die, Kendrick. It might change form for a while, but it will still exist."

Fresh tears spilled from her eyes. "You're right,"

He leaned over and pressed his lips to hers. When he pulled back, he asked, "What does that feel like?"

"Do you really want to know?"

"Yeah."

"Feels like somebody pressed an ice cube to my lips." She laughed gently. "But I love it because it's you."

"It kills me that I'll never be able to touch you."

"What would you do if you could touch me?"

Silas hesitated for a moment.

"What?" she asked.

"You know, I have endless time to think about such things," he said slyly. "And I've thought *a lot* about this particular subject."

"Is that so?" she asked flirtatiously.

He nodded. "For one thing, I bet you look *spectacular* when you're naked."

Kendrick smiled, feeling a blush creep onto her face. But she didn't want him to stop talking.

"I love to imagine stripping you of your clothes, nice and slow," he said seductively. "But if I got the chance, I don't think I'd be that patient." He laughed self-consciously. "In my fantasies, I'm a much better lover than I actually would be in real life."

"What makes you say that?"

"It's not like I'm all that experienced. I've been with a few women, but not many. With them it was, you know ..." He trailed off and looked away with uncharacteristic shyness. "Kinda quick. Was during the war when we would march through town after town. If the woman was willing, well then, so was I. Didn't happen often, so when I did get the opportunity ... yeah. It all happened *real* quick."

"I think you would be an amazing lover," she said.

Silas seemed bolstered by her confidence in him. "With you, I would take my time. I'd want to make love to you for hours."

"Mmmm," she said dreamily. "That would be incredible."

"Wouldn't it?" His eyes flashed and his voice grew huskier. "Can you imagine? The two of us in bed together. Me inside of you. Your legs wrapped around my back."

"Yes," she said quietly. "I can imagine."

"Have you ever … thought about that before? Being with me like that?"

"Yes, I have," she said shyly. "A lot."

"Really?" he said, eyes wide. Silas seemed so excited about the idea, she knew she should probably elaborate, but she couldn't bring herself to do it.

"Do you think of me when you're home, you know, alone?" he ventured.

Her chest tightened and her cheeks flushed with heat.

Just tell him the truth. It would make him so happy to know.

"I've thought about us having sex. And I—I've … t—touched myself."

Silas moaned deep in his throat. "Honestly? You really have?"

He sounded so hopeful, she nearly laughed. "I would never lie about something so embarrassing." Kendrick groaned and covered her face with her hands. She wasn't exactly sorry about her confession, but she felt humiliated all the same.

"Kendrick." His voice was so firm, she was forced to look up. "No matter how much you've fantasized about us having sex, it can't be anywhere near as much as me. My sweet, I've pictured us making love in every position there is."

Her face flushed deeper, but now it was due to arousal instead of shame. The sound of his deep, sexy voice was intoxicating.

"Our first time would be slow and sensuous. I'd force myself to be patient no matter how much restraint it might take. I'd make love to you just the way I mentioned before. Me on top, deep inside you, with your legs around me."

Kendrick nodded hungrily as she listened.

"The next time would be faster. After I'd gotten to know your body and learned how to pleasure you properly, I'd know just how and where to touch you. My God Kendrick, the visions I've had of you. Bending you over a table and having my way with you. Up against the wall. On the floor." He was practically salivating.

Never before had any man stared at her with such intense lust before. For the first time in her life, she felt sexy and desirable.

"I wasn't even sure if you had a sex drive anymore," she said.

"It's kinda like the food thing. I'm not exactly hungry, but I know what I'm missing. I remember the feeling of sexual sensation and release." Silas groaned again. "Can't help thinking how much I enjoy watching you eat food. Watching your pleasure. Good God, would I love to watch while you—"

Kendrick held up her hand to stop him from finishing his thought. "Well, you'll just have to imagine."

"Believe me. I will."

Her face became hot again as she felt his intense stare. Even she had to admit it would be rather erotic to have him watch her pleasure herself. It was the only sexual intimacy they could possibly share. Still, that was a step too far for her comfort. If nothing else, she was glad she had told him how much she desired him.

"I'm sorry I can't be a real boyfriend to you," he said somberly.

"You're more real to me than any other man I've ever known, Silas," she said, gazing into his eyes. "I've told you things I never thought I could tell anyone, and I'm not just talking about today's discussion. I mean everything. You understand me in ways I never thought anybody could."

"I know exactly what you mean. Over the course of hundreds of years, the only human contact I've had is casual conversations with tourists from a safe distance and interacting with people as a ghost. And with those people, they're either excited or terrified to have a ghost encounter. Nobody has treated me like a person—like Silas Murphy— since I was alive. Until now."

Silas closed his eyes, looking overwhelmed with emotion.

"Are you all right?" she asked.

He opened his eyes. "My biggest fear is that someday I'll cross over ... just disappear ... and I won't be able to say goodbye to you. In case that happens, I want you to know ... Kendrick, I will love you forever. Forever and always."

"I'll love you forever too, Silas," she said, voice trembling.

They sat together in silence for a few minutes.

"So tonight, when you get home from work. Are you gonna ... you know?"

"Ugh, please don't ask me about that. Be grateful I told you about it at all."

"Sorry, sorry. I don't mean to make you uncomfortable."

Without looking at him, Kendrick said, "Before I met you, it had been a long time since I'd been *inspired* to do that." A hot blush bloomed on her face again. "And that's the last thing I'm gonna say on the subject."

"All right. I promise I won't make you talk about it anymore. But I'm real happy you told me. Nobody's thought about me in that way in a really long time. Can't tell you how much it means to me."

"Trust me. I know exactly what you mean," Kendrick said fondly. Being the object of a man's sexual desire was a foreign concept to her.

"You are one damn sexy woman."

"I have to admit, I can't help feeling proud that I was able to turn on a *ghost*," she said.

Silas laughed. "You should be proud."

Kendrick sighed heavily.

"Time to go back to work, ain't it?"

"Yeah. That, and I've been putting off mentioning this, but I won't be around tomorrow through next week. I'm sorry, Silas."

"Why won't you be around?"

"Because of the holiday."

"Oh, I see. Thanksgiving."

"Right. I'm supposed to go visit my family in Maryland. My grandparents live there."

"I'll miss you, Kendrick, but I hope you have a good time with your family. Are you looking forward to it?"

"Yeah, kinda. It will be good to see my grandma and grandpa and be with my parents and all. But you know how it is. Holidays are still hard."

"Because there's somebody missing at the table," Silas said gently.

Kendrick nodded, her heart filling with warmth upon hearing his soft tone. "Yeah. But I'm gonna really try to focus on who is there and not just who's missing. I'm lucky to still have my grandparents with me and in relatively good health. And my parents. But now it kinda feels like there will be two people missing. I wish so much I could introduce you to my family. So weird that I'm in love with this wonderful man that I can't tell anyone about."

"You think your family would like me?"

"Oh, they would. I know they would. They'd see how nice you are and how well you treat me, and they'd be pressuring us to get married and give them grandchildren."

"Wouldn't that be wonderful?" Silas said longingly. "If we had a boy, we could name him after your brother."

Kendrick placed her hand over her heart to show how touched she was by his suggestion. She nodded.

"We'd be good parents, me and you," Kendrick said. "And I can't help thinking how much joy it would bring my mom and dad if they had some grandkids."

She swallowed against the bitterness and anger that threatened to rise up in her. It was all too easy to get sucked back into that pit of darkness and despair. No sense in dwelling on the sheer injustice of it all.

"I'm sorry you have to be alone here," she said. "I'll only be gone a week."

"Don't worry about me. You go have a good time with your family."

Wearily, Kendrick got to her feet and he stood up to face her.

"Just promise me one thing," he said, staring deeply into her eyes. "Kendrick, this is really important."

"Okay," she said, eyes wide with concern.

"When you come back, you have to tell me *every single thing* you ate for Thanksgiving. Leave nothing out!"

Kendrick laughed.

"I will, Silas. I make you a solemn vow."

"Good! I love you, my sweet."

"I love you too."

10

———————

Silas drifted through the battlefield feeling utterly euphoric as his mind went over the day's events.

Kendrick loved him. She had sexual fantasies about him.

He could hardly believe it. As he'd promised, he conjured up all kinds of new and exciting fantasies of Kendrick pleasuring herself while thinking of him. He hoped she'd gone home tonight and remembered everything he'd said about wanting to have sex with her against a table and the wall and in every position there was.

Silas groaned out loud as he imagined Kendrick naked under the covers, her hand slipping between her legs, her mouth open as she gratified herself while picturing him.

"That is so *hot*," he said as he wandered the battlefield. No one was around, but he remained invisible anyway. What he wouldn't *give* to be able to satisfy her needs himself.

Silas heard a crunching in the grass. At first, he thought it might be an animal or something. Then he saw it was a person. And not just any person. *His* person.

What in God's name is she doing here?

He used to love seeing Kendrick approach on the battle-field, but after what happened to her last time, he was horrified to see her. Quickly turning visible, he rushed over to her.

"Kendrick, you can't be here! You shouldn't be here."

"It's all right, Silas. I'll only stay a minute," she said, glancing apprehensively around, clasping her electric lantern. She was clearly frightened. Fortunately, the Battle of Yorktown wasn't an especially bloody one. Only a few hundred soldiers were killed across the miles-long battle-field, but still. Kendrick had already had the bad luck of standing on the site of one soldier's death, and it could certainly happen again.

"My sweet, why did you come—"

"Because I wanted to give you this," she said, holding up some sort of electrical device.

"What the hell is it?"

Kendrick laughed. "It's called a tablet. It's an old one of mine that I don't really use any more. Look, I loaded an audiobook on it for you to listen to."

With a few flicks of her fingers, she brought up a book cover on the device. It said *Killer in Queens* by Carolyn Penne.

"That's the book you told me about."

"Yeah, would you like to listen to it?" she asked, her eyes filled with hope. Not only did the book sound interesting when she had described it, Silas couldn't deny the woman anything when she looked at him like that.

"Sure, but how?"

"Quick, pick a place to sit. Like, a place you won't mind being for, like, several hours."

"Uh, okay. Doesn't really matter where to me."

Silas walked over to a tree and sat down in the darkness. Kendrick followed him and found a small crevice in a tree.

"The battery should last long enough for you to hear the whole book. Hopefully, it won't rain while I'm gone, but the tablet should stay pretty safe here. Ready to start? You'll have to listen to it straight through. Is that okay?"

"Yes, yes. Sure. Whatever. My sweet, you have to leave before you—"

"I know, I know. I just ... I love the idea of sharing this book with you so we can talk about it when I get back."

"Me too," he said with a smile. He felt honored that Kendrick wanted to share her passion for reading with him.

"Okay, here we go," she said excitedly. The audiobook began to play. "I love you, Silas."

"I love you too."

Kendrick blew him a kiss and dashed off.

"You're crazy!" he said.

"I know!" she said with a giggle.

Silas watched her until she disappeared from his sight and then turned his focus on the audiobook. He quickly understood why Kendrick liked the story so much. Silas had no idea how long the book was or how much time had passed because he was so engrossed in the story. He drew in a silent, literally breathless gasp when he got to the twist Kendrick had told him about.

Silas was shocked yet delighted at the way the novel had kept him guessing all the way through. The novel finished just as the sun was coming up. Now he really understood why Kendrick was desperate to discuss the book. A surprise ending was much more fun when you had someone to share it with.

He missed her so much already. It would be a long week without her. As the sun continued to rise, he made his way toward the river and sat down at the edge. Watching the sun shine on the rippling water, he felt a deep longing in his soul for Kendrick. He felt incomplete sitting here without her.

Silas struggled not to dwell on the things he couldn't change. So many things in his life he desperately wished he could undo or do differently, but that was impossible. Now he found himself incessantly ruminating over Kendrick and all the things he couldn't change with her. They loved each other, but it was only a matter of time until they were torn apart. How he would have loved to marry her and have children with her. It was so easy to picture being part of a family with Kendrick, their children, and her parents. His phantom heart squeezed in his chest when he imagined the happiness those children would have brought her mother and father after they had suffered so much. No child could ever replace the son they'd lost, but the love and laughter of new life might bring them some measure of peace.

Loneliness swept over him in a powerful wave. He hadn't felt so bereft since the early days after his death when he had wandered, lost and alone, with no one to turn to. The pain searing his heart from missing Kendrick now was nothing compared to what she would be forced to endure once Silas was gone. If he did manage to cross over, his troubles would be over. He would be at peace, while Kendrick was left behind to grieve and suffer.

Imagining her pain was too much. Silas began to weep tearlessly. He hadn't cried since Levi's death so many years ago. Silas recalled hiding away from his fellow soldiers for a few minutes to cry and grieve privately. Now he grieved for his own lost life and his eventual loss of the woman he loved so dearly.

Silas knew he had to be strong for her sake. Clearly,

Kendrick would never be able to move on as long as he was still around. As much as it hurt him to think of her marrying another man, it hurt his very soul to think of her living the rest of her life alone. She wanted to marry and have children. He couldn't let her deny herself that happiness because of him. The longer he remained here with her, the more he would hold her back and the worse her eventual grief would be.

I simply have to figure out how to cross over.

Recalling Kendrick's suggestion about speaking to his family and to the soldiers whose lives he had taken, he decided to give it a try. He was alone on the battlefield, but he would still feel silly talking out loud. So he spoke silently with his heart as he looked out at the beauty of the water and the sky.

I'm sorry, you know. I never meant to hurt any of you.

Without forming conscious words and thoughts, Silas allowed his emotions to take over. He pondered the indescribable agony his mother must have endured when he had died. He pictured his father, stoic as he received the news, trying to be strong for his mother. And there was Jenny, Abigail, and Gabriel, all younger than him.

Sharp pain pierced his heart as he pictured his precious brother and sisters, and he felt renewed empathy for Kendrick and the tragic loss of her brother.

"I'm so sorry," he whispered to his siblings as he gazed heavenward.

How he had loved and adored them. He wanted to cry out in anguish. They had trusted him to protect them. Little Gabriel, who looked so much like Silas, had wanted to grow up to be just like his big brother.

What a horrible role model I was.

Silas should have taught them to choose love, not pride.

Peace not war. Family and friends and hearth and all the things that made life worth living. To forget worrying about what others thought of you, and instead worry about what you could do for other people. Sure, everyone had thought of him as a war hero. Who the hell cared? He thought of all the simple shopkeepers and farmers who had stayed in Massachusetts to do their jobs and support their families. To be good neighbors and friends. Now that was a legacy worth taking pride in.

Gathering his emotional strength, he forced himself to consider all the men he'd killed in battle. Five that he knew of, but there could have been more struck down by the bullets he'd fired. With each of those deaths, Silas had left a trail of devastation. Broken-hearted parents, brothers and sisters, sweethearts, and friends. With his bullets, he'd blown open gaping wounds of grief for so many loved ones. Wounds that would never heal, no matter how much time had passed.

Silas knew no amount of sorrow and regret would help him truly repent or replace what he had taken. Slowly, his eyes traveled from one side of the river to the other. After all the long years of loneliness and torment, he had believed this time might be different. That confiding in Kendrick would help. That he might finally find peace.

But now, after having bared his soul to the people he had wronged so terribly all those years ago, he felt far worse than when he'd sat down by the river.

A fresh wave of hopelessness crashed over him. Nothing to do now but wait until Kendrick returned.

After that? He had absolutely no idea what to do.

11

    Silas showed up early at Market Square to wait for Kendrick on the day she was slated to return. Colonial Williamsburg was bustling, and the Christmas decorations were already up. Wreaths on the doors of the historical buildings, holly everywhere. As beautiful as it was, he had barely taken notice of the place. He'd have plenty of time to look at the holiday décor later. Right now, the only thing he was interested in was seeing Kendrick.

After finishing the book and making a few more feeble attempts to cross over, the ache of missing her had been unbearable. He'd simply vanished for the last few days, so when he returned to consciousness, he could see his beloved at last.

His ghostly heart nearly exploded with euphoria when he caught sight of her familiar stride. The excruciating wait was over.

Kendrick's pretty blue eyes lit up when she saw him, and her lips blossomed into the sweetest smile Silas had ever seen.

How joyous it is to be loved.

Silas had never had a sweetheart in life, and he was still getting used to the idea that he had one now.

She dashed over to him. Even after being dead all this time, it felt unnatural to Silas that she didn't rush over to embrace him. They were so much in love, yet they couldn't kiss or hold each other. He didn't think he would ever get used to that. After quickly spreading out her towel so she could sit under a tree, she turned to face him.

"I cannot begin to tell you how much I missed you," she said, gazing into his eyes. He could see the sheer relief on her face, and he knew the separation had been just as hard on her.

"Me too, Kendrick. It felt like forever. How was your holiday?"

"It was really nice," she said happily. "Great to see my family all together. I'm very lucky that we all get along so well, you know? I have friends with families who are really toxic and hypercritical and all that, which is awful. And I know lots of people who get in political arguments during the holidays. There's none of that with my family, so we just get to enjoy each other."

"That sounds perfect. I'm so glad."

He was grateful, but he felt lonely as she spoke. He missed his own kin, especially around the holidays; it would have been comforting to go with Kendrick and spend time with her family during Thanksgiving.

"Were you able to listen to the book?" she asked eagerly.

"Oh shoot! Well yes, I was. But darn it, I meant to go check on the device afterward to see if it was okay. I vanished for part of the time you were gone, so I'm not even sure if it rained."

"Oh, it's fine," she said with a dismissive wave. "I'm not worried about that old thing. What did you think?"

"Wow, that's what I think!" he practically shouted.

Kendrick laughed. "What did I tell you?"

"I had no idea how it was gonna turn out 'til the very end." The tale had begun with a string of unsolved murders in Queens, NY, and two detectives were put on the case. Detective Jerry Wallace and Detective Barry Dazing had been partners and friends for years. They had always had each other's backs as they worked to solve crimes that others thought were unsolvable. Then came the twist ending.

"I couldn't believe it was one of the detectives all along!" Silas exclaimed. It turned out that the serial killer was none other than Barry Dazing.

"Neither could I the first time I read it. I read it again after I knew the ending so I could pick it apart and figure out how the author was able to keep such a clever secret. Her writing is just incredible. I'm totally addicted to her books."

They chatted excitedly about *Killer in Queens* for a while, discussing their favorite parts, characters, and of course, the twist ending. Talking with Kendrick felt like being with a friend he'd known all his life.

"So, while I was away for the week, guess what I did?"

"That thing I'm not supposed to ask you about anymore?"

"No!" she said, a pretty blush blooming on her cheeks. With a shy laugh, she admitted, "Well, yes ... that too. But that's not what I want to talk about. I started writing a little."

"You did? Good for you. I'm so proud of you," he said.

"You're the only one I've told about it so far."

"Will you tell me about what you've written?"

Kendrick hesitated, but it seemed like she did want to talk about it. Still, Silas understood that writing was a pretty personal thing.

"Well, it's like in theory, I guess I would want it to be a series like Carolyn Penne's "Killer" series. Only in mine, the detective is a woman. I like the idea of adding a romance element to it, too. Like, she could fall in love at some point in the series."

"Perhaps with a sexy soldier?"

"Perhaps," she said with a smile. "I like that idea. There's definitely some stuff in there that's based on my life. Like the main character has a brother who died. He was murdered, and that's what drives her sense of justice to fight crimes."

"I love that," Silas said, his pride in his girl growing by the moment. "Think of all the emotion you could pour into your story."

"Exactly." She laughed gently. "Kurt would have *loved* the idea that I had him murdered in my book. The bloodier the better."

Silas laughed. "What a lovely tribute."

Kendrick smiled. "Yeah. Oddly enough, it really is."

"That's great. You'll be a famous author yet, my love."

"Maybe." She shrugged. "But I won't regret trying my hand at writing no matter what happens. Thanks for the great advice, Silas."

"My pleasure. And while you were gone, I tried some of *your* advice. You said I should try to talk to my family and to the soldiers and all that."

"That's great! What did you say?"

"Well, I didn't exactly talk to them out loud."

"I guess it was more like a silent prayer or meditation type thing?"

"Yeah. Like that."

"How did it go?" she asked.

"Not great," Silas admitted. "I'm not sure what I expected, but I actually felt kinda worse."

"Oh no," Kendrick said. "Well, it's gotta be tough to tear open all those old wounds. Maybe it's one of those things that gets worse before it gets better."

"Maybe," he said with a weary shrug. He watched as a young couple laughed together while they shopped. The man was about the age of many of the soldiers he'd killed.

"Are you willing to try it again?"

"Got nothin' to lose, I suppose."

"Do you want me to go with you?"

"No. I usually sit by the river 'cause it's peaceful there, and I don't want you going near the battlefield. Besides, I really worry about you spending so much time with me. You need other people in your daily life. *Living* people."

"I'm fine, Silas."

"No, you're not," he said firmly. "You're not gonna be fine if I cross over. And you're not gonna be fine if you're wasting time with me instead of living your life."

"How could you think that my precious time with you is a waste?" she asked, sounding offended.

"Because there's no future for us. We both know that. That's just the way it is. I worry about you all the time, Kendrick. About what's gonna happen to you. If by some miracle I'm able to cross over, I might be at peace, but you'll be the one left behind to suffer. And if I don't cross over soon, it's not doing you any good to be hanging around with me instead of moving on with your life. I'm scared that the longer you're with me, the more painful it will be when it's all over."

Kendrick fell silent for a little while, contemplating his words.

"I hear what you're saying. I guess I just want to make

the most of the time we have together since we don't know how long we're gonna have."

Selfishly, Silas would have loved if Kendrick would be with him every moment of her free time. After all, he had nothing to do and nothing to look forward to except seeing her beautiful face. But she had a life to live, and he was not about to stand in her way.

"You're supposed to be moving in with your parents soon, right?"

Kendrick looked down at the ground.

"Kendrick?"

"I'm still planning on moving and eventually getting my own house and all that …"

"But?"

"I'm just postponing it temporarily. My lease on my apartment is up, so I'm just paying month to month right now. I told both my jobs I can stay on longer than I thought."

"Did you have a job lined up where you were supposed to move?"

After hesitating a moment, she said, "There will be other jobs."

"Kendrick!"

"I'm not leaving you, Silas. I'm staying with you for as long as I can."

"As much as I love hearing you say that, you know that's not good. It's not healthy. You must realize that."

"All I know is that I'm going to be very unhappy without you, and I'm trying to put that time off for as long as possible. It's like being in love with someone who has a terminal illness, like cancer." Her voice began to quake. "I'm going to stay by your side until it's all over. Until you're gone. I'll deal with the grief when the time comes, but I'll never be sorry I loved you. And I'm not going anywhere as long as you're here."

"But I still don't think it's a good idea for you to spend all your time with me."

"I'm not spending all my time with you. I come here on my lunch hour instead of sitting at my desk or in my car. What's the big deal?"

"I'm scared you won't have anybody to support you after I'm gone. Seems like you shut a lot of people out of your life after Kurt died, and I'm worried you'll do that again."

"I grieve better by myself anyway."

The notion of Kendrick grieving his loss in total isolation was too much to bear.

"Don't you have friends? People you can go out with? Coworkers?" he asked, exasperation in his voice.

"My coworkers are nice, but they're not really friends. Just acquaintances. I have friends, but I haven't gone out with them in a while."

"You should go out more. Why don't you call them up and make plans to go out?"

Kendrick sighed. "I'd just rather be with you, Silas. I feel like I can talk about real stuff with you."

"You know I love our deep conversations, my sweet," he said with a smile. "Talking about life and death. Reincarnation. Heaven. All that important stuff. But it can also be fun to talk about other things. I lost track of how much time we spent talking 'bout that book. That was fun, wasn't it?"

"Yeah, it was," Kendrick said. The small smile on her lips encouraged him.

"My sweet, I want you to promise me you will make plans to go see your friends. It's too cold and dark to come see me in the evenings now anyway."

She turned her head to watch the shoppers at the

outdoor market. He watched her eyes as she considered his words.

"Kendrick, I need you to do this for me. I'm gonna try really hard to cross over. For your sake. My being here is holding you back."

"Silas—"

"It is, and you know it!" he snapped. He wasn't angry with her; he was mad at the situation they were both in. And he needed her to understand. "You're literally not able to move on with the rest of your life while I'm still here. You've already said you're not leaving Williamsburg until I'm gone. So I'm gonna do everything in my power to finally go where I'm supposed to. I'll go to the river and concentrate, meditate, all night long, every night if I have to. And if it works, it will mean I have to leave you."

Silas closed his eyes as fresh pain washed over him. Knowing Kendrick would suffer was the worst part of their eventual separation. But they'd both known from the beginning there was no hope for a happy ending. He opened his eyes.

"I have to go at some point, Kendrick. And there's no way I can ever rest in peace knowing you're here all alone. Please. Reach out to your friends. You don't want to admit it, but you're gonna need them when I'm gone."

Kendrick turned to meet his gaze, and he stared pleadingly into her eyes.

"Okay. I'll make plans. I promise. Now stop looking at me like that. You're gonna make me cry."

"Sorry."

She heaved a deep sigh. "The whole idea makes me tired."

"What idea?"

"Going out. Making small talk. Pretending to care about stupid things."

"Try to keep an open mind, okay? And you have to be patient with the non-bereaved. People who don't understand what you've been through. What you're *still* going through. You wouldn't understand either if it hadn't happened to you."

"That is true. God, I sound like such a bitch, don't I?"

"Of course not! You just sound … sad."

"I am sad," she whispered. "I can't bear to think about losing you."

"I know," he said mournfully. "I need you to promise me something else."

"You're awfully pushy today, my sweet," she said with a smile.

He grimaced. "I am. You're right. Feel like I'm making out my last will and testament. There's just no way of knowing how long I have, so I have to make sure I say everything on my mind."

"Okay, shoot."

"I want you to promise to be open-minded about getting married someday."

She scoffed bitterly.

"I know it's hard to think about right now, but I don't want you being a spinster your whole life 'cause of me."

"People don't say 'spinster' anymore. Back in your day, a woman was expected to get married and have kids. Things are different now. Women have options."

"I get that. You're gonna be plenty busy as a famous thriller author."

Kendrick rolled her eyes.

"Even so, you *do* want to get married and have children. You've said as much."

"I guess."

"It's not gonna be with me, Kendrick."

Her jaw grew rigid. "I don't want to talk about that."

"You have to at least promise me you won't close your heart to the idea of finding love again."

Kendrick gazed into the distance where the crowds had begun to thicken due to the festive season. Silas followed her eyes as she watched several excited children chatter to their parents about what they wanted for Christmas. The parents looked a tad weary, but happy. She said quietly, "There's nobody else like you. And there never will be."

Silas understood; he felt the same way. Though he wasn't about to say it out loud, the idea of loving anyone besides Kendrick felt impossible.

"Instead of me already being dead, think of it as if we got married and then I died in a car accident or something." He winced. "I'm so sorry, Kendrick. Bad example."

"It's all right," she said, smiling at him.

"Imagine it's like we loved each other and got married, and then I died not long after. Imagine I had cancer, like you mentioned. It would be all right for you to marry again. It's not like you're replacing me. But you deserve a second chance at happiness. Might seem impossible now, just know that if you ever meet another man, I'll be smiling down on you both."

Picturing Kendrick with another man was agonizing, but her happiness was most important.

"I can't imagine loving anyone else," she said.

"Promise me you will at least stay open to the idea."

Kendrick nodded sadly. "You'll always be the love of my life, Silas."

"And you will be mine, Kendrick. You will be mine."

12

———————

Kendrick kept her word to Silas. She called her friends and made plans to go out on Friday night. She'd met Deanna and Marie when they were teenagers, and they had become best friends. Kendrick had been fairly popular in high school, but all that had changed when Kurt died. Most of her alleged friends abandoned her once she was no longer the happy-go-lucky girl she had been before the tragedy. Deanna and Marie did their best to stand by her, but even they got tired of her constant grief after a while. Kendrick had found it too hard to do all the normal teenage things like hanging out at the mall, going to the movies, and attending school sports events. She'd had no interest in going to the prom, while most of the other girls were obsessed with it. Everything had felt trivial after her brother's death. Though Marie and Deanna's expectation that she should go back to normal angered Kendrick, deep down, she understood that it must have been a drag to be around her sometimes. It was probably like trying to be friends with Wednesday Addams. They'd kept in touch off and on since high school, but lately, their friendship had mainly been via text. Both women had sounded surprised but pleased to hear from her.

Since it was the beginning of December, Kendrick figured it would be practical to shop for Christmas while meeting with her friends. If nothing else, she could check that off her to-do list while fulfilling her obligation to Silas. She'd intended to shop with her friends for a short while, then call it a night.

However, upon meeting up with Deanna and Marie, she found herself having a lot more fun than she'd expected. Marie, petite with blond hair and blue eyes, still looked like the peppy cheerleader she'd been in high school. Now a successful pharmaceutical researcher, she defied the dumb blonde stereotype and was a hell of a lot smarter than people usually gave her credit for. Deanna, a tall brunette, was no slouch in the intellectual department either. She was currently in grad school pursuing her Ph.D. in psychology.

And yet, when the three of them got together, they got to giggling like they had as teenagers. Nobody was more surprised than Kendrick. Though she tended to disdain that kind of behavior, it felt good to laugh for once. Her evening turned out to be a delightful distraction from the things that weighed on her mind. Perhaps Silas's point on the benefit of talking about superficial stuff once in a while had some merit.

Kendrick was most surprised that she was getting into the spirit of Christmas for once. Like all other holidays, it would never be the same without her twin brother. Memories of them as children, clad in their pajamas and waiting up for Santa still loomed large in her mind. After all these years, her heart still felt empty when she hung up all the stockings except Kurt's. Yet, seeing the kids at the mall visiting Santa made her smile, reminding her that there was still life going on around her. Not everything was doom and gloom.

She even found the perfect gift for her mother—a delicate crystal unicorn. Actually, Marie found it, having remembered how much Kendrick's mother loved unicorns. Her friend's thoughtfulness was a sweet reminder of Kendrick's shared past with her friends—the Secret Santas they'd done in high school, and the shots of peppermint schnapps they'd had on Christmas Eve. So many happy memories; Kendrick found her heart swelling at the thoughts of making more.

As always, Silas was right. Kurt's absence still left a huge, empty hole in her heart that would never be filled. The impending grief of losing Silas would do the same thing, and she felt entirely unprepared for that loss. But Silas had helped her focus on what she *did* have. God willing, her parents would still be around for a long time. They'd share more Christmases, birthdays, celebrations. They would throw a huge party for Deanna when she got her doctorate. Maybe her friends would marry and have kids someday, and she would be Aunt Kendrick. There was still so much life to live.

After they'd made their way through the entire mall, Kendrick said, "I'm starving. Wanna grab some food and maybe a drink or two?"

"That would be great," Marie said with a smile. She eyed Kendrick curiously for some reason.

They headed over to one of the restaurants in the mall and, after a short wait, they were seated.

"Feels good to sit down," Kendrick said, setting her shopping bags under the table. The place was crowded, bursting with holiday shoppers. Kendrick had to admit it was rather nice to be among the living for a change. The brightly colored Mexican décor lifted her spirits.

"Sure does," Deanna said. "Ooh, we should get some nachos."

"Sounds great," Kendrick agreed. A sweet wave of nostalgia swept over her as she remembered the countless plates of nachos they had shared over the years.

When the server came over, Deanna put in the appetizer order and they all ordered drinks.

"Hey, we should get some shots of peppermint schnapps," Kendrick said.

"Great idea," Marie said.

"That shit tastes like mouthwash," Deanna said. "But it is tradition."

Kendrick laughed and held up three fingers at the server, who nodded.

Marie shot her that curious look again.

"What?"

"It's good to hear you laugh, Kendrick. And it's really good to see you."

"You guys, too. I'm sorry it's been so long," she said, feeling genuine regret at the lost time. "So catch me up. What's going on with you both?"

Marie filled her in on her job, and Deanna talked about grad school. When the schnapps arrived, they toasted each other cheerfully and downed the drinks, wincing and groaning as they did.

"So gross," Kendrick said, wiping her mouth.

"Like a liquid candy cane," Marie said with a grimace.

"Ahh, but it does take the edge off," Kendrick said. She sipped her glass of water to rinse her mouth before switching back to wine.

Soon, the nachos arrived, and they eagerly dug into the cheesy goodness.

"So what have you been up to, Kendrick?" Marie asked.

"Not a whole lot," she lied.

You wouldn't believe me if I told you.

"Why haven't you moved yet? Not that I'm in any hurry for that to happen," Marie said with a frown.

"It's not that far away," Kendrick assured her. "Um well, the job I wanted in Newport News fell through, so now I gotta make other plans."

"That's too bad," Deanna said. "What else is going on?"

"Well, I hadn't planned on telling you this, but I think the schnapps and wine are giving me courage," she began.

"Ooh, this sounds good already," Marie said, leaning in to listen.

"Don't laugh, okay? But I actually started writing a book."

"No way," Marie exclaimed. "That's great. But since when have you been interested in writing?"

"I've always loved mysteries and thrillers and that kind of thing."

Both her friends nodded, and Kendrick was comforted being in the presence of people who knew her so well.

"I don't know. Just thought I would try writing to see how it goes. I really like doing it. Kinda cathartic in a way. Similar to how I feel when I'm reading a good thriller. Takes my mind off things for a while."

Though she'd tried her best to keep her negative thoughts at bay, her mind drifted back to her sorrow over Silas and her brother. Over the years, she'd gotten used to the dull ache of life without Kurt, but the thought of losing Silas was raw and fresh.

Deanna and Marie watched her carefully.

"Holidays are still hard," Kendrick said at last. "But being with you guys makes it a lot better."

"We don't always know what to say," Deanna said cautiously. "But that doesn't mean we're not thinking of you."

Kendrick nodded. Her two best friends had been right by her side through Kurt's wake and funeral. They were scared, overwhelmed sixteen-year-olds just like she was, but they'd stayed strong for her sake. They rarely mentioned her brother anymore, but then again, neither did she. After a while, Kendrick just figured people didn't want to hear about him anymore.

"I know I'm not the same person I was before Kurt died," she said. The alcohol had dulled her senses, but it was also making her a bit weepy.

"Of course you're not," Marie said.

"Sometimes I feel like you expect me to be. I get the feeling everybody's like *It's been nine years. Get over it already.*"

"We would never say that," Marie said.

"Of course you wouldn't actually say that, but ..."

Marie lowered her head guiltily, and Deanna looked uncomfortable as well.

"But we've made you feel like that sometimes," Marie said, and Kendrick nodded.

"So hard to explain how I feel sometimes. Like some days, I'm fine. And then other days, I'll hear a song that reminds me of Kurt. Or I'll hear somebody say something that he might have said. And it's like ... it can knock the wind out of me. Just ... brings me to my knees, and I don't know how to keep going." Kendrick's eyes filled with tears as she spoke, and soon her friends were tearing up as well.

Wiping her eyes, she said, "I'm sorry. Didn't mean to put a damper on things. We can talk about something else."

"No," Deanna said gently. "I think it's important to talk about this. That's why we don't see much of you, isn't it? We make you feel like you can't talk about this. About Kurt."

Kendrick could see that even saying his name made Deanna wince. As if she was afraid of hurting her by speaking his name. She recalled Silas's words about being patient with the "non-bereaved." Maybe they didn't have any way of truly understanding what she was feeling, but that didn't mean they didn't care.

"It's okay to talk about him," Kendrick gently explained. "I actually like it. I think ... one of the things that scares me the most is people will forget him." Her voice trembled as she spoke. Fresh tears spilled down Deanna's cheeks.

"Oh, honey. Nobody will ever forget him," Deanna said. "But what you said about certain memories triggering your pain. I'm scared I'll do that to you if I talk about him."

Kendrick smiled gently at her. "I see what you mean. But speaking about him won't remind me that he died. Believe me, I never forget."

Deanna nodded.

"I am so sorry if we ever made you feel like you couldn't be open about your grief," Marie said. "As for me, I think it's pure selfishness on my part." She drew in a shaky breath. "He died so suddenly. He was here one day and then he was gone. I don't even remember the last thing I said to him. I don't like thinking about it, because if Kurt could die like that, anybody can. At any time. I have the luxury of putting it out of my mind because it wasn't my brother. Kendrick, I'm so sorry. I've always chickened out when you talk about him, so no wonder you've been avoiding me. I promise I will never do that to you again."

Marie reached over and squeezed her hand. "I want you to know you can talk to me about anything, okay? Always."

"Thank you," Kendrick responded, her voice nearly a whisper. She smiled. "I'm actually including him in my book. Well, a character based on him. I had him killed off. Murder victim."

Deanna and Marie giggled.

"Oh my God," Deanna said. "He would have *loved* that!"

"Yeah, he would," Marie agreed.

"Right?" Kendrick said, elated that her friends remembered Kurt so well. "I miss him so much."

"I know you do," Deanna said. Both women looked at her expectantly.

Kendrick laughed. "That's it! I don't have anything more profound to say. I miss my goofy-ass brother. Grief sucks."

Her friends laughed, and a sense of relief washed over her. She felt like she really could talk about Kurt the next time she felt the need to.

She took another sip of wine, allowing herself a few seconds to reorganize her thoughts and emotions. Her natural tendency was to focus on the negative, and it was still an effort to remember to think about the good stuff, too.

"How's Brody doing these days?" Kendrick asked Deanna, who smiled happily at the mention of her steady boyfriend. The two were very much in love, and it was pretty much a given that they'd get married. Likely after she got her Ph.D.

It wasn't long before Kendrick's mood began to lift again, and she found herself laughing with her friends once more. They discussed Brody, including some salacious details about his and Deanna's spicy sex life. The women huddled close and spoke in hushed tones so as not to scandalize the patrons of the family restaurant. Their raucous laughter drew some attention, however. They also talked about the hot guy at Marie's work. She had to make sure he was single and wasn't gay before she got too excited about the man.

"You know, Kendrick," Deanna said. "Brody has this friend who I think might be perfect for you."

"Oh, I don't know," she said, rolling her eyes. There was only one "perfect" guy for her. Nobody else would ever come close. Besides, she wouldn't even remotely entertain the idea of dating anyone else while Silas was still around. And probably not even after that, despite her promise to him to stay open-minded about the possibility.

"You sure? He's a really cool guy. Has a great government job. He's stable and steady, but also really fun, you know? He even likes to read!"

"Sorry. Just not interested."

"When was the last time you dated anyone?" Marie asked.

Kendrick sighed deeply. "I'm kinda seeing someone now."

As much as she didn't want to talk about her situation with Silas, she couldn't bear the idea of denying his existence.

"You are? Why didn't you tell us?" Marie asked.

"Who is he? Where did you meet him?" Deanna asked, looking excited and genuinely relieved. It was sweet to see how much her friends cared about her happiness.

"To say that it's hard to explain doesn't even begin to describe it. There's a reason that I hadn't planned on mentioning him to you guys. Ever."

Both women stared at her, understandably perplexed. It felt wonderful to have her friends back in her life, and the last thing she needed was for them to think she was crazy.

There was too much to explain, and they would never believe her. Besides, it hurt too much to talk about.

"Why? What's wrong with him? Does he treat you badly?" Marie's eyes flashed as she spoke. One of her old college boyfriends used to hit her, and it had taken a while for her to safely get away from that relationship.

"Nothing like that. I promise."

"Okay," she said quietly, still looking worried.

"There are things about him I just can't tell you. I have my reasons," she said, pleading with her eyes for her friends to understand. They both nodded uncertainly. "It has nothing to do with the way he treats me. He's wonderful. Gentle. Kind. The type of guy who's nice to everybody. And he gets me in a way nobody else ever has. He's lost somebody, too. More than one person, actually. I don't have to explain my grief to him because he knows."

"What's his name?" Deanna asked.

"Silas," she said with reverence.

"Unusual name," Marie said.

"Yeah well, he's an unusual man." Kendrick had to draw in a deep breath to steady herself. "I love him, and he loves me. He is *the* one. My soulmate. I really believe that. But sooner or later, we're not sure when, he's going to have to go away. And he won't be coming back."

Deanna opened her mouth to speak, but Kendrick held up her hand to silence her. She had to get through this fast or she would break down.

"I'm begging you. Please. Don't ask me any questions about it, okay? We knew from the beginning that it was over before it began. That we had no future together. That's why I wasn't going to say anything. I was gonna just try to deal with it all on my own, but now I'm kind of glad that I said something. All I can tell you is that when Silas leaves, I am going to completely fall apart."

Her eyes filled with tears. Marie covered her mouth, looking overcome with emotion at the intensity of Kendrick's raw grief. Deanna gazed at Kendrick with deep sadness.

"When that happens—when he goes away for good—I'm really gonna need to lean on you. No questions asked. Can you do that?"

"Kendrick, I promise you we will be right by your side for whatever you need," Marie said, reaching over to take her hand.

"Of course we will," Deanna affirmed.

"And I will do my best to respect your wishes," Marie continued. "But can you at least tell me, like... is this guy married or something?"

"Oh no. Nothing like that. There's no other woman or anything like that. It's just circumstances beyond our control," Kendrick said.

"Is he in the CIA? The Witness Protection Program?" Marie asked. Kendrick shot her a weary look. "Sorry, sorry. I can't help but be curious."

"I understand. I really do. It's just really complicated, and you wouldn't believe me if I told you."

"I promise we'll believe you," Marie exclaimed.

Kendrick sighed deeply but said nothing.

"Kendrick," Deanna said as she took hold of her hand while Marie still gripped her other one. "Of course we'll respect your wishes."

"Yes," Marie said firmly. "No more questions. I promise. We'll be there for you. No matter what. Okay, I lied. One more question but it's not intrusive, and I swear it's the last one."

"What?" Kendrick asked a bit testily.

"Do you have any idea of *when* Silas is going away?"

"Not really. But I will tell you that's the reason I haven't moved away yet. I gave up that job in Newport News because I'm not leaving Williamsburg until he does."

"Got it," Marie said with a quick nod of her head. "Whenever it happens, you just say the word and we'll be there to help you through it."

"Thank you," Kendrick whispered. She squeezed each woman's hand once before letting go.

"Thank you for letting us back in your life, Kendrick," Deanna said. "We've really missed you."

Kendrick smiled, feeling a little stronger knowing that her friends had her back.

13

Silas wandered the battlefield alone after dark, thinking of Kendrick, hoping she was having a good time with her friends. He worried about her more and more these days. The way she was putting her entire future on hold was awful. Perhaps her friends would encourage her to make that move to Newport News as she had planned. The best thing for Kendrick might be to reconnect with her old friends while also making new ones when she moved away. The idea of being without her was torture, but he reminded himself he likely wouldn't feel that pain if he crossed over. After having witnessed other souls move on, he truly believed there was no more pain and suffering where they went.

Which was why he was roaming around the battlefield, redoubling his efforts to cross over for Kendrick's sake if not for his own. Trouble was, he had no real inkling of what to do to make it finally happen after all these years.

Tonight, he would start where it all began—or ended, depending on how he looked at it. Silas visited the cluster of trees where he had died all those years ago and sat down underneath. He was still for quite some time, immersing himself in the silence. Since he couldn't possibly atone for the sins he'd committed in life in a physical way, he figured the answer must somehow come from within him. Sitting in the dark, he waited for inspiration or an epiphany to strike that would show him the way home.

After a while, he felt frustrated. Stupid, even. What had he expected to happen? Divine intervention?

Start at the beginning, he told himself. *Why are you still here?*

The answer was the same as it had been since the day he'd crawled under a tree and died.

Because I don't deserve to go to Heaven.

He'd learned one thing from the spirits who had gone before him: you couldn't make it to Heaven until you felt that you deserved to go there. He'd witnessed so many perfectly good men and women holding themselves back from paradise, believing they were not worthy. But that was different. In his case, he really didn't deserve to be at peace. But that's what each of those earthbound spirits thought as well.

Start at the beginning.

Silas suffered greatly the day he had died and had been suffering for some time. That constant, raw hunger he'd lived with day in and day out for so long had rendered him desperately weak, so that when he fell ill, he'd had little chance of survival. Yellow fever had ravaged his body, making his head and muscles ache. Worst of all was when he'd vomited up blood. At that moment, he realized he would likely die soon, and the thought had terrified him. The battle raged around him. Bullets flew, chaos reigned. He'd been entirely useless to his unit during that day's battle as he'd barely had the strength to stand. No one took notice when he staggered toward the trees all alone. His last thoughts were of his mother before he collapsed and died.

He thought back on that pitiable man who'd died all alone of a terrible, frightening illness. Had Silas witnessed such suffering in anyone else, he would have felt deeply for them. No matter what their crimes in life, nobody deserved such an ending. Perhaps he was too hard on himself. If his beloved mother and father and his precious siblings had made the same mistakes he had, surely he would have forgiven them. Kendrick still had occasional bouts of anger toward Kurt for having been reckless with his life, but Silas knew she had forgiven him. His family had likely forgiven him as well. Why was it so hard to forgive himself?

Kendrick had shed tears of fear and anguish, worrying that her dear brother could be a lonely spirit too. Stuck between worlds like Silas was. Surely, his own family would not wish this kind of existence on him. Why did he wish it on himself?

Then he did have an epiphany of sorts. Or at least an idea that might help him with his plight.

Kurt, he pleaded inwardly with his heart. *If you're there. If you are in Heaven and at peace, at one with the angels. I beg of you, please help me. Don't do it for me. Do it for Kendrick. Though I'll never understand why, she loves me. She'll be broken when I am gone, but I must leave. I cannot have her delay her own life, have her stay with me and my hopeless existence. She cannot—will not—move on while I am still here. Please help me to go so that I can set her free.*

In the stillness, Silas felt something stir deep in his soul. He somehow felt—knew for *certain*—that Kurt Banner had heard his cry for help. It was as if he could feel a connection with the boy, similar to the way he felt connected to Kendrick on a deeply spiritual level.

Silas let out a choked cry of emotion that was nearly a sob. But it was a cry of euphoria, not sorrow.

He's all right. I know it. Kurt is at home. At peace. Surrounded by love and joy and light.

Knowing the relief and elation Kendrick would feel at this knowledge made him happier than he could ever remember feeling.

And he felt as if he'd just taken one giant step toward crossing over.

∼

Silas sat with Kendrick at lunchtime the following Monday. At his insistence, they'd moved to a bench across the street from Market Square. It was slightly less private than their usual spot since there were more people walking by, but Silas didn't want her sitting on the cold ground.

"Did you have a good time with your friends?" Silas asked hopefully, watching Kendrick bite into her sandwich.

She nodded and swallowed before she answered. "I did, Silas. I really did. I'd intended to just go shopping with them for a little while, but we were having so much fun, we went out for some food and drinks after. It felt good to see them again. I honestly didn't realize how much I'd missed them, and I'd forgotten how much fun they can be. Funny how quickly we just fall back into our old ways when we get together." She smiled fondly as she spoke. "We get to talking and laughing like we did in high school."

"I'm so glad to hear you say that," Silas said.

"We even talked about Kurt. I was all emotional. Even more than usual, with the help of alcohol. I told them how I felt, and I think they kinda knew they were pushing me away, even if it wasn't intentional. They said I could talk to them about anything now, and that they'd be supportive."

Kendrick drew in a deep breath and let it out slowly. "It certainly helps to talk to people who knew him. It means so much to me to know they haven't forgotten him."

"Of course they haven't," Silas said.

"I mentioned you, too. Didn't give them any details about your situation, of course. They were talking about setting me up with some guy, and I wasn't about to do that."

Another way I'm holding her back.

As much as he truly wanted her to be happy, Silas didn't want to think about her being with another man. Not until he had left the planet, anyway.

"I wish I could tell them everything about you."

"Then why don't you?" Silas asked. Plenty of times he'd wished he could tell others the truth: that he was dead. But he couldn't without terrorizing people in the process, which was the last thing he wanted.

"They would think I was crazy."

"At first, maybe. But it's easy enough to prove. All they'd have to do is try to touch me. Then they'd know for sure you weren't crazy."

"I guess so. I don't know. I like keeping you to myself. I did tell them you would have to go away at some point and you'd be gone for good. Didn't tell them why, and I told them they weren't allowed to ask about it. But I said that when it happens, I'm gonna have a complete breakdown and I'm gonna need their support."

"Do you think they'll be there for you when the time comes?"

"I know they will," Kendrick said confidently. "No question."

"Good," Silas said, feeling immensely relieved. "I hate the thought of you dealing with it all alone."

"I went out because you forced me too, but I wound up being really glad I did. As usual, you know what's best for me better than I do."

"Sometimes you just need somebody who loves you to look out for you." Silas paused for a moment. "You're gonna be okay, Kendrick. No matter what happens with me. You're so much stronger than you know. You have your friends to lean on and your family. I truly believe you have a bright future ahead of you, even without me."

Kendrick closed her eyes and swallowed hard.

"You're stronger than you know," he repeated softly.

"Thank you, Silas. You're looking out for me, like always. I wish I could return the favor, but I feel pretty useless when it comes to helping you."

"But you have helped me, Kendrick. I think you were really on to somethin' when you told me to try to talk to the people I wronged. I wasn't sure at first, but the more I do it, the more it seems to help. Spent most of my week working on that. And I feel better. I really do."

"That's great," she said, her eyes shining.

"Tried talking to my family and all of that. You know what else I did? I tried talking to Kurt."

A sweet smile played on her lips. "I love that you did that, Silas."

"I honestly feel like he heard me, Kendrick. I really think he was listening to me."

She nodded, looking pleased but not necessarily convinced.

"You don't believe me?"

"It's not that I don't believe you. It's just that you don't *know* that he heard you. You feel like he did. I feel that way too, sometimes. Like I can feel his presence," she said wistfully. "There are times when it feels like he's standing right next to me. I'd love to believe it's real."

"But you don't."

"I can't be sure, that's all," she said sadly. "But I think it's wonderful that you tried to reach out to him. That means a lot to me, and I really hope it helps you."

Kendrick sighed.

"Time for you to go back to work, isn't it?"

She nodded wearily. "I hate leaving."

"I know. I'll see you tomorrow, my sweet."

"Keep up the good work, Silas," she said as they stood up. You're doing great. And say hi to my brother for me."

"I surely will."

With a sad smile, she turned and walked away.

14

Kendrick continued to meet with Silas daily during her lunch breaks, despite the considerably colder weather. She hated the chill of winter, but she never complained. She did her best to hide her discomfort from Silas lest he suggest they stop meeting until it got warmer again. Every moment with him felt precious, and she didn't want to lose any time with him.

Silas wasn't stupid, though. He could see her shivering and could tell by the bundled-up tourists that it was quite cold out. The weather did mean fewer people out on the streets, so they had more privacy to talk.

Christmas came and went. Kendrick missed Silas, but she had a lovely visit with her family during the holidays. She continued to see Deanna and Marie as well, which made her happy.

One day in January, Kendrick found Silas looking especially somber as he sat on the bench waiting for her. Her heart dropped as panic gripped her.

What if he's ready to cross over? Is this goodbye?

As if this week wasn't hard enough already. Kendrick

wanted him to cross over, of course. She wanted what was best for him. That didn't mean she wouldn't be utterly destroyed when it happened.

"Are you all right?" she asked, feeling shaky as she sat down on the cold bench beside him.

"Yeah," he said quietly. "I know what today is, Kendrick."

"Oh," she said, letting out a sigh of relief. "You looked so serious, I was afraid that—"

She stopped herself before she said something she'd regret. Silas would never let go of his ghostly existence if he was too worried about her. She needed to encourage his transition, not hinder it.

Today was January 10th. The date that was forever ingrained in her mind as the day her whole life turned upside down.

"Are you okay?" he asked, his brown eyes filled with concern.

"Yes, I'm doing okay, I guess. Thank you so much for remembering. I barely even remember mentioning the date to you," she said, genuinely touched at his kindness.

Kendrick took a moment to steady her nerves, still on edge after her brief scare about losing Silas. She'd done her best to prepare for that eventuality, but times like this made her realize she wasn't ready. She would never be ready. It truly did feel like Silas had a terminal illness. You knew ahead of time what's going to happen, but that didn't mean you would ever be emotionally prepared when it did.

"Ten years now," Kendrick said. She'd had no time to prepare for Kurt's death, and that really had been worse.

"Does it feel like it's been that long?"

"It's weird. Sometimes it feels like it. Then other times the pain is so raw, it might as well have happened yesterday. I will say that as the years go by, the anniversary of his death does get a tiny bit better. First two years were just ... awful. And yet, it feels wrong that I'm in my mid-twenties and he'll always be sixteen."

Silas nodded, watching her intently. It reminded her of the day they'd met, the way he was willing to hear about things nobody else wanted to talk about.

"I kind of dread the seventeenth anniversary, you know? When he will have been dead longer than he was alive."

"I can understand that," Silas said gently. After a moment, he asked, "Are you mad at him?"

"Why would I be mad at him?"

"You mentioned before that sometimes you feel angry with him for being so careless with his life. Are you still angry?"

The sudden flash of fury that shot through her took her by surprise. During this, the toughest week of the whole year, Kendrick realized she was angrier with Kurt than she had thought. One stupid decision on his part had sentenced her to a lifetime of grief. Sure, the razor-edge of grief had softened over time, but it was still there in the shadows of every birthday, every holiday, every milestone he missed. Damn right she was mad.

And yet, she had to take care with her response. Silas wasn't asking only out of concern for her. He was really asking if she thought his family had forgiven *him*.

"I guess sometimes I'm still mad," she said, struggling to calm her emotions.

"Tell me the truth, Kendrick. I really want to know how you're feeling."

Tears welled up in her eyes, both from anger and from the sheer beauty of having somebody who loved her and who understood her so well. Silas could tell when she was holding back, and dear God how she loved him for that.

"I am angry sometimes," she said, finally allowing her tears to fall freely. "He wasn't driving that night. My parents are still so goddamned pissed at the kid who was behind the wheel, but I'm not. Because I know good and goddamn well the same thing might have happened if Kurt had been driving. He was just as dumb and reckless as his friends. They were all being equally stupid. And Kurt wasn't wearing his fucking seatbelt."

Her hands shook with rage that she hadn't even known she'd had until that moment. Most of the time, she'd felt disloyal to her brother and disrespectful to the dead to be angry, *but she was mad as hell.*

"I *always* told him to wear his seatbelt. One time, he wanted me to drop him off at a friend's house, and he was sitting in the front seat. He wouldn't put his belt on, so I drove a few feet away and then jammed on the brakes and he slammed into the dashboard," she said with a bitter laugh. "He was like 'What the fuck, Kendrick?' And I said, *'Put on your seatbelt!'* And he did. He always did when he was with me. But I wasn't there to talk some sense into him that night. The other boys might have been stupid and reckless too, but they were wearing their belts. Those two guys are twenty-six years old now, and Kurt's in the ground."

Kendrick put her face in her hands and began to sob quietly. She felt a cold sensation on her back that was somehow still warm because it was Silas trying to comfort her. After calming down and wiping her eyes, she turned to face him.

"I guess I am a lot madder at Kurt than I realized. But I still love him. And I forgive him. I really do. If nothing else, I want him to be up in Heaven so I can give him hell when I get there," she said with a laugh.

"Good point." Silas looked relieved to hear her laugh again.

"Thanks again for remembering today. My friends remembered too. Both Marie and Deanna texted me to say they were thinking of me. Both of 'em said they didn't want to call in case I didn't feel like talking, but they wanted me to know they remembered. I'm glad they knew him, you know?"

"I wish I could have known him."

Kendrick smiled. "He woulda liked you."

"You think?"

"Definitely. Would have had a field day with sexual innuendos every time you and I were in the same room together," she said with a laugh. Then, her voice nearly a whisper, she added, "You'll probably see him before I do."

"I really might," Silas said. His words sounded like a warning.

"You think it's gonna be soon, don't you?" Kendrick asked, her stomach filling with dread.

Silas nodded slowly. "My sweet, the last thing I want to do is add to your pain right now ... but yes. I don't know why exactly, but yes. I have the feeling my time is coming soon. Very soon."

"Okay." Kendrick felt numb. It was all too much right now. Too much to process. There would be plenty of time for that later.

"I'm so sorry," Silas said mournfully.

"Don't be," she told him. "Please, whatever you do, don't hold yourself back for my sake. If you have a chance to cross over, grab it. I mean it, Silas."

Kendrick picked up her phone and sent a text message to her boss.

"I'm telling my work that I'm not feeling well, and I'll be

out for the rest of the day." She laughed weakly. "And it is the truth. Feel like I'm gonna throw up, even though I haven't eaten anything in a while."

Kendrick glanced distastefully at her brown lunch bag before tossing it in the trash.

"Let's walk for a while, Silas."

They spent the rest of the afternoon together, wandering around the historical district. It was a quiet, wintry day. No outdoor markets, little foot traffic. It felt as if they had the world to themselves. They talked about life and death as they frequently did, and they even shared a few laughs. There were even some moments where it was possible to forget the future for a while. Brief instants when they were just two people in love, strolling around, enjoying the day. But those moments didn't last, and all too soon the darkness of reality crept in.

Literal darkness fell, leaving Kendrick little choice but to call it a night. She was tempted to stay with him. To walk and talk for as long as possible, until God reached down and ripped Silas away from her. But of course, Silas would have none of it.

"You have to go home now, Kendrick. Go home to your warm bed and rest."

"I don't want to."

"I know, my love. But it's cold and dark. You can't stay with me."

His words hung heavily between them.

"I know."

Silas walked with her to the Visitor Center parking lot.

"I don't know what else to say, Kendrick. Except that I love you. Forever and always."

"I love you too, Silas," she said, feeling too wrung out to cry. "Forever and always."

Silas blew her a kiss, and then he did something he rarely did. He disappeared.

Kendrick knew he was still there. She could feel his presence. But she respected his wishes by getting into the car and driving off.

The next day, when she arrived at their usual spot in Colonial Williamsburg, she stood still and simply stared.

The bench was empty.

15

———

Kendrick went to their usual spot in Colonial Williamsburg every day that week, but there was no sign of Silas. She'd sink down onto the bench, hardly feeling the cold, hard wood and the chill of the wind whipping around her, still and alone for the entirety of every lunch break. Though she desperately hoped Silas would show, deep in her heart she knew he wouldn't. Feeling numb, she would manage to stagger back to her car and drive back to work on autopilot. Each time, she'd weep in the car as she drove back to work.

The numbness of his loss began to subside, making way for the raw pain she'd known was coming. The intensity of her grief was horrible and yet so familiar. But ten years ago, nobody went back to work or school the next day, pretending that life was normal after Kurt died. Her mother had taken a leave of absence from work, and Kendrick couldn't remember how long she had been out of school. At least a week, maybe two. This time around, nobody in her family knew that Silas had even existed, so nobody knew what she was going through. Her soulmate, her true love, her best friend was gone. It was as if she had gone to the hospital to visit her sick husband only to be told he had died, then she had to go back to work and regular life like nothing had happened.

Perhaps it was a mercy that she'd lost Silas on the anniversary of the day she'd lost Kurt. Those who knew about Kurt would understand why she wasn't herself around this time of year. She wouldn't have to pretend she was all right every time the awful date approached.

Kendrick somehow made it through the week, though she'd been a complete wreck. Several coworkers at the law firm noticed the dark circles under her eyes and asked if she was all right. Even Sweet Pregnant Lady expressed her concern while shopping at Milligan's on Friday evening.

"I'll be all right," was Kendrick's reply to anyone who asked. She refused to say "I *am* all right," because she sure as hell wasn't. Her tone made it clear that she wasn't about to elaborate on her problems, but she did thank everyone who asked about her welfare. Their kindness and concern brought her some measure of comfort.

After wrapping up her Friday night shift at Milligan's, Kendrick went to the battlefield, even though she knew Silas wouldn't have wanted her to go there. It was pitch black out and the frigid January air burned her throat and lungs. Worst of all was the risk of visiting the battlefield with no one there to help her if she suffered another phantom gunshot wound. She found it hard to care about the danger. In her despair, she wouldn't have cared if someone shot her dead for real. Might end her pain once and for all. Or she might wind up as a ghost, wandering for centuries all alone.

Kendrick first went toward the tree where she used to sit and talk with Silas. A strangled cry escaped her throat when she saw the tablet still stuck in the crevice where she'd left it. There was no way it would still work after enduring the wintry weather for so long. Hugging it to her chest, her silent tears fell.

Gripping the tablet and the electric lantern, Kendrick made her way toward the river. The wind near the water was even colder, chilling her to her bones. The temperature had been hovering near the 30s, below average for Virginia.

It figures. Why should anything be easy?

She set the lantern down so she could wrap her arms around herself in a feeble attempt to warm up. She was half tempted to hurl the useless tablet into the water, but there was no sense in polluting the river that Silas had loved so much.

Silas would be so mad at me if he knew I was here.

Kendrick could practically hear him demanding she go home and get in her warm bed. The thought made her smile. She closed her eyes and breathed in deeply. Concentrating hard, she held onto a shred of hope that Silas was still here. She really had wanted him to cross over and to be at peace, but now that he was gone, the pain was so intense she just wanted it to stop. She wondered if this was how people felt when a loved one finally passed away after a long and painful illness. Relief at first that their wife or husband was no longer in pain, but then the reality of their loss set in.

Try as she might, Kendrick could not feel Silas's presence.

"I can't be selfish," she said out loud. "I hope you're all right, Silas. I truly hope you're at peace. And I hope you're with Kurt now."

Kendrick's voice cracked as she spoke, and warm tears spilled down her cold cheeks.

Glancing skyward, she said, "You two behave yourselves until I get there, okay?"

Though the thought of Silas and Kurt being together in Heaven brought her a measure of comfort, the heaviness of their absence crashed down hard as she made her way back to her car in the dark. Not since Kurt's wake had she experienced such brutal devastation. That moment when she'd fixated on his scar and the reality of his death had slammed into her with blunt force. She'd understood then that Kurt wasn't coming back.

And neither was Silas.

THE DRIVE HOME from the battlefield was treacherous. Kendrick was sobbing so hard that she'd had to pull over twice in order to compose herself. The second time, she'd been so distraught and distracted that she'd nearly slammed into the car in front of her at a stoplight. Most frightening of all, she'd found it hard to care if she survived the drive home. She'd known then that she was in a dangerous, vulnerable place and had to get ahold of herself.

After the near accident, she moved onto the shoulder of the road to try to pull herself together. As her thoughts and emotions threatened to spin completely out of control, thinking of Silas helped to center her. He would not want this for her. He would want her to take good care of herself. In this bleak moment, it was difficult for Kendrick to give a damn whether she lived or died, but she did care about other people. Good God, what would happen to her parents if she died in a car accident just like their son?

It would destroy them completely.

Silas had spent hundreds of years regretting what his death had done to his family, and Kendrick wasn't about to make that same mistake. That, and she reminded herself it was okay to practice some self-care right now.

Quit being a goddamn martyr.

Perhaps it had been a mistake to force herself to work at both her jobs this week. She had sick days she could use at the law firm, and there was no reason not to use them. Kendrick decided she could call in sick all next week. It would actually be bereavement leave, but nobody there needed to know that.

The time had come to call in the cavalry for some more assistance. Kendrick was afraid she wouldn't be able to speak coherently on the phone, so she texted Deanna and Marie and told them she needed them to come to her apartment right away. She rolled down the windows and cautiously drove the rest of the way home. The cold air kept her alert and focused.

Marie showed up at her place about a half hour later. Her eyes flew open wide, and she gasped when Kendrick opened the door.

"Kendrick? What's wrong?"

"He's gone." She couldn't summon the strength to say anything more.

It took Marie a few seconds to register her words.

"Oh," she said quietly. A crease formed on her forehead. No doubt she wanted to ask what the hell happened to this mysterious guy, but she held her tongue. Instead, she walked into the apartment. Placing a hand on Kendrick's back, she gently led her into the living room and sat down on the couch with her.

A short while later, there was another knock on the door.

"That's probably Deanna," Kendrick said.

Marie nodded and got up to answer the door. Kendrick

heard the women speaking in hushed tones for a moment before they came into the living room together.

Deanna sat down next to Kendrick and pulled her into a hug. "Everything's gonna be okay," she said. She released her, and the three sat together on the couch.

"I know you don't want us to ask any questions," Deanna said. "And we won't."

"Right," Marie said with a firm nod.

"But it is a little hard to know what to say to help you since we don't know anything about what's going on. Still, we're here for whatever you need."

"Thank you," Kendrick said wearily. She'd cried so much and so hard that she was out of tears, at least for the moment. "I don't even know what I need right now."

Silas. That's what I need.

Her friends gazed at her with such deep concern that she felt the tears already threatening to return. What a tough situation Kendrick had put them in. They were supposed to provide love and comfort without having any real clue about what the hell was going on. And yet, here they were anyway. Kendrick loved them so damned much.

"I might not know exactly what's happening," Deanna said. "But one thing I know for sure is that you're a survivor. I know you're in terrible pain right now, but you will get through this. I've seen you do it before. Somehow, you made it out of the darkness when Kurt died. Might not feel like it now, but there will be light again."

Kendrick laughed gently. "That's what Silas told me. To never stop searching for the light."

She pictured Silas walking toward the light of Heaven and felt comforted by the notion. He'd said that when spirits crossed over, he could tell by the joy on their faces that they were going somewhere incredible that was beyond our understanding.

If Silas and Kurt were together now in that place of perfect love and peace, then any amount of pain Kendrick endured was worth it. That thought made her feel slightly stronger. Given the choice, she would gladly be the one left behind to suffer, as long as they were all right.

"We'll stay with you as long as you want," Marie said. "Do you need anything? Are you hungry?"

"No, I don't think I could eat right now. I could use a drink, that's for sure. I've got some wine and other stuff in the kitchen."

"On it!" Marie said, jumping up.

"Tell us what else we can do," Deanna said. "I'm just not sure. It's like, if the guy dumped you, we would sit here and trash talk him all night, but ..."

Kendrick laughed. "You're right."

"And if you dumped him, we'd be all like, there's plenty of fish in the sea!" she said so perkily that it made Kendrick laugh again.

"I know. I'm not making this easy on you guys." She sighed. "I guess distraction is what I need right now. This is just one of those things where there's really nothing anybody can do to fix the situation, so taking my mind off it is all we can do."

"Okay," Deanna said, sounding more confident, having some instruction on how to proceed. She grabbed the remote and turned on the TV. They both called out when they caught sight of one of their favorite comedy movies while she scanned the channels.

"Perfect," Kendrick said. The flick was truly perfect—funny with lots of quotable lines and devoid of romance.

Marie came in with the wine and glasses, and they settled in to watch the movie. When that film ended, they found another good one to watch. Between the funny films and alcohol, Kendrick was able to laugh, which provided the small ray of light that Silas had always urged her to reach out for. She still felt terrible, but no longer totally alone and despairing.

Kendrick drank way too much and she knew she would probably be sick in the morning, but it was hard to care. Alcohol dulled her pain for the moment, and she welcomed the relief.

Sure enough, she woke up the next morning with a dry mouth and a queasy stomach. It took her a moment to figure out where she was. Squinting at the bright light of morning, she realized she'd slept on the couch. She heard someone moving in the kitchen.

"Deanna?"

"Yeah, I'm here." She walked into the living room with a tall glass of ice water. "Marie's here too. In the bathroom."

Kendrick gratefully accepted the water and gulped half the glass. "Aw, man. You guys didn't have to stay over."

"We certainly did," Deanna said, "considering how much you drank. We had to make sure you were okay."

"I'm fine," she said, sitting up on the couch. Her head began to clear. It would be a little while before she was ready to eat anything, but other than that, she didn't feel too bad. She'd had far worse hangovers.

"Are you all right?" her friend asked.

"Yeah," she said weakly as a fresh wave of grief washed over her. She recalled that horrible feeling after her brother's accident. For days, weeks, even months afterward, she would wake each morning and remember all over again that Kurt was dead. Now it was happening again.

Deanna eyed her cautiously. She seemed even more worried now than she had been last night.

Marie came in from the hallway. "You're awake," she said with false cheerfulness. She, too, seemed quite concerned. "How are you doing?"

"I'm okay, I guess. I'm sorry you guys got stuck here last night. You don't have to hang around. I'm sure you've got stuff to do today."

Marie sat in one of the living room chairs, and Deanna perched on the couch next to Kendrick. Neither seemed to be in any hurry to leave. They stared at her.

"What?" Kendrick asked, suddenly feeling self-conscious.

"I know you don't want us to ask you anything," Deanna said. "But I have to at least ask ... This guy, Silas. He didn't kill himself, did he?"

"What? No! What makes you ask that?"

"We know he died, Kendrick," Deanna said.

"How did you—"

"You were *really* drunk last night, hon," she said. "You were crying really hard, and you kept saying 'He's dead, he's dead, he's gone.'"

Oh no ...

Her stomach roiled with fresh nausea. She grabbed the ice water and downed the rest of it.

"We figured if he had some kind of terminal illness or something, you would have told us," Marie said. "All we know is this guy died, and you obviously knew he was gonna die."

"You're not in some kind of legal trouble, are you?" Deanna asked nervously.

"No. Nothing like that."

"Then, Kendrick, what in hell is going on?" Deanna

demanded. "We're trying to respect your wishes here, but you're really freaking us out."

"We've never had secrets between us," Marie said, sounding hurt. "Why start now?"

"You know you can trust us," Deanna said, equally wounded.

Kendrick groaned deep in her throat. She realized at this point she had absolutely nothing to lose by being honest. And yes, she did know she could trust them.

"It's not that I don't want to tell you," she said. "It's that you won't believe me."

"Of course we'll believe you," Deanna exclaimed.

Kendrick scoffed. "You say that now. Once I tell you, you'll probably try to have me committed."

Both Deanna and Marie stared at her eagerly. She had to give her friends credit. They had been incredibly patient with her. But now that they already knew Silas was dead, she might as well tell them the truth about him. Otherwise, they might think he was in the mafia or something.

"All right. Fine. You win. I don't like talking about it, but you guys know that I go ghost hunting sometimes, right?"

Both women nodded. Though they'd listened politely when she'd talked about her ghost hunts, Kendrick got the feeling that they thought it was silly, that they didn't believe in ghosts.

"Silas is dead. He was dead when I met him. He's a ghost."

Deanna and Marie stared at her silently.

"After Kurt died, I guess I wanted to find some kind of reassurance that there was life after death. That my brother wasn't gone forever, and that maybe I'd see him again."

"That makes sense," Marie said gently.

"That's why I was looking for ghosts. I can sense the

presence of spirits. Always could. I can't explain it; I just get this weird feeling when a ghost is around, and now I've got the ghost-detecting equipment. I'm almost always right when I get that feeling. My thermal camera confirms it. Anyway, turns out ghosts aren't just orbs and mists and flashes of light caught on film. They can look just like anyone else. If you didn't know any better, you would think they were alive. You can't tell the difference. Well, I can. Usually, I get this sensation of death when ..."

Her friends continued to stare. Kendrick plowed ahead.

"So anyway, ghosts can look just like the living, only they're wearing the clothes they died in, so they can kinda stick out if they died a long time ago. But in a tourist district like Colonial Williamsburg, they can pass as reenactors and most people don't know the difference." She drew in a deep breath and let it out. "Silas was a Revolutionary soldier. He died in the Battle of Yorktown. Wears—or wore—a soldier's uniform, tricorn hat, the whole deal. We met during a ghost hunt, and we fell in love. He's been wandering, mostly alone, since he died in 1781. I tried ... I wanted to help him cross over ..."

Kendrick knew her words must have sounded stupid and crazy and unbelievable. But every word was true, and it hurt like hell to talk about it.

"I always knew I would lose him. Someday he would cross over and leave forever. I—I—I just hope he's with Kurt now," she managed to say before breaking down in sobs. Wiping her tears, she kept her head down so she wouldn't have to look at her friends who probably thought she was nuts. "It's—it's funny. I told Silas about you two, and he said I should tell you about him. While he was still around, it would have been easy to prove I was telling the truth. All you'd have to do is try to touch him. Your hand would go right through his body, and you'd see for yourself he was dead. Too late now. He's gone."

Grabbing some tissues, she wiped her eyes and tried to steady herself before facing Deanna and Marie. At last, she lifted her head.

Neither of them spoke. If they thought she was out of her mind, they hid it well. Mostly, they just looked worried.

"Silas and I used to meet up every day in Colonial Williamsburg. I'd drive over on my lunch hour and we would sit and talk. Always had to stay far enough away from the tourists so nobody would accidentally touch him. That used to make him sad. He loved talking to people, and tourists liked to interact with him because they thought he worked there, you know, playing a soldier." Kendrick thought back over all the conversations they had shared. "I could talk to him about anything. But with him being dead and me being alive, we knew there was no hope for us to stay together. So I decided to try to help finally set his spirit free. He'd been stuck here long enough. I wanted to help him make it to Heaven. It's funny. He sure helped me. Helped me see things ... life ... differently. He showed me how to focus on what I did have instead of always dwelling on what I had lost. I doubt I helped him much at all really, but somehow, he made it anyway. Silas knew his time was coming. He could feel it. He warned me that it might be soon. And then, one day I went to our usual spot during lunchtime and he wasn't there. Of all days ... January 10th was the last time I saw him."

"That must have been really hard for you," Deanna said. "When you realized he wasn't coming back."

She couldn't tell if Deanna believed her wild tale or if she was simply humoring her, but she appreciated her words, nonetheless. She spoke softly in her best therapist voice; she was an expert in psychology after all.

"Silas and I always talked about how it felt like he had a terminal illness. We always knew it was only a matter of time. But when it happens, no matter how much you were expecting it, you're never really ready. I'm not sorry I met him. Even now, even with all this pain. But still, I don't think I'll ever understand why I met my soulmate only to have him taken away from me."

"I can't imagine what you're going through," Deanna said. Marie remained silent, her expression tight.

"Do you actually believe what I'm telling you?"

"Yes."

"You do?"

"Kendrick, I've known you for a long time. You're a stable person. If anybody else told me something like this, I probably would think they were crazy. But you're not crazy. And you're not a liar, and you're not some attention-seeking drama queen. I have no reason to doubt anything you say."

Deanna gazed at her with love and concern.

"I don't blame you if you don't believe me," Kendrick said to Marie. "I don't know what I would think if I was in your shoes. All I can do is swear that everything I've said is true."

Marie stared at Kendrick for a moment, and then whispered, "I believe you."

"Really?"

"Not gonna lie," Marie said, shaking her head, "this whole thing sounds totally insane. But you can't fake the kind of pain you're in. Last night ... My God, Kendrick. You were so upset. And you were way too drunk to have had any kind of filter."

To Kendrick's surprise, Marie's eyes filled with tears.

"The way you were crying and wailing. It was just like when you totally lost it at Kurt's viewing." Marie's voice shook with emotion. "Nobody should have to go through something like that, never mind going through it twice. Oh honey, I'm so sorry." She got up from her chair and rushed over to the couch, pulling Kendrick into a hug. Soon, all three of them were hugging and crying.

Kendrick's grief was raw and piercing and horrible. It would be a long time before she felt close to normal again.

But at least she wasn't alone.

16

Kendrick took the week off from work as she had planned. It helped to have that time to simply rest her mind, heart, and soul without having to pretend that her life wasn't utterly shattered. After that, she did her best to press on. She began searching for a job in Newport News now that there was nothing keeping her in Colonial Williamsburg. Besides, she believed being close to her parents and far away from all the painful memories would help. Silas wanted her to move on with her life, and knowing that gave her some measure of strength.

No stranger to grief, she knew the drill. When her brother had died, she'd read lots of books on coping with loss. Life would never go back to normal. She learned that she wouldn't be the same person after suffering a devastating loss, nor should she expect to be. Most importantly, she wouldn't *want* to be the same person. The new Kendrick would be stronger and wiser, and it was good to embrace that rather than fight it.

Many of those books referred to this unique type of

suffering as "grief work." She'd always liked that because it described how it felt.

These days, getting out of bed took a huge effort. Grief wasn't just something that happened to a person. It was something they frequently had to work through. Kendrick learned to be patient with herself, reminding herself to take everything one step at a time. She worked hard at healing her heart, partly because she knew that was what Silas would have wanted for her.

As she went about her daily life, Silas was never far from her mind. She hoped he was at peace, and she wondered if he was watching over her. She knew for sure that he loved her, forever and always, as he had promised. Knowing that helped immensely.

Kendrick had her good days and her bad days. There were times when the darkness of grief threatened to swallow her whole, but she never stopped searching for the light. The light of hope.

The wintry weather gradually fell away, and springtime made its return. Her search for a job in the Newport News area had been half-hearted; she hadn't found anything yet. Kendrick still visited the riverbank on the edge of the York-town Battlefield. Several times, Kendrick felt an other-worldly presence nearby. However, she'd learned not to get too excited about it. Hundreds of men had died on that battlefield, so it could be any number of spirits she was sens-ing. Over time, she'd stopped hoping that Silas would suddenly appear. He was gone for good, and she had to accept it.

Sitting by the water's edge made her feel at one with nature. It made her feel closer to Silas. She still grieved for him deeply, but watching the river made her think she might actually be okay. She was determined to live her life to the fullest in memory of him. For his sake. And for her own. He had once told her that she was stronger than she knew. On good days, she even believed him.

Life overall became slightly more bearable, even pleasant once in a while, now that the warm weather and light had begun to return. The month of June was lovely in Williamsburg, and Kendrick liked seeing so many tourists around. Even that thought made her heart twinge a little, knowing how much Silas would have enjoyed seeing so many people visiting the area. Things were always busy at Milligan's these days, which certainly made the time go by faster.

One Saturday morning, she looked up and smiled when Sweet Pregnant Lady entered the shop in a lovely flowing blue maternity dress that brought out the blue in her eyes.

She looks so beautiful.

Kendrick realized it was silly to think nice things about someone rather than say them out loud.

"You look beautiful," she said to the lady as she got closer to where Kendrick was stocking steak sauce on the shelves.

"Thank you for saying that," the woman said with a sweet smile. "I don't feel beautiful these days, but it is nice to hear it."

"Doesn't your husband say you're beautiful?"

The woman nodded, a fond look crossing her face. "Every day," she said softly.

"Good," Kendrick said with a laugh. What a lucky kid she was carrying. He or she would have two parents who clearly loved each other dearly, and no doubt would share that love with their new arrival. "I don't think I ever asked you. Do you know what you're having?"

Rubbing her belly, she said, "Funny you should ask that

now. We just found out the sex yesterday. Made it all this time without knowing, but we finally caved. My husband had a daughter with his first marriage, so we wanted to know what to expect."

"And?" Kendrick asked enthusiastically.

"This one's a boy," she said, her eyes shining.

"Oh, that's exciting!"

"Yeah. Honestly, neither one of us had a strong preference. We just wanted to know."

"Hey, before I forget, we got some more imported chocolates in today."

"Perfect," Sweet Pregnant Lady said happily before making a beeline toward the sweets section. She had been eating lots of chocolates these days, saying it helped make up for all the soft cheese and wine she couldn't have.

The brief interaction with her favorite customer brought Kendrick some joy.

Another ray of light.

Thinking of the new baby was a lovely reminder that beautiful things were still happening in the world. Naturally, she thought of Silas and how much she would have loved to have had his child. But then, so many things made her think of him.

Kendrick glanced out of the window at the front of the shop and thought she saw him for a moment. That wasn't uncommon around here. Her heart still dropped into her stomach whenever she caught sight of a man wearing a tricorn hat. Despite the heartache it caused, she had learned to try to laugh it off when that happened.

But this time it was different.

This time, it *was* Silas.

Kendrick let out a loud gasp.

Calm down, get a grip. It can't possibly be him.

And yet, it was. The man's eyes opened wide as he locked his gaze onto her. She would know those brown eyes anywhere in the world. He put his hand over his mouth in shock. Well, he put his hand near his mouth because he was dead, after all. Not only was Silas actually standing outside the shop, it was clear by his expression that he had not meant for her to see him.

What in God's name is going on?

Somehow, she had the presence of mind to say, "Sallie, you gotta cover for me. Family emergency. I'm sorry, I have to go!"

"Okay, hon," Sallie yelled from the back. "Hope everything's all right."

Shaking, Kendrick dashed out of the shop on legs so rubbery, she nearly fell down.

"Silas," she gasped.

Silas glanced around. There were tourists everywhere.

"Come with me where we can talk," he said.

He took off in the direction of the College of William and Mary, walking so fast, Kendrick had to practically run to keep up. Terror struck her heart as she feared he might disappear all over again. Or maybe this was a dream, and she would wake up cold and lonely in her bed. That had happened many times in the last few months.

The last few months when Silas had apparently abandoned her.

Maybe the man didn't love her, forever and always, as he had promised. Perhaps he had simply tired of her and vanished to get away from her.

At last, Silas stopped power walking when they reached the college campus. He found a private spot behind one of the school buildings where they could talk.

Kendrick's breath came in gasps, both from exertion and the pure adrenaline surging through her body.

"Silas!" she shouted. "What in the hell is going on?"

"Oh, my sweet. I'm so sorry. I didn't mean— I forgot to go invisible. I didn't want you to see me."

"So you just *left* me? On purpose? And you got caught by *mistake*?"

"No, no. Nothing like that. I swear. I couldn't stay away from you. I tried. I really tried, but—"

"Why? Why did you go away?" Kendrick asked, tears in her eyes. They were tears of rage, grief, and confusion.

"Because I was *ruining your life*," Silas said sadly. As Kendrick stared deep into the eyes of her soulmate, she saw what she desperately needed to see. His everlasting love for her. It was still there.

"No you're not!"

"Kendrick, I've been trapped here for hundreds of years. There was no reason to think that was gonna change anytime soon. I was doing better, making progress. That wasn't a lie. I've been feeling better, reaching out to my family, to Kurt. And it's been helping. But I could be here another hundred years for all we know. And I couldn't have you waiting around for me. You have to go and live your life, and you weren't gonna do that as long as I was still around."

She knew everything he was saying was the truth, and she understood why he had done what he had done. But she was still furious.

"I grieved for you for months. You put me through absolute hell, and for what? I'll have to go through it all over again the next time you go away!"

"My sweet, I'm so sorry," he said, reaching out to touch her face. She closed her eyes and wept at the familiar, ice-cold touch. She had missed him more than she knew how to say. "I was trying to do the right thing. And I took the cowardly way out. I vanished for a lot of the time so I wouldn't have to feel the pain of losing you. But when I would return to consciousness, I just couldn't stay away. I had to see you. I saw you visit the river sometimes."

"You did?"

"Yes, but I couldn't stay long because you would feel me there. You would turn around and look in my direction."

"So that *was* you I felt!"

Silas nodded. "It's easier to come by the shop to see you. With so many people around, my presence gets lost in the shuffle."

"Do you have any idea what you've put me through?"

Nodding somberly, he said, "I know exactly what you've been through. Losing you was like dying all over again. Worse. I'm sorry I went away, Kendrick."

"I thought you were at peace. I thought you might be with Kurt."

Sharp pain stabbed at Kendrick's stark reminder of everything she had lost. Her twin brother had gone away suddenly, too. Silas had done his best to warn her, make her think that his time was coming.

"I didn't know what else to do, my sweet," he said mournfully. "I wanted to be with you on the anniversary of your brother's death. I couldn't bear the thought of you being alone on that day. And I thought that you already had such a bad time in the month of January ... I didn't want to ruin another time of the year with my disappearance."

In a warped way, that made sense. Like when you heard about somebody dying on their birthday. Perhaps that made it easier on the loved ones left behind. Their birthday would still be hard but there wouldn't be a separate death day to mourn as well.

"God, you have no idea how much I hated leaving you. I just kept having these terrible visions of you hanging out with me here for years."

"Oh yeah," she scoffed. "That would be terrible, wouldn't it?"

"Not for me, it wouldn't. But for you. I pictured you staying here, growing older. Not living closer to your parents where you belong. Stuck at a day job you have no interest in. Giving up any chance at marriage, children. Any kind of future. Have you even done any writing lately?"

"No, Silas. I have not," she said sharply. "I suppose that makes me a horrible, lazy person with no ambition, but I was too busy trying to summon the strength to get out of bed in the morning."

"I didn't mean it that way," he said. "I just didn't want you to throw your future away for me. I have absolutely nothing to offer you. There's barely anything left of me," Silas said, holding out his ghostly arms. "Spending too much time with me is a waste of your life, and I love you too much to sit back and watch that happen."

"I know," she said wearily. "If I was the dead one, I don't even know what I would do. I'd probably feel the same way."

"We both want what's best for each other, Kendrick. Sometimes we just don't have any clue what that is."

Silas gazed helplessly into her eyes. "Please don't hate me."

"I could never hate you, Silas. I love you."

"You can't know how hard it was for me to leave like I did. In a way, I felt like I was doing the same thing to you that I did to my family," he said, his voice breaking with emotion.

Kendrick's heart ached as she gazed at him.

"I know you only did what you thought was best," she told him.

"I did, Kendrick. I really did! And I hated every agonizing moment."

"I know. I forgive you, Silas."

He made a motion with his chest like he was sighing with relief. "Thank God."

"Silas, you have to promise me you won't leave me again. Not until you absolutely have to."

"I feel like I'm destroying your life no matter what I do," Silas said, gazing somberly into her eyes.

"Promise me," Kendrick pleaded tearfully.

"My sweet, you're asking me to wreck any chance of happiness in your life. How can I—"

They both turned their heads as they heard footsteps approach. Kendrick was stunned to see Sweet Pregnant Lady walking, staggering really, toward them.

Gasping heavily, she pressed her hand against the brick wall of the building to steady herself.

"You two ... don't make it easy ... for a pregnant woman to catch up to you," she said.

Silas's eyes opened wide as he glanced down at her swollen belly.

"Are you all right, ma'am? Do you need us to call for help?"

"Oh no. I'm just fine," she said. "Just need a minute."

Kendrick stared at her, wondering why the woman had followed them.

"Actually, I'm here to help *you*," she said with a smile. Gazing fondly at Silas, she slowly dragged her hand *right through his shoulder* before either of them could stop her.

Silas jumped back as if stung. Kendrick braced herself

for the woman's scream of fright, but she didn't seem scared in the slightest.

"I know this is going to sound totally crazy," the blue-eyed mother-to-be said, "but it is possible to come back to life even when you've been dead for a really long time."

It took Kendrick a moment to let the woman's words sink in. And yes, that did sound totally crazy.

"You can't be serious," Kendrick said at last.

"It's true," the lady said, affectionately rubbing her pregnant belly. "You should meet my husband. He died in the battle of Gettysburg."

17

———

S ilas stared at this mysterious woman, trying to figure out who she was and what in blazes she was talking about. She seemed a nice enough person, but it also seemed she was completely out of her mind. Like Kendrick, she had no fear of ghosts.

"It's funny," the woman said, gazing at Kendrick. "I'd heard the rumors that a Revolutionary soldier had fallen in love with a living woman around here. I just had no idea it was you, Kendrick."

So Kendrick already knew this strange woman?

"How did you hear about that?" Kendrick asked.

"I own a bed and breakfast in town. Well, me and my husband own it."

"Right. I know. O'Rorke's."

"Yes, that's the one," the lady said. "Like most places in town, it's haunted."

She said the words like it was no big deal.

"We know the spirits who haunt the place. Dear souls," she said fondly. "They keep watch over the place for us. And they tell us what's going on in town, including what some of the ghosts are up to."

"No kiddin'," Silas said, shaking his head. A ghostly rumor mill. The thought struck him as amusing.

"I'm embarrassed to admit," Kendrick said, "in all the time I've known you, I never actually caught your name."

The lady smiled. "That's all right. I only know yours because you wear a name tag. My name is Remy. Remy O'Rorke."

"Remy, this is Silas Murphy."

"Lovely to meet you," Silas said, touching his hat, or at least appearing to. "Do you need to sit down?"

"Oh, no," Remy said, looking around at the grassy area. "Believe me, I won't be able to get up."

"What did you mean when you said it was possible to come back to life?" Kendrick asked. Silas was grateful his beloved had gotten straight to the point. It was killing him to make polite small talk when all he wanted was answers.

"I know it sounds crazy, and if I hadn't seen it for myself, I wouldn't have believed it either. But my husband, Avery, was dead when I first met him. He came back to life, flesh and blood. And he's not the only one. I know of another soldier who died in Gettysburg who is now alive and well. And I've heard of at least two spirits here in Williamsburg who made it back as well."

"Seriously?" Silas asked.

Remy nodded. "As you know, spirits are trapped here because there's something wrong. Usually, it's some kind of strong emotion that keeps them earthbound. Could be guilt, anger, regret, those kinds of things."

Silas glanced at Kendrick, and they both nodded. That certainly described his situation.

"And then when they figure out how to work through

those difficult emotions, they cross over. Usually. But once in a while, they stay. And it's usually because they have someone to stay around for," Remy said, smiling at Kendrick. "For instance, I've heard about a ghostly woman who was trapped here since the 1700s. She fell in love with a man who works in one of the buildings over in the historical district. When she somehow found the answers she needed in order to cross over, she was able to come back to life so she could be with him."

"That sounds wonderful," Silas said doubtfully.

"But hard to believe," Remy finished for him.

"Yes," he said with a grin.

"I understand. But what I'm telling you is the truth, and I want you both to know that I would be happy to help you in any way I can. As I mentioned, my husband, Avery, was a soldier in the Civil War. I'm sure he could relate to some of the things you've been through, Silas."

Remy looked sadly at Silas's uniform, and he found her presence comforting. After so many years of being deprived of much human contact, how lovely it was to have a new friend.

"And Kendrick, I want you to know that I understand your situation too. I know how hard it is to love someone and not even be able to touch him. To want to help him but sometimes not knowing how."

"Yes," Kendrick said. "That's exactly how I feel."

"We should exchange numbers," Remy said. "So you can get in touch with me any time you like."

"Damn, I left the shop so quickly I left my phone there. And my purse, come to think about it."

"Why don't we all walk back there to get your things?" Silas suggested.

"Good idea," Kendrick agreed.

Silas watched Remy carefully. It would not do to have a woman in her condition stumble while she walked through the grass. He felt better once they'd reached the sidewalk that would lead them right to Milligan's.

"I really think having Silas meet with Avery might help," Remy said. "I knew a woman back in Gettysburg who spent a lot of time counseling some of the soldiers who were left behind there after the war. She had professional psychology training, but I think talking to anybody who's willing to listen—especially someone who understands what you've endured—could make a big difference. Also, her husband is a soldier who suffers from PTSD, and he found talking to other soldiers really helped."

"I think it's a wonderful idea to have Silas meet your husband," Kendrick said.

"You should know, though," Remy said cautiously. "Even if it works ..."

"What?" Kendrick asked, sounding concerned.

"There's still a good chance that Silas will cross over. Though I've known of several people who have made it back, plenty more go to the other side and stay there."

Kendrick drew in a deep breath and nodded. Silas's heart ached just looking at her. He knew she had endured months of grief when he'd disappeared; she must dread the idea of having to do it again.

"I understand," she said softly. "But it will be worth it if we can help Silas, one way or another. He can't stay here, as he is now, forever. He's suffered alone long enough, and it's time for his pain to end one way or another."

"Oh, sweetie," Remy said. She stopped walking and pulled Kendrick in for a hug. "That's exactly how I felt about Avery."

After squeezing her tight for a moment, Remy released her.

"You've got a good woman here, Silas."

"Don't I know it," he said with a smile.

When they reached the front of the store, Remy said, "I think I will sit down for just a minute."

She sank down into a chair at one of the outdoor tables and let out a groan. Then she picked up a paper menu from the table and fanned herself to get some relief from the early June heat.

"Do you need anything?" Kendrick asked.

"A bottle of water would be lovely," she said.

"You got it."

Kendrick walked to the front door of the store with Silas close on her heels.

"I'm gonna get her some water and then I'll grab my stuff and we can go somewhere and talk."

"No, Kendrick."

"What?" she asked, eyes wide. His ghostly heart squeezed when he saw the panic in her face.

"My sweet, I want you to finish your shift. There's no reason you can't go back to work. We can talk afterward. It'll still be light out after the store closes."

"Silas, I just got you back! How can you—"

"I will not have you put any part of your life on hold for me any longer. We have no way of knowing what's gonna happen with me." With a quick glance in Remy's direction, he said, "I've got no idea what to think 'bout what she's telling us."

"Me neither," Kendrick said, shaking her head. "It's so crazy."

"The only thing I know for sure is you *must* go on living ... and prepare for the possibility of life without me."

Seeing her eyes fill with tears was gut-wrenching, but he knew he must stand firm. It was in her best interest.

"I understand," she whispered. "All right. I'll go back to work. But *only* if you swear to me that you will *never leave me again* unless you have to."

Silas carefully considered such a vow. He worried that Kendrick would remain here in Williamsburg with him, forgoing all her plans for her future if he promised he would stay until he was forced to go.

"Silas," she said in a shaky voice.

"I promise," he said at last. Perhaps he could somehow convince her not to wait around forever if this whole crossing over continued to drag on for years. Seeing her pain made him realize that abandoning her was not the answer. He would keep his promise and never leave her willingly, ever again.

"Now go get that dear woman some water and do your job," he said in a stern, boss-like voice that coaxed a laugh from her. "When you're done, I'll be here."

"Okay," she said. "I love you."

"I love you more than you could possibly know."

Kendrick wiped her eyes and seemed to calm down a bit. She should know by now that he would never lie to her. Though he still wasn't sure he *should* have vowed not to leave her, he'd said it. And he would honor his promise.

Silas walked over to where poor Remy was melting in the sun.

"Are you all right?" he asked her.

"Oh yes, I'll be just fine," she said with a smile.

"I want to thank you for offering your help. I 'preciate it very much."

"I'm glad to do anything I can," she said. "It's impossible to know what will happen. But Silas, I want you to know that I will be there for her, no matter what. As one of the few people who knows what she's going through, I can be a shoulder to cry on if that's what she needs."

"Thank you," he said.

"I can see how much you love her. And I know this has been hard on you, too. I'm hopeful that we can get you through this. One way or another, you won't have to be like this anymore."

She gazed at his ghostly form and then back up to his face.

"Avery and I ... We'll take care of her as best we can if you have to go away, Silas."

He nodded.

"And if you make it back, you can have a romantic getaway with Kendrick at our bed and breakfast."

He laughed. "Now *that* is my idea of Heaven."

Glancing at the door of the store, he said, "Well, I best skedaddle. Tryin' my best not to interrupt her daily routine, you know?"

"You're a good man, Silas. Take care of yourself."

"And you as well! And take care of that sweet baby," he said, before rushing off when he saw Kendrick open the door of the shop with a plastic water bottle in hand.

SILAS MADE sure he was waiting outside Milligan's before closing time so Kendrick wouldn't have to worry about him showing up. He had caused her enough heartache already.

"Hello, beautiful," he said when she came out of the shop.

"Hello, Silas." She carefully locked the door, then tugged on it to make sure it was secure. Kendrick looked tired, and not just from working all day. Shoulders slumped, she seemed emotionally weary, and he knew it was his fault. He considered himself fortunate that she didn't hate him for leaving her the way he had.

"Should we go to our usual spot?" she asked.

"Market Square is closed, so there won't be too many tourists there. Even so, how 'bout we go to the Governor's Palace Garden? Feel like I never take you anywhere new anymore," he said in a feeble attempt at a joke.

"I don't care where we go as long as I'm with you."

"I'm glad to hear you say that," he said, shoulders drooping with relief. "How have you been?"

Kendrick sighed deeply. "I think you know how I've been."

"My sweet, I'm so—"

"I know you're sorry, Silas. You're lucky I didn't move to Newport News while you were gone."

"No, I'm not lucky. I was hoping you would be able to move on. It's what's best for you."

"Maybe," she said with a shrug. "But I'll never be sorry that I got to have more time with you."

"My hope was that you would find a job and start a new life with your family in Newport News, and that I really would cross over. I tried, Kendrick," Silas said, hearing his own frustration and anger in his voice. "I really did. When I wasn't vanishing, I tried talking to Kurt. To my family. To God. To anybody who might listen to me. I begged and pleaded for help. You know what I wanted more than anything?"

Kendrick shook her head, looking at him with deep concern and sadness.

"I wanted to cross over so that I could come back and visit you in any way that I could. Like when you said you sometimes feel Kurt's presence. I wanted you to feel *me*. I wanted you to know I was there and watching over you, forever and always."

She wiped the tears that had formed in her eyes. "That's beautiful, Silas. I love that."

When they reached the Palace Garden, they sat on an ornate bench overlooking the tulip garden. With flowers blooming all over the place, it was the perfect, romantic spot to kiss the woman you loved. But that was not to be, of course.

"What do you think about what that Remy woman said?" Silas asked.

"I think it sounds too good to be true."

"Right."

"The whole thing sounds so insane, but then, I never thought I would fall in love with a ghost. I mean, it's like everything that's happened over the last year in my life seems crazy. Impossible."

"Right," Silas said again.

Kendrick turned to look into his eyes. "I'm afraid to hope that what she's saying is true."

"Me too."

"But would you even want to come back to life, Silas? Even if that were possible?"

"Of course I would. How can you even ask a thing like that?" he said. "I love you."

Kendrick smiled, and he was relieved to see more affection than hurt in her gaze. "It's not about loving me, Silas. You've existed in one form or another for a very long time. I honestly wouldn't blame you if you just wanted to go to your eternal rest."

"What I want is to be with you."

"You say that now, but you could very well change your

mind once you see that light. I think about that sometimes," Kendrick said in a faraway voice.

"Think about what, exactly?"

"I've read a lot about near-death experiences. You know, when somebody dies and is then resuscitated. They say they see this wonderful, bright, loving light, and they feel compelled to walk right into it. I often wonder if, after Kurt's accident, he saw that light and had a choice. You know how much I miss him, Silas, but I can't blame him if he wanted to go into that loving light and be at peace. As angry as I get at him sometimes for not being careful that night, I can't be mad at him for choosing to cross over instead of staying behind in some broken, injured body. When it comes down to it, I just want him to be okay." She didn't seem to notice the fresh tears that had begun falling down her cheeks. "And I feel the same way about you."

"Kendrick, if what Remy says is real—if it's at all possible to come back—I will fight with everything I have to stay with you. God's gonna have to drag me to Heaven kicking and screaming."

She laughed, and what a glorious sound it was.

"Silas," she said, gazing into his eyes. "I'm just saying that if the time comes, it's okay if you choose to go."

"I won't," he said stubbornly.

"Okay." She sounded like a mother who was humoring her toddler.

"Remy seems like a nice lady. I mean, she doesn't *seem* crazy, so who knows?"

"Oh, she's always been very sweet. Comes into the shop all the time. Though I'm still not sure what to think about the whole coming back from the dead thing, I do think it would be a great idea for you to speak with her husband. I mean, if she was telling the truth about him fighting in the Civil War."

"I agree with you there," Silas said. As much as he loved Kendrick, there were plenty of things about the war he didn't want to talk to her about. She'd endured enough violence and death in her life. He needed her to focus on the good things in life.

"I missed you so much," she said.

"I missed you too, my love. But, my sweet, I've never seen you look so tired. You've been through a lot today. Why don't you go home and get some rest?"

"I will soon. But I want to sit with you for a while longer."

Silas nodded. He wasn't ready to let go just yet either.

"Then that's what we'll do."

18

Kendrick asked Deanna and Marie to lunch at the King's Arms Tavern in the historical district on a Saturday afternoon. She requested they meet her in front of Milligan's, even though she didn't have to work that day. The two women were already seated on one of the benches outside the shop when she got there.

"Finally," Marie said. "I'm starving. Should we have made reservations? Hope we don't have to wait too long."

"Well, we might have to wait just a little bit. I actually asked you guys to come here for a reason," Kendrick said.

"Lunch isn't enough of a reason?" Marie asked. "So hungryyyy."

"We'll eat soon. I promise. There's someone I want you to meet first."

"Really?" Deanna asked. "Who?"

"This guy I've been seeing."

"You're kidding," Marie said, sitting up straight on the bench. "You met someone? Where did you meet? What's his name?"

"Come on. Let's just go, and you can question him to

death when you meet him," Kendrick said, nearly laughing at her own joke. She knew she should probably warn them, but when else could you spring this kind of surprise on people?

Kendrick started in the direction of the college campus, and Deanna and Marie followed.

"Is he coming to lunch with us?" Marie asked.

"Probably not." Kendrick felt bad about making her friends wait to eat, but she suspected they would forget all about food once they met Silas.

"Does he work around here?" Marie asked.

"No."

"Where did you meet him?"

Kendrick almost answered the question, but she realized if she said Yorktown Battlefield, she'd give away the secret.

"I told you, you can ask all the questions you want when you meet him."

"Where are we going?" Deanna asked, looking behind her as they left the Merchants Square area.

"I asked him to meet us on the college campus."

"Is he a student at the College of William and Mary?" Marie asked. Kendrick shot her an amused look but didn't answer. "Sorry. Forgot I'm supposed to hold all questions until the official Q and A session."

"Please do," Kendrick said. Her stomach tingled with excitement. She couldn't wait to see how her friends would react to meeting the man she loved. If nobody screamed or passed out, she would consider the meeting a success.

She led them around the back of the same school building where they had spoken to Remy. As previously arranged, Silas was standing under a tree at a safe distance. Kendrick wanted to give her friends a few moments to adjust to what was happening before they dove right in to speaking with a ghost.

Deanna spotted him first. She stopped walking, and her eyes grew wide as she stared at him from several yards away. Clad as always in his tricorn hat, black boots, tan breeches, and long blue jacket, he smiled and nodded carefully. He stayed where he was, not wanting to make any sudden moves to frighten anyone.

"Is that ... Is that ..." Marie asked, frozen in place.

"Yes," Kendrick said. "That is Silas Murphy. The man I love more than I ever thought possible."

Deanna stared at him in confusion, while Marie simply went white. For once, Marie had no questions. Only stunned silence. Kendrick allowed her friends a moment to let the truth sink in, knowing she needed to explain some things.

"Turns out he didn't really cross over. He just went away for a while."

"Why would he do that?" Deanna asked.

"He only wanted me to *think* he had crossed over."

"What?" she asked harshly, her initial shock replaced by anger.

"He did it because he was worried about me. Believe me, I was really upset when he came back. Especially since I don't think he ever intended to tell me he was still around. See, ghosts can become invisible whenever they like. When I first caught sight of him a few days ago, he had forgotten to turn invisible."

"So he was *hiding* from you? Does he have any idea the hell he put you through?"

Glancing over at Silas, she saw he looked worried. Still, he waited patiently until they were ready to approach him.

"Yes, he does. Because he went through the same thing."

"But it was his fault," Deanna snapped.

"I know, but he really thought it was what was best for me."

Her friend considered her words but didn't look convinced.

"That's—that's really him?" Marie asked, staring at Silas.

"Yes. Are you ready to meet him?"

"I sure am," Deanna said.

Kendrick had only thought about how her friends would react to meeting a dead guy. It hadn't occurred to her that they might not get along with him.

She started toward Silas with Deanna right by her side. Marie followed behind.

"Hello, my sweet," Kendrick said when she reached Silas. He smiled at her. As they'd planned, they held up their hands. With one quick motion, she swiped her hand right through his. His ghostly image wavered for a moment, before becoming firm and solid-looking again.

"Wow," Deanna said.

"Yeah," Kendrick said with a chuckle. Together, she and Silas had decided it would be best to prove to her friends right away that he was a spirit. No sense in dragging it out.

"Oh my God," Marie said, looking frighteningly pale. She staggered back for a moment.

Concerned, Silas took a few steps away from her to give her space.

Looking like she might faint, Marie placed her hands on the trunk of the tree to steady herself. Then she gingerly turned herself around and slowly slid down to the ground and sat with her back against the tree. She drew in several sharp breaths, like she was trying her best not to pass out.

"Are you all right?" Kendrick said, rushing over and crouching down by her side.

Marie nodded her head rapidly. "Yes. Yes, I think so. I just need a minute."

Kendrick stared into her friend's blue eyes, trying to get her to focus. That seemed to help; the color began to return to her face.

Marie risked a glance in Silas's direction. He had taken several steps back in an effort to make her feel safer. "I'm really sorry. I didn't mean ..."

"Oh, please don't be sorry," he said, his brown eyes filled with tender concern. "Hardly the first time this has happened. I've seen just 'bout every reaction there is to seeing a ghost over the years. But you don't have to be afraid, ya hear? I won't hurt you. I *can't* hurt you," he said with a smile, slowly holding up his ghostly hands.

"Silas, this is Marie."

"Very glad to meet you," Silas said, carefully sitting down beside her.

Marie nodded, seeming much calmer now. Silas had that way about him. He was so kind and gentle that it was nearly impossible to be afraid of him.

"I thought you believed me about him, girl," Kendrick gently teased. She took a seat near Marie and Silas.

"I did. At least, I thought I did. But it's different actually seeing it. S—sorry—not it. *Him.* It's different seeing *him.*"

"Sorry we didn't give you any advance warning 'bout this," Silas said, shooting Kendrick a wry look. He had been in favor of giving them a heads-up, but Kendrick had disagreed.

"It's all right," Marie said, smiling at him. "It really is nice to meet you, Silas. Never thought I would get the chance to."

Deanna eyed him curiously but said nothing.

"Deanna's a little ... um ..." Kendrick said, struggling to

find the right words. It would break her heart if Deanna wound up disliking Silas. "Upset about the way you went away."

"Ah, I see," Silas said, looking apologetic. "I don't blame you for that."

"How could you do that to her?" Deanna demanded, hands on her hips.

"Deanna, please don't—"

"No, no. It's all right. These are your friends. And they're loyal friends. I can see that. Deanna, if anybody hurts Kendrick, you've got every right to give 'em hell, and there's no reason it should be any different with me. I want you to tell me 'zactly what's on your mind."

"Kendrick was utterly destroyed when you left," Deanna said in a shaky voice. As much as Kendrick hated conflict, she couldn't help being touched by her friend's concern.

Silas nodded sadly.

"She was hysterical," she said, eyes flashing. "I've never seen her so upset. Well no. That's not true. There was only one other time I saw her so completely shattered."

"When Kurt died," he said quietly.

"Yes."

"I'm so grateful Kendrick has friends like you looking out for her," Silas said. He glanced over at Marie. She smiled sympathetically at Silas. "I understand why you're so angry, and you're not wrong. Trouble is, I knew Kendrick was going to have to go through that ... that grief ... sooner or later. It's too late for me. More than two hundred years too late. I could not abide having her waste all her time—waste her *life*—on me. I've spent centuries tryin' to figure out why I'm stuck here, and I have no reason to believe that's gonna change in another hundred years."

Kendrick's heart ached as Silas spoke. He sounded so tired.

"Last thing I wanted was this beautiful woman to be trapped here with me, getting old and gray and throwing away any chance at happiness." Then, in a voice rife with sorrow and grief, he whispered, "So I felt I had to let her go."

That last part got through to Deanna. Silas had spoken with such passion and sorrow and deep love that it was impossible not to believe him.

"If she thought I was at peace, she thought I'd moved on, then maybe she would move on with her life too," he said. "I left on the same day as Kurt died because I didn't want to ruin another date, another season for her. She's been through so much ... Believe me, it tore me up to add to her anguish."

"I see," Deanna said softly. "I understand. I'm sorry I gave you a hard time, Silas." She sat down to join the rest of the group.

"I'm not," he said firmly. "Makes me know for sure you'll always be there for Kendrick. To defend her, protect her, support her. That's all that matters to me."

Deanna nodded. "And I can see how much you love her," she said. "That you're looking out for her too."

"I love her very much," Silas said, gazing over at Kendrick.

"And you can't even touch her," Deanna said, shaking her head.

"Believe me, I'd like to do more than just touch her," he said, raising an eyebrow.

Deanna laughed, and everything felt right in Kendrick's world.

"Can I ask questions now?" Marie asked.

"Of course you can," Silas said. Kendrick nodded her approval.

"What's it like ... you know ... being dead?" she asked cautiously, as if she feared she might offend him. Kendrick had no such worries. Silas loved talking to people, and he never got upset about questions about his death or anything else.

"Welp, it was pretty dang boring until I met this lady over here," Silas said with a wink. He went on to talk about his "life" after his death. The things he could and couldn't do. The loneliness, the few bright spots. Marie and Deanna listened with rapt attention, learning about concepts like vanishing and walking through walls. Much to Kendrick's surprise, Silas even told the unvarnished truth about how he died. Though he talked about being a soldier, he made it clear he hadn't died a hero.

"Well, I think you're a hero," Kendrick told him. He shrugged and smiled at her.

"So did you tell them about, you know, the stuff Remy told us?"

She shook her head. "I thought that might be information overload for them. One step at a time, you know?"

"Makes sense. Still, they've handled everything else pretty dang well." Silas grinned at Deanna and Marie, who smiled warmly back.

"Who is Remy and what did he tell you?" Marie asked.

"Remy is a she, actually," Kendrick said. "She's that pregnant lady, that customer I mentioned to you guys?"

"Oh yeah. I remember you talking about her," Deanna said. "So wait, she knows about you, Silas? Like *all* about you?"

"Yep. Sure does," Silas said. Then he looked questioningly at Kendrick.

Shrugging, she said, "Why not? Go ahead and tell them."

"So this Remy lady follows us one day. To right around here, actually," Silas said, looking around the campus. "Then real quick, she puts her hand through me like it's nothing. Not scared and not the least bit surprised. She already knew I was dead."

"That's odd," Marie said.

"Said she heard rumors, from other ghosts mind you," Kendrick said with amusement, "that a Revolutionary soldier had fallen in love with a woman around here. When Remy saw us, she put two and two together. That's how she knew Silas wasn't just a Colonial Williamsburg employee."

"So she knew about you guys," Deanna said with a shrug.

"There's more," Silas said with a twinkle in his eyes.

"Remy said ... she *claims* that her husband—her living husband and the father of her baby—was a soldier in the Civil War."

The confused looks on Deanna's and Marie's faces made both Silas and Kendrick laugh.

"I know," Kendrick said. "According to her, she met the man in Gettysburg while he was still dead. The guy, Avery, died in battle. Not sure which side he was on. But anyway, he died and was stuck here for a long time just like Silas. And, like all ghosts, he had something that was keeping him trapped here. Then, once he figured it out, instead of crossing over, he came back to life."

"Just came back to life," Deanna deadpanned.

"Apparently so," Silas said with a chuckle.

"Wow. Do you think that's possible?" Marie asked.

"We don't know what to think. The idea seems totally

crazy, not to mention too much to hope for," Kendrick said, looking over at Silas. He agreed with a sad nod.

"So that could mean there's, like, formerly dead people just walking around here?" Marie asked with fascination.

"According to Remy, there's at least two in Williamsburg."

"Damn. So you might actually be able to come back?" Marie said, eyes wide.

"You mean, you really believe her story?" Kendrick asked.

"Well, right now I kinda feel like I'm on another planet, considering everything that's happened today," she said with a laugh. "I don't really know what to believe. The only thing I know for sure is you guys have absolutely nothing to lose by staying open to the idea. Did this Remy lady tell you what you have to do to make this happen?"

"Nothing specific yet," Kendrick said. "I've got her phone number so I can reach out to her. She did say it would probably be a good idea to have Avery meet and talk with Silas. If Remy is telling the truth and Avery really was a soldier, there's a chance he might be able to help Silas with the issues that are keeping him here."

"And then he might cross over," Deanna said gently.

"Yes," Silas said. "That could happen as well."

Marie let out a deep sigh. "This is really rough. I'm glad you guys found each other, but I'm sorry this is so damn hard."

"Yeah well, everything happens for a reason," Kendrick scoffed. Marie gave her a sympathetic smile, knowing how much she'd hated when people told her that after Kurt died. She didn't believe it, but even if she did, it didn't help.

"I want to let you both know," Silas said, addressing her friends, "that I've made a promise to Kendrick I'd never go away ever again unless I really have to. Everything is so uncertain, never knowing one day to the next what will happen. So all three of you need to know that if I ever suddenly disappear again, well, it's for real."

The women nodded. Kendrick's eyes teared up, and Deanna reached over and squeezed her hand.

"We'll be here for you through it all, honey. Whatever happens," she said.

"Damn right we will," Marie said.

"And I can't thank you both enough for that," Silas said. "Now weren't you all supposed to go to lunch?"

"God, I'd forgotten all about that," Marie said.

"And you said you were starving, like, an hour ago," Kendrick said. "Let's get you fed before you nearly pass out again."

Marie laughed, blushing a little.

"Can you come with us, Silas?" Deanna asked. "Is there a way you could at least sit with us? Or ..."

"It might be possible, I suppose. But you girls go on ahead."

"You probably could join us, Silas," Kendrick said. "Would be easy enough if we sat outside."

Shaking his head, Silas said, "No, no. I want you all to go without me. Not that I don't enjoy your company, 'cuz I surely do, and I hope we meet up again real soon. But like I told you, I worry 'bout her spending so much time with me. Time alone with her friends is important too."

"That's very gracious of you, Silas," Marie said, her voice thick with emotion. Silas was the total opposite of her abusive and controlling ex-boyfriend who'd tried to cut her off from her friends. "And I do hope to see you again soon."

Kendrick stood up, as did her friends.

"Have a nice lunch, my sweet. I'll catch up with you

tomorrow," he said, locking eyes with her. They shared a loving smile of mutual relief that today's meeting had gone well. "And you know the rules ..."

"Tell you everything I ate," she said with a laugh. "You know I will."

19

———

While the women were having their lunch, Silas strolled around the historical district. He was elated, utterly grateful that Kendrick had such wonderful friends in her life. Though he felt a twinge of sadness at not being able to join them at the restaurant like a normal boyfriend would have, he was glad that she could go out and enjoy herself.

What sweet ladies Marie and Deanna were. Deanna was fiercely protective, and Silas was truly grateful for that as well. Kendrick had said they'd all been friends since high school, so he knew they'd seen her through the worst time of her life. He was confident they would take care of her if he did have to leave for good.

Silas reveled in smiling at the happy tourists on such a warm, bright day, appearing to tip his tricorn hat to them. Children in particular always seemed fascinated by his military uniform, and he was always pleased to chat with them. Interacting with people was always risky, but he couldn't help it. He simply adored being among the living.

Silas made a right turn onto Botetourt Street and turned

to stroll down Nicholson Street. As he wandered aimlessly, he caught sight of a woman in the distance who looked slightly familiar. The lady wore a bluish-gray sundress and had light brown hair that fell almost to her shoulders. Silas couldn't explain the odd sensation that he most certainly knew her from somewhere. He hurried down Nicholson Street, remembering not to float toward the woman since he was visible, and it would not do to incite a panic from nearby tourists.

The woman looked up as he rushed toward her. She stopped walking, slightly alarmed, but who could blame her with some strange man coming straight at her?

Her gray eyes flew open wide.

"Silas!"

"Rebekah!" Silas said, eying her up and down. In ghostly lore, she was the one known as the Weeping Woman. To him, she was a fellow spirit, trapped eternally in the Colonial Williamsburg area. "It's been years since I've seen you around here. It's lovely to see you, but I'd been hoping you crossed over."

Rebekah smiled warmly at him. She shook her head.

"Or I thought maybe you'd vanished or ... But ..." Silas realized why it had taken so long to recognize her. "I see you got your hair cut ... somehow. And your clothes are different."

"Yes," she said softly. "It's a bit difficult to explain." Rebekah glanced around at the tourists who were strolling down Nicholson Street. "Come with me. I know where we can have some privacy to talk."

Silas's ghostly heart hammered as though he was alive and overexcited. He was afraid to hope what Rebekah would tell him, but he was pretty certain he already knew.

She was alive.

Though he didn't know her well, their paths had crossed many times over the last several hundred years. They'd chatted, but they'd never shared details of their personal experiences. Silas knew Rebekah wasn't thrilled about being known as the Weeping Woman, yet he never knew *why* she wept or what had kept her here as a spirit. Likewise, all she knew about him was he died on the battlefield. She probably assumed he'd fallen in battle, and he'd never said otherwise.

In all the time Silas had known her—those lonely nights when he'd drifted past her and they'd shared a sad, knowing smile at their mutual plight—Rebekah had always appeared the same way. Her light brown hair cascaded down her back, and she wore a light dress with a floral pattern on it. Not anymore.

As they walked down the road, Silas realized he could hear her footsteps, and his heart caught in his throat.

Oh dear God, I think it might really be true. Remy said she knew of at least two spirits in Williamsburg who had come back to life. Rebekah Jennings must be one of them.

Rebekah led him to a quiet area behind Hay's Cabinetmaker's Shop, with a wooden bridge that covered a small, trickling stream. She stopped on the bridge and turned to face him.

Smiling, she said gently, "I'm not even sure where to begin."

"You're alive, aren't you?" Silas burst out excitedly.

She laughed. "Well, that was easier than I thought. Yes, I am."

"I've heard that it was possible. A lady that owns a bed and breakfast around here told me that her husband came back to life."

"Really? How fascinating," Rebekah said, her voice filled

with wonder. "So far, I only know of that happening to me and one other woman. I've often wondered if such a miracle happened more than we know."

Silas nodded rapidly. "Well she said—Remy, that's her name. The bed and breakfast lady," he babbled on. "She said she met her husband in Gettysburg, and he was a soldier like me, and then he died and came back."

Rebekah laughed, her eyes sparkling with amusement at Silas's enthusiasm.

"Rebekah, *how*? How did you do this? How did you make this happen?"

"Do you want to come back, too, Silas?" she asked, sounding surprised. "Instead of crossing over?"

"Yes," he said. "You have no idea how much."

"You always did enjoy being around the living," she said. "Many spirits around here just want to be left alone. But you? You always loved talking to people."

"I do, but it's more than that. So much more."

"What else?"

"I'm in love with a woman who's alive."

"Oh, Silas," she said, her eyes filled with sympathy. "I understand. Goodness knows, I understand how that feels. Who is she? I wonder if I know her. You must have met her somewhere nearby."

"Her name is Kendrick Banner. She works at Milligan's Wine and Cheese Shop over at Merchants Square."

Rebekah nodded thoughtfully, but the name clearly didn't ring a bell with her.

"She's my soulmate," Silas said as if pleading with her to understand his desperation. "All this time, we couldn't understand why we had to meet like this. When there was no chance of us being together."

"And now you know there is a chance," she said, looking at him in a way that told him she did understand.

The back door to the cabinetmaker's shop opened, and a man with dark brown hair and brown eyes peered at them. He wore a black button-down vest and a white, flowing shirt.

"Thought I heard your voice out here," the man said. He smiled at Rebekah and then glanced at Silas curiously.

"Gregory," Rebekah said. "Is anyone in the shop right now?"

Gregory shook his head.

"Good. Come on in," she said to Silas as she hurried into the building.

Once they were inside and Gregory shut the door behind them, Rebekah gestured at Silas.

"Gregory, I would like you to meet my friend, Silas Murphy."

"Well, it's very nice to meet you," Gregory said with a smile. Then he extended his hand.

"Silas is ... Well, he's like I used to be."

"Oh, I see. Well then I shall greet you with a wave instead," he said with a chuckle and a wave.

"Nice to meet you as well," Silas said with a nod. He tried to appear calm, but inside he was screaming for answers. He desperately needed to know how Rebekah had made it back to the land of the living, and how he might do it too.

"I was just telling Silas about what happened with me," Rebekah said.

Eyes wide, Silas nodded with childlike enthusiasm.

"If it's at all possible, he wants to come back too."

"Really?" Gregory said thoughtfully, scratching his chin. Silas noticed the wedding band on his finger. His gaze snapped to Rebekah's left hand, where he saw a diamond engagement ring and a wedding band.

"Is he your husband?" Silas asked incredulously.

"Yes," Rebekah said as she gazed lovingly at Gregory. "We've been married about three years now."

Silas stared at the two of them, struggling to wrap his mind around what he was seeing.

"Do you have children?"

Rebekah and Gregory exchanged a knowing look.

"Not yet," Rebekah said. "But I'm expecting."

"You are?" Silas said, glancing at her belly.

"We haven't really told people because I'm not too far along yet, but yes," she said, her eyes lighting up as she looked at her husband. Gregory grinned, looking every bit the proud father he would soon be.

"My God, my God," Silas muttered. It all seemed so impossible, too good to be true. He felt a wave of physical dizziness, as if he needed to sit down. How strange. Dear God, everything was strange right now.

"I know. It's so crazy, isn't it?" Gregory asked. "If it wasn't happening to me, I would never believe such a wild tale."

"You don't understand, Gregory," Rebekah said as she watched Silas try to comprehend everything he was hearing. "Silas is in love, too. With a living woman."

"Oh, I see," Gregory said, his dark brown eyes filled with compassion that equaled Rebekah's. "That's why you want to come back."

"Yes," Silas said. "I'd heard tales that it was possible, but I didn't really believe it."

"Until now," Gregory said.

Silas nodded numbly.

"Well, the universe certainly works in mysterious ways," Gregory warned. "We don't know for sure what the grand plan is or why anything happens. We can't know for certain what will happen in your situation. But I promise you this, Silas. If there is absolutely anything we can do to help you, you can count on us."

Rebekah nodded. "Anything."

"Then you must tell me," Silas pleaded as he looked back and forth between the married couple. "How did you make this happen?"

THE MOMENT SILAS left Hay's Cabinetmaker's Shop, he turned invisible. He wanted to move as fast as possible in the hopes of catching Kendrick before she left the historical district. When he reached the King's Arms Tavern, Silas floated through the walls to have a look.

To his relief, Kendrick and her friends were still there. With empty plates and glasses in front of them, they had clearly finished their meal and were chatting and laughing together. Silas had no intention of eavesdropping on their private conversation, so he drifted back out right away. Kendrick had turned her head and looked around the moment he'd arrived, clearly sensing a presence; he couldn't have listened in undetected even if he'd wanted to.

Nothing gets by my girl.

My girl. For the first time, Silas began to hope that perhaps Kendrick wouldn't just be his girl. Good God, perhaps someday she could be his *wife*. And she might even carry his child, just as Rebekah was carrying Gregory's. The woman had been *dead* and now she was growing a new life within her. The wonder of it all!

Now that Silas was back out on the crowded street, turning visible was no easy feat. He ducked behind the

King's Arms building and found a large tree that would conceal him well enough. After carefully looking around, he faded back into visibility. As nonchalantly as could be, he made his way back to the busy street.

He worried that he might have missed Kendrick and her friends leaving. Looking up and down the street, he saw no signs of them. Surely, they couldn't have paid the check and walked all the way down the street in the brief time Silas hadn't been looking.

After a few tense moments of staring at the tavern door, he finally saw Marie come out, followed by Deanna and his beloved Kendrick. He was struck by how beautiful she was; such pretty reddish hair and a smile that lit up his whole world. Seeing her laugh with her friends filled him with joy. Still, he felt there wasn't a moment to lose. He wanted to be part of the living world—*her* living world—as soon as possible. *If* it was possible. He could easily imagine Kendrick as his lovely bride with Deanna and Marie looking pretty in their bridesmaid's dresses. If there was *any possible way* to make that fantasy a reality, he good and goddamn would.

"Kendrick!" Silas called out.

"Silas." She looked confused as she walked down the stone steps of the restaurant. Her confusion turned to worry, as she could see how worked up he was. "Are you all right?"

She rushed over to him, a safe distance away from the tourists who were gathered, waiting to be called when their table was ready.

"Yes, I'm all right. But I need to talk to you right away!"

"Silas, would you like us to ..." Marie tactfully gestured with her hand as she glanced at Deanna, indicating they would give them privacy to talk if he wished.

"No, no. I'd love for you ladies to hear this too. Come with me."

With that, he led them to the same grassy area behind the King's Arms Tavern where he'd briefly hidden to become visible. He sat underneath the tree and the women did the same, looking at him expectantly.

"What's going on?" Kendrick asked, her pretty blue eyes open wide with curiosity and not a little concern.

"I went for a stroll while you ladies were at lunch. Walking around, people-watching, you know. And I ran into this woman that I've known for a really long time. Didn't know her well. Just seen her in passing over the years. The ghost tours call her the Weeping Woman."

"Oh yes. You've mentioned her before," Kendrick said.

"Did I?" Silas asked.

"Yeah, when I asked you if you knew other ghosts and you were telling me some of their stories."

"Right, yes. I do remember that. Anyway, her real name is Rebekah Jennings."

"As in the Jennings Tavern?" Marie asked, gesturing toward the general direction of the historical tavern. The Jennings Tavern was one of the historical buildings available for touring, as opposed to a functioning restaurant like the King's Arms.

"Yes, exactly," Silas said excitedly. "Her family owned that tavern back in the 1700s. Rebekah must have died, I don't know, in the 1750s or 1760s maybe."

"Wow," Marie said, shaking her head. Clearly, she was still adjusting to the idea of dead people walking around. But now she wasn't pale and ready to faint. She simply looked fascinated.

"Okay, so it's nice that you saw your friend …" Kendrick gently prodded, trying to help him get to the point.

"My sweet," Silas said, his face breaking into a huge grin. "I hadn't seen her in a long time, and I'd hoped, for her sake, that she'd crossed over. But that's not what happened. Rebekah looks different now. Got her hair cut, wears modern makeup, and got some new clothes. *Because she's alive.*"

Kendrick gasped and covered her mouth in shock.

"What?" Deanna exclaimed. "Are you serious?"

Silas nodded rapidly. "Remy told us that there were at least two spirits that she knew of that came back to life. Rebekah must be one of them."

Kendrick slowly lowered her hand and stared at Silas. He understood exactly what she was feeling: that sudden surge of thrilling hope that it was possible for them to stay together after all.

"My sweet," Silas said. "She's *married*. Rebekah *married* a man that works here at Colonial Williamsburg!"

"Oh my God," Kendrick said, finally finding her voice.

"She introduced me to her husband. Works over at the cabinetmaker's shop." He stopped himself before he added the fact that Rebekah was pregnant. As much as he wanted to share that additional piece of miraculous news, Rebekah had said they hadn't told many people yet. As honored as he was that they'd told him, he felt it wasn't his place to announce their blessing to others.

"You're sure, Silas," Kendrick asked cautiously. He understood what she was feeling now, too. Hope was a scary thing sometimes. And the notion of coming back to life, that their love might not be doomed after all, definitely seemed too much to hope for.

"I've known Rebekah for hundreds of years, my love. I know absolutely for certain that she was dead. And I've seen with my own eyes that she is alive. Breathing, walking—"

"Oh my God," Kendrick cried out as she finally grabbed hold of the euphoria that Silas was feeling.

"I know!" Silas shouted, making all three women laugh.

"How did this happen for her? What did she do?" Kendrick asked.

"I asked her about that, and she told me everything. Strangely enough, we never talked about why we were stuck here before. Lots of ghosts don't like sharing our private pain, you know? But she did tell me today. Rebekah explained to me what happened in her life," Silas said, treading carefully.

Rebekah had not sworn him to secrecy or anything, yet he still didn't feel right telling others about her personal life. With Gregory gently massaging her back as she spoke, Rebekah had confided that she had been responsible for her little brother's accidental drowning death. And then, compounding the tragedy, she had taken her own life.

"With Gregory's help, she was able to confront her pain and move past it. Then, because she and Gregory were in love, she was permitted to stay with him."

"I see." Kendrick drew in a deep breath and let it out.

Silas's mind whirred with possibilities, and yet he knew there was still at least one huge problem. He'd been here for hundreds of years. What made him think he could suddenly overcome all the things that had kept him stuck here?

"What ... what ... what do we do now?" Kendrick sputtered, looking as overwhelmed as he felt.

"If I were you," Deanna said, "I would call that Remy woman as soon as possible. She might be able to figure out how to make this happen for you."

Silas and Kendrick gazed into each other's eyes.

"Yes," Kendrick said. "That sounds like a plan."

20

Kendrick had called Remy as soon as she'd arrived home from Colonial Williamsburg after learning about Rebekah's situation. Remy had been incredibly patient as Kendrick cried her way through the emotional phone call. When Silas had first told her what had happened, she'd been too stunned to really react. Once the news had sunk in, she'd been an emotional mess.

Given her own situation, Remy clearly understood what Kendrick was going through more than anyone else ever could. When she had fallen in love with the man who was now her husband, she had known that coming back to life was possible. She also knew there was a chance that Avery would cross over and she would lose him forever. Or at least, she would lose him for the rest of her lifetime on Earth. Remy knew the uncertainty, the anguish, and the hope that Kendrick was feeling.

Kendrick felt guilty about dumping her emotional baggage on a woman in Remy's condition, but what choice did she have? Ever the Sweet Lady, Remy assured her that she would do everything in her power to help. They decided their next move should be to have Silas speak with Avery right away. After all, Avery knew exactly how it felt to be a ghost, *and* he knew what it was like to be a soldier.

After confirming that O'Rorke's Bed and Breakfast was located only a few miles away, and therefore, within traveling distance for Silas, they had agreed to meet there. Kendrick had told Silas the plan the next time she met up with him in the historical district. They would meet on a Saturday afternoon after her morning shift at Milligan's.

When Kendrick arrived at O'Rorke's, Silas was waiting for her at the front gate. He had never been inside the place before either, and he'd said he wanted to go in together.

That, and it wasn't like he could knock on the door.

Kendrick smiled at Silas and then turned to look at the tavern. The lovely brick building with its red shutters had the delightful, old-fashioned feel that permeated the historical district. With a glassed-in sun porch on the side of the building and a lush garden out front, the inn was warm and inviting, yet also incredibly romantic.

"This place is gorgeous," Kendrick gushed. "And it's so romantic that a husband and wife own it, don't you think?"

"I do," Silas said. "Shall we go in?"

Walking side by side with Silas up the brick walkway to the quaint tavern felt so natural. For a moment, she could pretend they were a couple here on a weekend getaway. Tears sprang to her eyes at the mere thought. She wanted the fantasy to be true so much, it physically hurt.

"You all right?" he asked.

"Yes," she whispered.

"Everything's gonna be okay," Silas reassured her.

Kendrick drew in a deep breath and reminded herself that everything would be all right. Eventually. As much as she desperately wanted a life together with Silas, if he crossed over instead, she would find a way to deal with it. All that really mattered was his happiness and that his long years of endless, lonely suffering as a spirit would finally come to an end.

They walked up the stone steps to the front door and Kendrick knocked. The door swung open, and a tall, handsome man with light brown hair and warm gray eyes greeted them with a smile.

"Hello. You must be Kendrick and Silas," the man said.

"Yes," Kendrick responded.

"Come on in," he said, opening the door wider and stepping aside to allow them both in. "It's lovely to meet you."

Remy had failed to mention that her husband had an absolutely gorgeous Irish brogue. Kendrick had always been a sucker for a man with an accent, but what woman wasn't?

"Avery O'Rorke," he said, offering his hand to Kendrick.

"I'm so pleased to meet you," she said, shaking his hand. She was suddenly struck with a familiar sensation, and she knew there was an otherworldly presence nearby. At first, she thought it was one of the spirited residents Remy had mentioned that frequented the tavern. Then she suddenly realized … It was *Avery* she was sensing. He had come back from death, and she could sense it. It was extraordinary.

Avery turned to Silas and nodded his greeting. It was such a relief to be in the company of someone well aware that Silas was a ghost. There was no need to keep a safe distance.

"Glad to meet you, Avery," Silas said. "Thanks so much for meeting with us."

"Oh, it's our pleasure, I assure you. Remy can't wait to give you the grand tour."

Avery led them out of the small parlor and into a cozy sitting room that featured a red velvet couch, several chairs, and an ornately carved wooden coffee table. On a table against the wall, a coffee and tea service was set up, complete with fancy china cups and saucers.

"This is so lovely, Avery," Kendrick gushed as she walked over to the fireplace in the center of the room. A gold-plated mirror was mounted just above it, and she caught sight of Silas's reflection. She'd always meant to ask him if his image would appear when in front of a mirror. Now she knew. *Fascinating.*

"Thank you," Avery said. "This room is quite popular with our guests. We pride ourselves in giving folks a chance to get away from the busyness of life 'round here. This room is a great place to just sit and relax."

Kendrick glanced up at Avery while he was speaking. He looked past her, and she could tell by the look on his face that Remy had entered the room behind her. Her husband's face took on such an expression of pure love and adoration that it took Kendrick's breath away. Truly, this was the face of a man who had managed to defeat death to be with his soulmate.

"So glad you two could make it," Remy said as she stepped—or waddled—into the room. She wore that brightly colored blue maternity dress that brought out her already stark-blue eyes. "Ugh, sorry. I don't move so fast these days, seeing as I'm big as a house," she said with a grimace.

Avery went to her immediately and put his arm around her. After kissing her cheek, he said, "Nonsense. You look bey-yuutiful," Seriously, a girl could swoon just hearing that sexy Irishman talk.

"Let's show them the rest of the place," Remy said.

"You sure you're up to it?" he asked, putting a protective hand on her swollen belly.

"Oh yes, I'm fine. Been sitting all day and I need to move around a bit," she said.

Kendrick breathed in deeply and told Silas, "This whole place smells like spice and cinnamon. Just like Williamsburg. I love that. Wish you could smell it."

Silas grinned and nodded. "That sounds nice."

Remy and Avery proudly took Kendrick and Silas around and showed them the rest of their charming inn. The sunny breakfast nook featured brick walls and several windows that looked out onto the backyard garden. A one-bedroom suite upstairs was currently unoccupied, so they were able to tour. The small but lovely room had a canopy bed, a window with a bench seat, and a small bathroom.

"Oh, this is so pretty," Kendrick exclaimed.

"I already told Silas that, you know, if everything works out, you two are welcome to come and stay for free," Remy said.

"Perhaps for a honeymoon," Avery said with a grin.

Placing her hand over her heart, Kendrick said, "Oh, can you imagine?"

"Yes," Silas said after she'd barely finished her sentence. Kendrick's heart caught in her throat when she gazed at him. His face held the same expression Avery's had when looking at his wife.

They finished their tour, and Avery gingerly helped his wife back down the narrow staircase.

"If you like, you boys can go somewhere and talk privately," Remy said. "Kendrick and I can sit in the parlor for a bit, if that's okay with you?"

Kendrick nodded.

"Aye, that's a good idea," Avery said. "I love you." Then he tenderly called her something that sounded like "a keeshla," then he turned to Silas. "Shall we go outside for a bit, my good man?"

"Sure," Silas said, blowing Kendrick a kiss as he followed Avery out the back door into the garden area. Kendrick hoped it wouldn't be too awkward for him since he didn't know Avery well. But then, Kendrick had connected quickly with Remy, given their common, yet insane, life circumstances.

Remy eased herself into one of the chairs in the picturesque sitting room.

"Can I get you something?"

"Water would be great, thank you. Please, help yourself to tea or coffee. Anything you like."

Kendrick grabbed a bottle of water from the mini fridge on the table and handed it to Remy. Then, surveying her options, she said, "Normally, I drink coffee. But these dainty teacups are so cute, and I feel like spiced tea is the perfect choice to drink in this gorgeous place!"

Remy laughed. "Many of our guests say the same thing."

After preparing her drink, Kendrick took a seat in one of the plush chairs across from Remy.

"You feeling okay?"

"Yeah, overall I am," Remy said, sipping her water. "I shouldn't complain. I've been pretty lucky as far as nausea and all that. And most importantly, the baby is developing well. Healthy. That's all that matters. I just can't get used to being so *big*, you know? I've always been petite, and now it can be hard to get around. And if one more person asks me if I'm sure I only have one in here ..."

"Ugh. What makes people say such stupid things?" Kendrick said with annoyance.

Remy laughed. "I'll never know. Okay, for real. I'm done complaining. When I first met Avery, I never dreamed I'd be able to marry him and carry his child." Rubbing her belly with affection, she said, "This is a miracle, and that's all there is to it."

"You must be so excited about the baby."

"I am. Oh, I really am. But ..." Her features darkened for a moment, taking Kendrick by surprise.

"But?"

"But I'm really scared," she said.

"Of course you are. But everything's gonna be just fine. Like you said, the baby's healthy. And thank God they have all kinds of things for pain management and all that these days."

"It's not that I'm scared about the delivery. I mean, I am. But even more ... I'm scared I won't be a good mother," Remy said, her eyes tearing up.

Kendrick was shocked. Remy exuded maternal warmth and love.

"Why would you say that? You're gonna be a wonderful mother."

"I didn't have the best upbringing," she said, her voice taking on a hard edge. "Was pretty much neglected. Had to raise myself for the most part."

The thought of Remy's painful childhood saddened Kendrick. She deserved so much better.

"Then you know what not to do," Kendrick said firmly. "I can see how much you and Avery love each other, and you're gonna love your little boy like crazy. Like all parents, you're bound to make mistakes. But your son will always know how much you love him. And you'll provide him the loving home you deserved but never got to have."

"Thank you so much, Kendrick," she said, wiping her eyes. "I didn't know how much I needed to hear that."

"And you have a stepdaughter, right? Didn't you say

Avery has a daughter?"

"*Had* a daughter."

Kendrick's eyes opened wide in horror.

"No, no. It's not as tragic as it sounds. Avery had a daughter, you know, the first time around."

"Oh, I see," Kendrick said with relief.

"She was just a little girl when Avery went off to war," Remy explained. "Charlotte was one of the reasons he was stuck on Earth for so long. He felt terrible about going off to war and leaving her behind."

"Silas struggled with the same kind of thing! Going off to war and leaving his family."

Remy nodded. "Another reason why it's important that those two have a talk."

Kendrick's heart felt lighter already. Yes. Maybe Avery truly could help to ease Silas's pain.

"You didn't tell me your husband had such a sexy accent," she said, raising an eyebrow.

"I swear, even after all this time, I never get tired of hearing him talk," Remy said with a laugh. "Was one of the first things that attracted me to him. That voice. When I first met him, I had no idea he was dead."

"Really?"

Remy shook her head. "Nope. Thought he was a sexy Civil War reenactor."

"That's so funny. I'm sure I'd have thought the same thing if I had just met Silas on the street. We actually met at the battlefield when he appeared right in front of me."

"He did? Weren't you frightened?"

"Not at all." With a shrug, she said, "I was ghost hunting."

"Ah, I see."

"What was that Avery called you? A keeshla?"

Remy's pretty face lit up. "*A chuisle.* An Irish term of endearment. The full phrase is *a chuisle mo chroi.* Literally, it means you are the pulse of my heart. He first called me that when he had no pulse, no beating heart."

Kendrick gasped softly. "Oh, that's so beautiful."

"It truly is," Remy said, gazing toward the garden where Avery had gone off with Silas.

Kendrick took a sip of the tea, which was full of spicy, flavorful goodness. Sitting with Remy and talking had a calming effect on her. Being with someone who understood what she was going through helped immensely.

"Do you think ... this can really happen for us?" Kendrick asked.

"I hope with all my heart that it does, Kendrick. I want this so much for you. For you both. I'm hopeful that having Silas talk with Avery will help. Avery's such a gentle soul. He has a way with people. A way of understanding them, empathizing with them. I really think he might be able to help Silas find peace. And if that happens ..."

"Silas might be allowed to come back. Or he might go to Heaven," Kendrick said, reminding herself to hope and pray for what was best for Silas, not what was best for her.

"Yes," Remy said quietly. "If he does cross over, that doesn't mean he'll stop loving you. You know that, right?"

She nodded. "I do know that."

Sipping her tea, she looked toward the garden and wondered what the two men were talking about.

"As much as I love talking with you, Remy, I can't help feeling jealous of Silas right now. He gets to sit out there and listen to Avery's brogue."

Remy laughed. "I understand. Believe me."

I know you do. You understand everything, and I am so incredibly grateful for that.

21

───────

Silas watched Avery draw in a deep breath as they both stepped outside. The garden was lush with flowers and the grass freshly mowed. Though Silas had a vague recollection of what flowers smelled like, he'd never experienced the scent of a lawn after it had just been cut. Every year, when the weather turned warm, people talked about how much they loved that smell.

But maybe someday he would find out what fresh-cut grass smelled like.

"After going so long without being able to smell anything or to feel the wind on me face, I learned never to take it for granted," Avery said with a sympathetic smile.

"I can believe that," Silas said. "Feels strange, having someone else know what this is like, you know?"

Avery nodded.

Turning back to look at the brick house, Silas said, "This inn here is incredible. Did you ever imagine you'd wind up in a place like this? With *her*?"

"Never. Many miles and more than a hundred years

from where I started, yet here I am. Every single day feels like a miracle."

Avery led him over to a small table and chair that were set up in the garden.

"Shall we sit?" Avery said.

"You know it makes no difference to me," Silas said with a wink. "But yes."

Avery pulled out a chair slightly for Silas, and he marveled at how convenient it was to be around somebody who knew he was a ghost. Silas couldn't pull out the chair himself, yet he needed to appear to be sitting in case one of the inn guests wandered out back.

Once they were seated, the atmosphere grew a tad awkward. After all, the men barely knew each other.

"I know it must be strange to sit here and talk about things ... personal things," Avery said tactfully. "But unfortunately, facin' up to your past is the only way to escape your existence. The only way out is through."

"I know," Silas said, thinking of all the spirits he'd encountered over the years. His heart squeezed in his chest when he recalled Rebekah's harrowing tale about seeing her little brother's body floating in the river. She'd been momentarily distracted, and he had drowned.

Dear God, I cannot begin to imagine that woman's pain.

Kendrick had nearly been destroyed when her brother had died. How would she have felt if she'd been responsible for his death?

"It's never easy to confront your past," Avery said. "But I'm sure Kendrick is worth it."

"Of course she is," Silas said. That was one thing he was absolutely sure about.

"There is something I wanted to ask you. Silas, I want you to know that anything you tell me stays between us."

Silas nodded. Though he barely knew Avery, he already trusted him. Both he and Remy were so eager to help, and there was nothing in it for them whatsoever. They were just good people, and that's all there was to it.

"As you likely know, everybody's situation is different. And you also know there's no guarantee how this is gonna play out. I can tell you that in my case, when the time came, I was given a choice about whether or not I wished to come back. To live again. The same choice was given to my soldier friend back in Gettysburg. Once we sorted through our personal problems, it was up to us on what would happen to our bodies, our spirits. We could go on to our reward or we could remain," Avery explained.

"I spoke to a woman in Williamsburg recently. She came back too. She told me that she was given a different choice."

"Is that so?" Avery asked with interest.

Silas didn't want to share too many personal details, but for the sake of discussion he did want to talk about it. At the very least, he wouldn't divulge her name.

"In her case, she had taken her own life. Because of that, there were things she hadn't done while she was living. Lessons she needed to learn and so forth. Her choice was different. She was supposed to come back and live again. Normally, she would have been born all over again, but since she was in love with a man who was still alive, she was given the option to come back now."

"Ah, I see. She must be the woman who married the woodworker?"

"Yes," Silas said. So much for concealing her identity.

"Fascinating. There is a chance that you will be given a choice, Silas. My question to you is, are you sure that coming back to life is what you really want?"

"Of course. I want to be with Kendrick. I love her."

"I know you do, my friend," Avery said kindly. "But you've been around this old Earth for such a long time. I know you don't want to hurt her, and I know how much you long to be with her. I just want you to know that it's all right if you want to go to your rest when the time comes."

Silas knew he would never leave Kendrick unless he had absolutely no choice.

"Silas, just between us now, do you really want to live again?"

He considered Avery's question.

"As I said, every situation is different. When my time came, my daughter came and spoke to me."

Silas watched the man's gray eyes as they clouded over with emotion.

"I'd been terribly torn between staying with me darlin' Remy and goin' home to be with the daughter I hadn't seen since I went off to war. Charlotte came and told me it was all right to stay."

If Avery got to see his child, did that mean Silas might see his loved ones as well? Perhaps Levi would come to greet him.

"In Jesse's case—Jesse is the soldier I mentioned—he got a glimpse of the other side. He loves his woman, Lucy, every bit as much as I love Remy. But Silas, he told me that in that moment, the choice was not easy. It's perfect over there, my friend. Filled with pure love, peace, happiness. I just want you to know that it's all right if you choose to go into the light."

Silas gazed around at the garden, watching the wind gently blow the leaves on the trees. The cheerful chirping of birds was the only sound to be heard. Avery had given him much to think about.

"I want to live, Avery. The most important thing will

always be Kendrick. I want to build a life with her. Yet it's more than that. I want to be around people again, and I'll never take a single moment for granted. Goddamn it, I want a chance to do things right this time."

"That sounds lovely. I just want you to understand that if you're given a choice, it truly will be your choice. And there is no one right answer. It's all right to do what's best for you."

"I 'preciate you sayin' that. I truly do."

"Now. As to the matter of why you're still here in the first place," Avery said. "Do you know why?"

"I think I do. Trouble is, it's not just one thing. One mistake I got to get past. More like I feel like I screwed up my whole life in every way possible."

"You're a good man, Silas. I could tell that 'bout you straight away."

"I try to be a good man now. Back then, I wasn't."

"What did you do that you think was so terrible?"

"Turned my back on my family to go to war."

Avery smiled, which should have been an odd response, but it wasn't. Silas could see it was a smile of understanding.

"Me darlin' daughter was only six years old when I went off to war. I always feared it was a mistake, joinin' the war and leaving a wife and child behind."

"Your wife—your first wife—did you miss her when you left for battle?"

"I did," Avery said. "She was a good friend, a dear woman. But she wasn't me soulmate. Even so, I felt leavin' her with a little girl to raise on her own wasn't the right thing to do. And leaving my daughter ..."

Silas could see the pain in Avery's eyes.

"All this time," he continued, "you never do stop missing your loved ones, now do ya?"

Silas shook his head sadly. "No. You carry them with you. Always. Then why did you join the war?"

"I felt it was the right thing to do at the time. Only second-guessed it once I got into battle. And when I didn't make it back."

"Why did you feel it was the right thing to do?"

"America was my adopted country. Despite the way the Irish were treated back then, the country was still good to me. Felt I had to defend it. From what, I'm not even sure anymore. I fought alongside my brothers in Alabama."

"You fought for the South?"

"Yes. Which brings lots more complications, as you know. We felt we were fightin' for our rights, our land, our families. Who the hell really knows what we were really fightin' for? Most wars are stupid, I'm afraid."

"But you fought because you truly believed you were doing the right thing."

"Yes, indeed."

"Well, I didn't. Not me," he said bitterly. "Hell no. I fought because I had to be a goddamn big shot. A war hero."

"A young man's hubris," Avery said with a shrug. "You think you're the only one who joined a fight for that reason?"

Silas was surprised by the casual nature of the man's response. He spent so much time judging himself harshly that he'd come to expect others to do the same.

"You know how many men I fought alongside that were only there 'cause they wanted to prove how tough they were? Enlisted so they could kill themselves some damn Rebels or Yanks? Lot of 'em died, too. And crossed over. So what makes you so terrible, Mr. Silas?"

"I abandoned my family."

"You think those other guys didn't?" he asked without missing a beat.

"My parents, my sisters, my brother. They needed me back home," Silas said, feeling a fresh wave of shame and regret threaten to consume him.

"You made a mistake," Avery said matter-of-factly. "And if you had it to do over again, you wouldn't. Do you really feel you should be condemned to eternal damnation, in the form of being trapped here as a ghost forever, because you made a mistake?"

He had to admit the idea did sound rather ludicrous when he heard it out loud.

"You feel that leaving your family was a terrible choice, and you're heartbroken over it. To me, that means you're a good man with a good heart. You cannot change the past, you can only go forward."

"You make it sound so easy."

"Six years old. My baby girl was six years old when her daddy went away and never came back," he said, his voice choked with emotion. "I regretted my choice to fight every day of the battle. When I lay dying on the hill of Little Round Top, my last words were 'Charlotte, I'm so sorry.'" Avery paused a moment to wipe his eyes. "I made a mistake when I went to war. It wasn't the right thing to do, and I paid the price for it. And so did my family. Do you think I'm a terrible person, Silas?"

Silas saw Avery for who he was. A kind, flawed man and loving father. A good friend.

"Of course not."

"For a long time, I felt like a terrible person. I don't anymore. You need to have the same revelation. And don't just do it for Kendrick. Do it for yourself because you deserve better than torturing yourself until the end of time."

Silas met Avery's gaze and saw a man so much like himself. It was impossible to hate Avery, so why did Silas hate himself so much?

"This does help me, Avery. Thank you."

"Plenty of people in this world do harm to others intentionally. That's not you."

"I've done plenty of harm. During the war. So many things ..."

"You killed people," Avery said in that now familiar casual tone.

"Yes. Did you?"

"Yes. And I used to spend many nights roaming around all alone thinking of those men. Their children, whose fathers never came back either. Sweethearts, wives, parents."

Silas's ghostly heart ached as he listened to Avery describe his own pain so vividly.

"So many regrets," he said in a faraway voice as he gazed at the garden. Turning back to Silas, he repeated, "The only way out is through. I've been thinking about your situation, and I have an idea on what may help."

"Yeah?"

"I'm not the only one who understands what it's like to fight and kill and die in war. I would like to suggest that you meet two friends of mine. Jesse, the Gettysburg soldier I mentioned, and a man name Sean. Sean didn't die in battle. Hasn't died at all, you know, yet." Avery chuckled at the absurdity of his words, and Silas joined in. "But Sean is active military. A sergeant. The man's been through hell and back in battle. Like me, those men understand. I'm sure you considered those you fought with as your brothers."

"Yes. I surely did."

"As did I. And Jesse and Sean are me brothers as well. Together, I think we can help you. Are you game?"

"I am. Let's do it."

Ripping open the raw, emotional wounds of battle would be a new kind of torture. But if it brought him closer to being with Kendrick, he was all in.

Avery stood up, and they both headed back into the inn. To Silas's delight, the first thing he heard was Kendrick's laughter. She and Remy seemed to be having a wonderful time together. Remy looked up at her husband and smiled from where she rested in the chair with her feet up. Then she turned to smile at Silas.

"How are you boys doing?"

"Very well, thank you," he responded.

"I told him my idea, and he's agreed to do it," Avery said.

"Oh, that's great," Remy exclaimed.

"What idea?" Kendrick asked.

"He thinks I should meet with two of his friends. One formerly dead, one who's just plain alive. Both soldiers. Avery thinks having us talk about things—tradin' war stories and such—might help me."

"Oh, that is a good idea," Kendrick said. She got up and walked over to him.

"Perfect. We'll set it up as soon as possible," Remy said, absently rubbing her belly. "Fortunately, both guys live in Maryland so it's not too far for them to travel. If we do this right away, Silas, you might be able to hold our son not too long after he's born."

"My God, what an honor that would be," Silas said, his heart filling with hope. Kendrick looked at him lovingly, and he almost expected her to put her arm around him.

Soon, my sweet. Perhaps soon I'll be able to hold you, and I will never, ever let go.

22

———————

Kendrick met up with Silas at their usual spot at Market Square during her lunch break. She still couldn't believe he was really here after she'd endured so many months without him. It felt so good to be near him. Still, with everything going on, her emotions were constantly in flux. Euphoria at the thought of him being alive someday. Despair at the possibility of losing him all over again. She had been devastated by grief when he'd disappeared; she knew exactly how painful it would be if it happened again.

Silas seemed optimistic, his eyes lighting up as he watched the tourists. He was probably hoping he'd soon be among the living again, no longer having to physically stay away from people. He turned to watch her as she ate her chef salad.

"What's on your mind?" she asked.

"What would you do if I came back?"

"What do you mean?"

"Like, what would *we* do?"

"Lots of things," Kendrick said. "First of all, I like to think we wouldn't leave the bedroom for days."

"Ohhhh, that sounds *heavenly*," Silas said, gazing at her with desire. "I like the way you think, my love. But I mean, what would we do for the future? Stay here? Move near your parents?"

"I don't want to talk about things like that."

"Why not? You're not changing your mind about being with me, are you?"

"Of course not, you silly man," she said with a smile. "I'm just very wary about talking too much about the future."

"In case it doesn't happen."

"Exactly," she said. "Trust me, it's been hard to keep myself from imagining all kinds of scenarios about what we would do if we were lucky enough to share our lives together. I can't allow myself to get wrapped up in things that might not happen."

"Will you do it for me?"

"Do what?"

"Indulge me, Kendrick. I really want to know what you would want to do if we were able to stay together," Silas said earnestly. "I like thinking about our life together. It makes me happy."

"You're so sweet," Kendrick said with a sigh. She took a sip from her water bottle before continuing. "Well, I do want to make you happy."

Silas's eyes flashed with excitement, and she realized how eager he really was to hear what she had to say.

"I would want to marry you, of course. I want to have children with you, but not right away. Having children shakes up your entire life, and I don't feel ready for that yet. I want to get things settled down first. I still want to buy a house and all that. After everything we've been through, I would want some time for just the two of as husband and wife."

Silas smiled fondly at her words.

"What would you want to do?" she asked.

"Well, I agree with everything you said. First thing I'd want to do is marry the hell out of you."

Kendrick laughed.

"I would marry you and we would have a lovely honeymoon somewhere. As much as I do want to stay at O'Rorke's sometime, it wouldn't be for our honeymoon."

"Why not?"

"Because I wouldn't want to scandalize our friends, not to mention their poor innocent guests, with the loud noises coming from our bedroom suite," Silas said, gazing at her with such raw desire and intensity that it took her breath away. "Kendrick, the things I would do to you if I could ... I'd give you so many orgasms, you'd lose count."

Kendrick held her breath as Silas's voice took on a deep, sensual tone of sheer lust. He so rarely spoke to her that way. She loved it.

"If you don't want kids right away, you'd better stock up on every kind of birth control there is, my sweet. Because I would pound you so hard and so long, we just might break the headboard on the bed."

"Thank you for giving me that image to use during my ... private time," Kendrick said, blushing hard. Silas groaned deep in his throat, making the somewhat embarrassing admission worth it. "You know, until we can make that fantasy a reality."

"And then, after we finally leave the bedroom, and after you'd regained your ability to walk," Silas continued, making her laugh again, "I'd find work somewhere ... somehow ... and we'd save up money for a house. We could live anywhere you like. Near your parents or here or anywhere."

Kendrick wrinkled her nose. "Would you even want to live here? After being trapped here so long, I figured you'd want to go as far away as possible."

Silas shook his head. "No, I like it here. I like the busyness of it all. The people, the activity. Most folks that come here are on vacation and they're having a good time. They're happy. I love that. I mean, if it were possible for me to travel, I would. I'd like to visit Massachusetts to see how much it's changed since I've been there. Travel to other places just for fun. But I kinda like the idea of living around here. Feel like I've been on the outside looking in for so long that I'd love to be a real part of this place."

"That's beautiful, Silas. I love that."

"But if you wanted to move closer to your parents, that would be just fine."

"Newport News isn't that far away from here. I could easily visit them all the time if we lived around here."

"And I know it would be really expensive and might not be possible," Silas said as he watched the tourists milling around. "But I'd love to own a shop in the Colonial Williamsburg area."

"Really?"

"Yeah. I've always wanted to be a shop owner, silly as it sounds. Well, not *always*. Just since I died. Had plenty of time to think about what I would do if I was alive. As you know, in life I was a total asshole."

"Agree to disagree," Kendrick said, and he laughed.

"Fine. But this time around, I'd love to be a shop owner who has regular customers but also lots of tourists who might pass my way and I never see them again. Sounds dumb, but to me there's something special about being a tiny part of a stranger's life, if only for a few minutes."

"It's not dumb, Silas. Hearing you talk like that just makes me love you more."

Silas smiled gratefully. Kendrick watched the busy outdoor shoppers as they pored over the merchandise. The cashier, located inside a large tent, happily joked around with one of the kids who was buying a small drum. How easy it was to imagine Silas smiling and joking with his own customers.

"And it would be nice seeing the same faces over and over again. Getting to know them personally and know what they like and don't like."

"Brie, Irish cheddar, crackers, sourdough bread, and garlic olive oil," Kendrick said with a smile. "That's usually Remy's order."

"You see? That's marvelous. And look how that relationship turned out. Once she was a regular customer, and now she's gonna be a lifelong friend. I really believe she will, Kendrick. No matter what happens with me."

"I believe that too," Kendrick said. She looked forward to introducing Remy to Deanna and Marie. They both would go crazy over Avery's sexy Irish accent.

"You could help run the store with me. I mean, only if that's what you wanted."

"I would love that, Silas. I could do all the money stuff, the accounting and all that."

"Yes, you could!" he said excitedly. "But only when you're not writing. Naturally, my store would feature my wife's thriller books on the shelves."

His thoughtfulness overwhelmed her, and she found herself fighting tears. Silas's words were so filled with hope and promise for the future.

"You've got it all figured out, now don't you?"

"Mind you, that's my ideal version of life. A successful store, a wife who's a published author, a nice house, and children at some point. But Kendrick, it won't have to be the ideal version, will it? If the business fails and we can't afford a big house, who the hell cares? The future will be ideal anyway, because it will be with you."

"Silas, I want to be with you so much it hurts," she told him.

"I know, my sweet. I feel the same way."

Soon enough, we'll find out how our story ends.

Kendrick's stomach roiled again with churning emotions.

God, please let this be a happy ending.

23

———

Kendrick's hands shook on the steering wheel as she drove toward Yorktown Battlefield. Remy and Avery had arranged for their friends to come to Virginia on Saturday. With the baby coming soon, there was no time to waste as far as the mother-to-be was concerned. Not that Silas's progress couldn't continue without her help, but she seemed determined to get everything settled before she gave birth. As far as Kendrick was concerned, she couldn't have Silas in her arms fast enough, so that timeline worked just fine for her.

That, and she wasn't sure how much more emotional upheaval she could take. The not knowing what was going to happen was extremely stressful, and she felt like she was on the verge of a nervous breakdown. Kendrick was doing all she could to stay strong, but it wasn't easy.

They'd all decided it would be best for Silas to speak with Avery, Jesse, and Sean on the battlefield near where he'd breathed his last, so long ago. Both Avery and Jesse had said they'd felt compelled to return to the place where they'd died when they were given the choice to come back to life. Hopefully, being near where Silas had passed would help him on his journey back to life.

Or his journey to his final, eternal destination.

Kendrick felt physically sick just thinking about that. She forced herself to breathe slowly and deliberately in an effort to stay calm as she pulled into a parking spot at the battlefield Visitor Center. She'd deliberately parked far away from the main entrance so she could have some privacy with Silas for a moment while they waited for the others to arrive.

She got out of her car and looked around. Then she turned her head sharply to the left when she felt a presence. Sure enough, Silas faded into view.

"Are you okay?" he asked.

"Not really. I'm terrified. This could be it, Silas. This could be the day you ..."

"This could literally be the first day of the rest of my life, Kendrick," he said in a soothing voice. "A life with you."

"Yes, or it could be the last day of—"

"Let's not talk about that. My sweet, I wish there was some way to make this easier on you. You know that whatever happens, I will love you. Forever and always."

"I love you too," she said, her voice quavering.

Silas gazed at her with concern but kept quiet for a moment. He probably knew if he said anything else, she would lose it completely.

A car pulled into the lot, and Kendrick saw Avery behind the wheel. She waved at him, and he drove over to a spot near where she stood with Silas.

As they watched Avery tenderly help his pregnant wife out of the car, Kendrick knew she and Silas were thinking the same thing.

That could be us someday.

Visions of happy Christmases and birthdays with Silas and their own children flooded her mind. She pictured her parents gleefully spoiling their adored grandchildren, with Kurt watching over them all from above. She drew in an audible, gaspy breath.

"It's all right, Kendrick," Silas said softly. "Everything's gonna be all right."

Remy took one look at Kendrick and rushed over to her. Throwing her arms around Kendrick, she wrapped her in a warm and loving embrace. There was simply no need for words.

Avery and Silas spoke quietly together for a few minutes. Soon enough, another car pulled up with two men inside. Remy's face lit up in a pretty smile, and Kendrick knew these were the guys they were waiting for. She watched as they got out of the car. One man was tall and somewhat slender, with brownish-blond hair. The other was equally tall but had a much more muscular physique, with dark brown hair and stunning hazel eyes. Both men were quite attractive, and it was easy to tell which one was the farm boy soldier from Texas and which was the military sergeant.

"Remy darlin', lemme have a look at ya," Jesse said, his blue-gray eyes filled with warmth.

"Ugh, I'm huge," Remy complained.

"You look *luuuvely*," he said in a charming southern drawl. "You're the second most beautiful pregnant woman I ever laid eyes on."

Jesse was dead once, too. And now he's a father.

Kendrick's emotions threatened to spiral out of control again, but she forced herself to get a grip.

"Jeez Remy, do all the guys you know have such beautiful accents?" Kendrick asked.

"Fraid not," Sean said in a deep voice. "Though my midwestern-ness does sneak out once in a while. You betcha, dontcha knooow."

Kendrick laughed. "You must be Sergeant Stone."

"Sean," he said with a grin. "Nice to meet you, Kendrick."

She was about to shake his hand, but he nodded and bowed slightly instead. Kendrick understood why when she glanced at his hands. He was missing several fingers. Remy had told her he'd been hurt during an explosion in battle, and Kendrick felt bad that Sean was clearly self-conscious about the injuries he'd sustained.

"And I'm Jesse Spenser," Jesse said, walking over to her and extending his hand. Kendrick held out her hand and he took it in both of his. "I'm so glad to meet you."

"You too."

"I know this must be a hard time for you," Jesse said, his tenderness nearly setting off a new flood of tears in her. "But I want you to know we're gonna do everythin' we can to bring Silas back to you."

"Thank you," she managed to say in a whisper.

"I know the waitin' is terrible," Jesse said. "And as you know, we don't know for sure if anything's gonna happen today or ..."

Kendrick nodded, feeling wrung out already.

"But I'm thinkin' it's best if you ladies stayed kinda close by," he said, glancing over at Remy. "Maybe there's a café you can go to or somethin' like that. Avery can text ya if anything happens ... or if it seems like anything is *going* to happen."

"Great idea," Remy said. "That makes sense."

"I just want to thank you all so much for everything you're doing to help us," Kendrick said, her heart full as she took in all the loving, friendly people who had gathered today.

"Our pleasure to help," Sean said. "Believe me."

"Let's just ..." Kendrick said, feeling herself losing control, "get started so we can get this all over with."

"Right," Jesse said with a firm nod.

"Silas, I—I can't ... I can't say goodbye, or I will completely fall apart," Kendrick said, her tears finally falling. Remy covered her mouth, clearly upset at seeing Kendrick's pain. Not just seeing it but *understanding* it.

"It's all right, my sweet," Silas said, looking her in the eye. "I know what's in your heart, and you know what's in mine. Besides, you know that whatever happens, *this isn't goodbye.*"

Kendrick nodded, holding her breath as she watched Silas, Jesse, Avery, and Sean walk onto the battlefield together.

Fear seized her heart.

What if only three of them come back?

24

With his ghostly heart pounding, Silas walked through the battlefield with the other three men. He was grateful the weather had cooperated with a warm and sunny day. Remy's husband and friends were so kind and seemed so determined to help him that he got the feeling they'd have sat out in the rain if necessary.

"We might want to go to the exact place where you died," Jesse suggested.

Silas nodded, feeling a renewed sense of dread. These men with him were *real* soldiers, no doubt having signed up for battle for noble reasons and then dying as heroes. Well, save for Sean. He was an active hero in the U.S. military. Now Silas would be forced to admit his shameful secrets about joining the war for stupid pride and his death by illness, not bullets.

He pictured Kendrick's face, reminding himself what this whole ordeal was about.

In silence, Silas led the men to the group of trees where he had died.

"It was here," he said simply.

Silas sat under one of the huge trees, and Jesse, Avery, and Sean sat down in a circle with him. Fresh anxiety stirred in his ghostly stomach. How strange this all was, being with guys he hardly knew in the middle of the battlefield where he'd passed away. He felt incredibly weak, both physically and emotionally, being around such strong, living men. God, he was sick of being dead. Sick of this existence. And beyond sick with concern over the woman he loved. It pained him to think of everything she'd endured since the day they'd met on this very field.

"How are you doing?" Jesse asked him. Such a simple question, but Silas could tell by the concern in his tone and expression that it was more than just a pleasantry. He actually wanted to know.

"Doing all right, I suppose. More worried about Kendrick than anything else."

"I understand," Jesse said, and the others nodded.

"You know we'll all take care of her," Avery reassured him. "No matter what happens."

"My wife is a therapist," Sean said. "She can always help find a grief expert for Kendrick if it comes to that."

"My God," Silas said. "She's suffered so much grief in her life already. I can't stand the thought of causing her any more pain."

"There is a good chance you will be able to stay with her," Jesse said. "In every case that I know of where a spirit came back to live again, it was because there was somebody on Earth who loved them dearly. But if you do ... go on to eternal rest ... Kendrick won't ever be alone."

"Me Remy is a mother hen already," Avery said with a laugh. "She'll look after her for sure."

"Good," Silas said. "That helps. It truly does. I guess I

need to stay positive here and hope for the best. So how do we even go about this? Where do we start?"

"Welp," Jesse began. "How 'bout you tell us what you know so far. I gather from Avery that you have a good idea why you're here."

As hard as it was to talk about, Silas knew it was best to plow forward and spill all his secrets. No sense in playing it coy—it would only waste time.

"I made a lot of terrible mistakes in my life," he said. "Avery mighta told you, I left my family to go to war."

"Same as I did," Avery said, which helped bolster him to continue.

"But at least you joined the war for the right reasons. You believed you were doing the right thing. Standin' up for your country and fightin' for your rights." Turning to Jesse, he asked, "Is that why you joined the war effort?"

"Yeah, it is. Hated leavin' my mama and daddy all alone, but I felt like it was the right thing to do. At the time, anyway."

Silas could see the regret on Jesse's face. Even after all this time, he clearly still had his doubts.

"Well, I didn't join for any noble reasons at all. Pure, stupid pride; that's all there was to it. Joined up to prove what I was made of," he said with disgust.

Sean chuckled. "You have any idea how many guys I serve with that are like that?"

Silas considered his words. He, too, had known soldiers like that. Yet somehow, he still felt like the only jerk who had done such a foolish thing.

"I guess I know I wasn't the only one, but that doesn't make it any less stupid and selfish. Even after all this time, I can't believe how badly I managed to mess things up. I wasted my whole life, and it was only after I was dead that I really understood that. I see the living people roaming around and it's like, I get it now. Every single day you have a choice to do good or bad. Every day is like a new beginning. I really do want a second chance. Kendrick is the number one reason, of course. I want a chance to love and care for her the way she deserves. I want to do things right for once."

"That old sayin' about you don't know what you got 'til it's gone is the darn truth," Jesse said. "I remember feeling that way, Silas. That awful, helpless feeling that nothin' you do matters. You can't touch anything. Can't do anything. Can't help anybody no matter how much you wish you could."

"Yes, *exactly*," Silas exclaimed. "These life lessons I finally learned don't do much good if I don't have a life anymore."

The men chuckled and nodded.

"And as terrible as I feel about abandoning my family, joinin' up with the war was just the beginning. Hard enough to think 'bout forgiving myself for being so careless with my life." A sudden painful image of Kendrick's grief over her brother's recklessness flashed in his mind, making him wince. "But then there's stuff that happened —stuff I did — when I was a soldier."

The others nodded at that too, but now their expressions were grim.

It should have felt strange and awkward to tell relative strangers about his life, but these guys didn't feel like strangers. Something in the way they simply sat and listened made him feel they understood his words. They already felt like friends, kindred spirits. Two of them had literally been spirits once, and they'd all been through the horrors of war. Somehow, being with them felt like being with his brothers in the war.

"That's the life of a soldier," Sean said. "Whatever your reasons might be, that's what you sign up for when you join. Then, in battle, it comes down to kill or be killed. You do what you have to do to survive."

"As much as I know I can tell Kendrick anything ..." Silas said.

"There's things you saw, things you've done in the war that you don't want to tell her," Sean finished.

"Yes," Silas admitted quietly. "It's not that I've deliberately kept things from her. I worry about giving her too much gory detail, even though God knows she's familiar with death."

"Remy told us about her twin brother," Jesse said. "I'm so sorry."

"Something like that can make you want to protect her even more," Avery said. "You may want to confide in her, but you don't want to upset her."

"I know I'm old fashioned," Jesse said. "But I come from a time when women were 'sposed to be protected from stuff like that."

"Only natural to protect the woman you love from the ugly stuff you've seen," Sean said. "Believe me, I've served with some tough women in the service who can handle that kind of thing as well as any man. But our wives—our women—are civilians."

"I didn't protect my sweet Lucy as well as I should have," Jesse said mournfully. "She's real sensitive to ghosts. Always has been. When I was dead, even when I was invisible, she could sense my presence. Poor thing could always sense when ghosts were around, and she used to be so frightened. 'Til she met me, anyways," he said with a weak smile. "Trouble is, you can pay a price when you're that sensitive. She had the bad fortune of being at Devil's Den at the same time of day when I died, and she felt my death. She actually experienced it … felt … what happened to me."

"That happened to Kendrick!" Silas said. "Wasn't my death, but it was on the battlefield here. Felt like she'd been shot. It was scary as hell."

Jesse nodded, looking pale and grim. "Horrible thing to see, isn't it? Talk about feelin' helpless."

"Yeah," Silas said, his heart aching as he remembered Kendrick's suffering. "She's already been through so much in her life. I don't want to add to her pain by telling her more awful stuff."

"But you can tell us," Avery said. "We've seen war. We've killed people. And we know what that does to your soul."

"Kendrick knows I killed people in the war. But I don't talk about it much with her. I'd be lyin' if I said it was only to protect her."

"You don't want her thinkin' less of ya," Jesse said, while Avery and Sean nodded in agreement.

Silas was overwhelmed by the understanding displayed before him by these soldiers. There was no judgment. After spending hundreds of years feeling like he was the worst person who ever lived, he got the feeling there was nothing he could say that would rattle these guys. What a relief that was to know.

"Those people I killed …" Silas said, unsure of how to express what he wanted to say.

After a moment of silence, Jesse helped him along. "You never forget their faces, do you? 'Specially when you're a spirit, and you've got nothing but endless time before you. Time to think, regret, and second-guess every move you ever made in life."

"You think of their families," Avery said. "You have that empty, gut-wrenching feeling of loss when you're missing your own family, and you know their families endured the same thing. You think of the mothers, the fathers, the sweethearts. The children," he said, his voice catching. Silas knew he was thinking of his own precious baby girl.

"And you wonder what the hell you were even fighting for in the first place," Sean said. "No matter what your reasons were for fighting, you still wonder. I'm active military, Silas. I joined up because I love my country, and I don't regret serving. But sometimes I still wonder what the killing is really about. And whether or not it's worth it."

Jesse, Avery, and Sean had just voiced some of Silas's own private thoughts as clearly as if he'd spoken them himself. Not just one person, *but all three of them* felt the way he did. Had done some of the horrific things he'd done. Yet, he didn't think less of any one of them. This rather did feel like the sudden epiphany he'd been searching for.

These men are flawed human beings just like I am. Just like we all are.

The thought was simple yet momentous. His revelation felt so powerful, he nearly expected a white light to appear. But nothing happened. Yet.

Silas gazed out at the battlefield for a moment. It was quiet here. Peaceful. The wind blew the leaves in the trees, and he heard the cries of birds in the distance. And yet, in his head, he could still hear the guns. The cannon fire. Terrible visions still filled his head, and he knew he'd never be rid of them.

"You never forget what it feels like to shoot someone," Silas said in a dull monotone. "The blood splatter ... the brains ..."

Yes. Those were things he wasn't about to tell Kendrick. Death wasn't always peaceful. Sometimes it was ugly and violent and horrible.

"The mangled bodies lyin' on the ground," he continued. "You see a dead man and you think that was somebody's little boy once. Mighta been somebody's father," he said, gazing sympathetically at Avery.

"There's somebody's darling," Jesse said. "That's what we used to say. You just knew that was somebody's whole world lyin' there in a puddle of his own blood."

"And when you're the one who took that world away ... How do you ever recover from that?" Silas said. Despite thinking he had it all figured out just a few moments ago, he again felt hopeless about his situation. But somehow Avery and Jesse had made it back. And they'd clearly felt the same way he did.

"The fact that you're this torn apart over it after all this time shows how much you care," Sean said. "Shows you're not some kind of monster."

"Like a lot of things in life, you don't ever totally recover," Jesse said. "Kendrick hasn't 'recovered' from the loss of her brother. But she got through the worst of it and somehow was able to move forward in her life. That's what you need to do."

"Like I told you before, the only way out is through," Avery said. "And you are going through by talking about these things. And you just may make it out the other side after all."

Silas reflected on Rebekah's pain over the accident with her brother. She wasn't "over it" either. But she had healed immensely since those dark days of despair. The thought gave him renewed hope that a complete recovery wasn't necessary. He merely had to let go of the deep guilt he'd held onto for so long. Forgiving himself, just a little, might be enough to unite him with Kendrick at last.

From that moment forward, Silas held nothing back. He

spoke freely about his guilt over his parents and siblings and talked more about the people he'd killed in battle. He talked about what it had felt like to watch his best friend die violently. Sean spoke candidly to him about having suffered through the same trauma. His friend, too, had been blown up right before his very eyes by a suicide bomber in Afghanistan. Silas hadn't even noticed until Sean held up his hands that he had lost several fingers on that tragic day.

Sean had felt the deep guilt and survivor's remorse Silas had when Levi died. Both Avery and Jesse understood the pain of leaving behind a family in order to head to war. All of them understood what it was like to love a woman more than life itself. These soldiers didn't just listen. They *knew* what he was feeling. In so many ways, they *were* him.

The entire experience, speaking with these men, was truly transformative. Something deep within Silas began to change.

His time was coming.

25

Remy had patiently waited with Kendrick for hours while the men talked on the battlefield, and for that she was grateful. The two sat at a corner table in a restaurant a few blocks away. Thankfully the place wasn't crowded, and they had an understanding server who told them they were welcome to stay as long as they liked. In return, the women had promised a very generous tip.

Kendrick's nerves were on edge, and she jumped every time Remy's phone buzzed with a notification. Remy was always quick to shake her head each time, to let her know it wasn't Avery with any news yet.

"I hope it's going okay. I wish so much I could be there with him," Kendrick said.

"I know you do. But it's probably best to let them talk privately. There's still some things about the war that Avery has trouble talking about with me. Without us there, they won't have to hold anything back."

"I guess I'm just afraid he might ... go ... and I won't be there to say goodbye."

"That was always Avery's greatest fear. That he would disappear without any notice. I used to go visit him at Little Round Top almost every day. Toward the end, when we knew he was making progress, he was really afraid that one day I'd show up and he'd just be gone. Scared him so much. The idea of me being left alone."

"And from what you told me, it's not like you had family to lean on. You really would be alone."

"Right, but I had Jesse and Lucy, as well as Sean and his wife, Theresa. And you have a lot of people here to support you too, Kendrick."

The phone buzzed again, giving Kendrick another mini heart attack.

"Just another email," Remy said, shaking her head. "Did I ever tell you how Avery came back?"

"Silas told me he got to see his daughter."

With a lovely smile, Remy said, "Yes, he did. Oh, that made him so happy. He was torn between wanting to stay with me and wanting to cross over to be with his little girl. What a painful choice." She stroked her belly as she spoke. "I can't imagine how much he missed Charlotte. She was only six years old when he left for war. When she appeared to him when it was, you know, his time, she appeared as an adult."

"Oh, wow."

"Yeah. He said she appeared to be younger than he was, but still all grown up. She said she lived to be sixty-four years old." Kendrick could hear the joy in Remy's voice as she spoke. "Did Avery's heart so much good to know she turned out okay. That she was happy and at peace. She even said she would have been proud to have me as her stepmother. Can you imagine? I'm so honored."

"So she knew all about you?"

"Yes. She knew about us, and she knew my love for Avery was pure and real. Best of all, she gave him her blessing. She said, 'Be happy, Daddy.'"

Kendrick placed her hand over her heart. "Oh, that's so beautiful."

"Isn't it? The greatest gift Avery could ever get was knowing his child was at peace."

Remy's phone vibrated again. This time, her eyes flashed when she looked at the screen.

"What is it?" Kendrick said, her panic rising.

"Avery said they're done. That's all he said."

Kendrick jumped up, and Remy eased herself out of her chair as quickly as she could. They'd paid the check hours ago in case they needed to make a quick getaway. As promised, they each left a huge cash tip on the table before they rushed back to Kendrick's car.

Kendrick's pulse pounded as they raced back to the Visitor Center. She feared that Avery's lack of detail in his text was a bad sign.

Maybe Silas is already gone.

"It's gonna be all right," Remy said. "Everything's gonna be fine."

Her words were soothing, but she sounded as unsure as Kendrick felt.

Kendrick had to watch where she was driving, but Remy had the luxury of looking out the window.

"Silas is there, Kendrick! I can see him with the guys."

"Oh, thank God," she said, nearly bursting into tears. Hands shaking on the wheel, she managed to pull into a parking spot. She jumped out of the car, forgetting poor Remy immediately. Out of the corner of her eye, she saw Avery walk over to the passenger side of the car to take care of his wife.

As she rushed over to Silas, she wondered if he was already alive. She still felt that familiar sensation of a spiritual presence, but then, that was present when she was near Jesse and Avery, who were no longer ghosts.

"Hello, my sweet," Silas said. He seemed happy to see her, but he didn't have the elated expression of a man who had just come back to life. Also, he didn't reach out to hold her.

"How did it go?"

"It went well, Kendrick. Truly, it did. It's strange; I really did feel like I had a breakthrough, you know? I feel, I don't know ... *different.*"

"Different better?"

"Yes," Silas said, his voice filled with frustration. "But I'm still here. And I'm the same as I was."

"I'm disappointed, but I can't help being relieved that you're still *here* at all," Kendrick said. She started to cry, finally releasing the crushing stress and roiling emotions she'd been trying to control all day. "Silas ... Silas ..." was all she could manage to say.

"Kendrick, darling, I'm so sorry for everything I've put you through," he said mournfully. He tenderly caressed her cheek. She relished the frigid chill of his ghostly touch because it was still *him*.

They gazed helplessly, hopelessly into each other's eyes for a moment. Even without looking around her, Kendrick could feel the love and support of their new friends literally surrounding the two of them. The uncertainty of their future together felt unbearable, but knowing they had people who truly cared about them helped ease the pain.

Silas frowned, and it took Kendrick a second to understand why. They both turned around when they heard the faint sound of crying.

It was Remy. Looking tearfully up at her husband, she said, "Avery, we have to do something to help them." Her shoulders shook as she wiped her eyes.

"*A chuisle mo chroi,*" Avery said tenderly as he pulled her into his arms. "Don't upset yourself."

"I—I just ... I remember what it's like, Avery. I remember having to leave you ... to watch you disappear into the dark every night, and I had to go home without you. I know what it's like when you can't even touch the person you love more than anything in the world."

"I remember too," Jesse said. "You never forget what that feels like. Even now, Lucy and I will be sittin' at dinner with the kids, and I'll hook my foot around hers under the table, just to be able to touch her."

Kendrick smiled at Jesse's charming admission. She knew nobody here took for granted what they had.

"I'm sorry you have to go through this," Remy said as she looked over at Silas and Kendrick where they stood close enough to touch, yet they couldn't.

"Avery's right, Remy," Kendrick said. "Don't get yourself so upset. Can't be good for the baby or for you."

Remy nodded, massaging her belly while Avery gently rubbed her back.

"I still think there must be something more we can do to help," Remy insisted. She scanned the area for a moment, then she turned back to the group.

"What if we all met again on the battlefield together?" she asked.

"Why?" Avery asked, still looking concerned as he tried to calm his wife.

"What if we got as many people as we can together on the battlefield where Silas died, and we simply lifted him up in prayer and asked for a second chance for him? Kendrick,

I know you said you have a couple of friends who know about your situation. Silas, you could maybe bring that friend of yours, the woman who came back to life, too. If we could all get together, surely God or the Universe or whatever might answer such a sincere wish for their love to survive death?"

As lovely as the idea was, Kendrick wasn't particularly optimistic that it would work. Her heart was so utterly worn out from careening wildly between hope and despair, that she was losing faith that anything would ever be resolved with Silas. It felt as if they would exist in this permanent state of limbo until Kendrick herself finally died.

And yet, considering the one making the request was a deeply emotional and weeping pregnant woman, it was pretty much impossible to say no.

"It's worth a try, Remy," Silas said. "If everyone is willing."

"Would you two be able to come back next weekend maybe?" Remy asked.

Kendrick nearly laughed when she looked at Jesse's and Sean's expressions. Neither one could possibly turn her down. Like most men, they didn't know what to do when a woman started crying.

"Of course we can," Sean said.

"Maybe you can bring Theresa and Lucy."

Jesse shook his head vehemently. "No. Not my Lucy. I won't have her set foot anywhere near a battlefield."

"Oh, of course," Remy said. "You're right."

Kendrick was baffled by the exchange, but then Silas said, "Jesse's wife is really sensitive. Like you are. She can feel the soldiers the way you did."

"Which also means we need to be very careful with

Kendrick as well," Jesse said. "If you're gonna be there with us."

"You're damn right I'm gonna be there," she said. "I don't care what happens to me."

"But I'll wager Silas does," Jesse said, and Silas nodded. He looked worried.

"Well, worst case scenario," Sean said, "if anything happens, me and Jesse and Avery will be here to protect her."

Jesse nodded, his face taking on a look of tremendous sadness. "That's true. When it happened to my Lucy, I was still dead. I couldn't help her."

"I know exactly how you feel," Silas said grimly. "I couldn't help Kendrick either."

"I'll be fine, guys. Really," Kendrick said. She'd die a thousand deaths on the battlefield if it meant she could stay with Silas.

"Next Saturday, then," Remy said. "I only hope I make it 'til then."

She gazed down at her precious baby bump.

I hope so too.

26

———————

A week later, they managed to gather quite a group of people for their little prayer circle. No matter what happened today, Silas knew he would never forget how it felt to have so many people come together to help him. Before he'd met Kendrick, he'd been utterly alone. Now, it seemed his list of friends was growing on a daily basis. How incredible that was.

Remy and Avery were in attendance, of course. Thankfully, their unborn son had stayed put, as they'd hoped he would. Sean had brought his wife, a feisty yet friendly redhead named Theresa. Jesse arrived solo, both to protect his wife and because Lucy needed to stay behind and look after their three children. Proud papa that he was, he loved showing off photos of his family to everyone in attendance. Silas could see the love radiating from Lucy's gentle brown eyes in each photograph.

Kendrick had recruited Deanna and Marie to come, and Silas had also gotten Rebekah and Gregory to attend. Like Remy, Rebekah had a special place in her heart for ghosts who were physically separated from their soulmates. She'd been more than eager to help, and she managed to get several other people to join the cause. She knew another woman by the name of Jackey who had come back to life. Rebekah got Jackey and her husband, Anthony, to come and help out.

Now they knew of *four* people who had been miraculously resurrected from the dead to be with their loved ones. Jesse, Avery, Rebekah, and Jackey had managed to cheat death for love's sake. Surely a fifth miracle might be possible ... right?

Most surprising of all was that Jackey had managed to get two of her friends to actually fly to Virginia all the way from Los Angeles, California to be with them. *Two strangers,* neither of whom had died yet, simply hopped on a plane to help people they'd never met. They were due to arrive here any minute. The man, an actor by the name of Orlando, had known Rebekah and Gregory when they'd first fallen in love. Apparently, he had supported Gregory through the tough times when he and Rebekah had thought their situation was utterly hopeless. They'd had no idea that it was even possible for Rebekah to return to the land of the living until it happened. Later, he and the woman who was now his wife, Paige, helped Jackey and Anthony on their journey to stay together.

"I've seen you before in Milligan's, where I work," Kendrick said after being formally introduced to Jackey. She stared at the woman with fascination for some reason.

"Oh, probably so," Jackey said with a smile. She was a rather glamorous-looking woman with dark skin and expressive brown eyes. "I love that place."

"And I *love* your artwork," Kendrick exclaimed. "Remy

told me about it, so I went and browsed in the store where you sell your drawings. They're stunning."

"Thank you so much," Jackey said. "That was one of the things I missed so much when I was dead. Not being able to draw or paint no more."

She smiled sympathetically at Silas. It was always such a comfort to speak to other ghosts, even former ghosts. They knew what it felt like to endure the helplessness and hopelessness of being a spirit.

"It's so funny," Kendrick said quietly after Jackey had walked away to talk to Rebekah and Gregory. "The first time I saw her in the store, I got this super ghostly vibe from her. I couldn't understand it, since she was obviously alive. It is so strange how I can not only sense ghosts, but I can sense former ghosts!"

It certainly was strange. How lovely yet utterly bizarre this whole thing was. It was like some secret gathering of the back-from-the-dead club. The best part was, the more you looked at this gathering of people—this mix of formerly dead and living people—the less crazy it seemed.

And the more possible it felt that things might work out after all.

Kendrick could feel it, too. He could see renewed hope and excitement on her face as they stood with all these people together in the parking lot of the Yorktown Battlefield Visitor Center.

"This is incredible," she whispered as she watched the people milling about.

"I know. How did we ever get so lucky as to have this many beautiful friends?" Silas asked in wonder.

Sudden, high-pitched squealing startled Silas. He and Kendrick turned around to see a pretty woman with dark hair and green eyes running into Jackey's arms.

Laughter rippled through the group as everyone turned to watch the happy reunion. Silas figured the woman must be Paige Blake, and the tall strapping man walking behind her must be Orlando.

"They sound like us when we get together," Deanna said with a smile.

Once the women had calmed down, more introductions were made. It took a while.

"I remember you," Silas said, walking right up to Orlando.

"You do?" Orlando asked, eying him curiously.

"You used to work in Colonial Williamsburg."

"That I did," he said with a grin.

"You wanna hear something funny?" Silas asked.

"Always," Orlando said, folding his arms and looking fascinated. Silas took an instant liking to the guy. He seemed funny and charming. But then, he had always enjoyed the man's costumed performances in the historical district.

"I got into a mock debate with you once in front of the courthouse," Silas said. "That day, you were playing a British character and I started an argument with you about the cause of liberty."

Orlando's eyes flew open wide. "Oh, my God, I totally remember that! That was so much fun. It was so crazy and unscripted. We got into that huge fight, and the audience was laughin' like crazy."

Silas laughed and nodded.

"I tried to find you later because I thought it would be fun to do it again," Orlando said. "But I never saw you again. *Wow.* Even after everything that's happened with Jackey and Rebekah and everything I know now, it never once occurred to me that I mighta been talking to a real soldier."

"Now you know."

"That, sir, is pretty damn cool."

"I'm glad you think so."

"Of course he does," Paige said, rolling her pretty green eyes. "He'll take any chance he can get to ham it up."

"She's not wrong," Orlando said proudly.

"I can't tell you what it means to us that you came all this way," Kendrick said, looking at the two of them in wonder.

"Kendrick, I know we just met, but can I give you a hug?" Paige asked earnestly.

"Of course! I'll take all the love I can get," she said, opening her arms.

"You got it honey," Paige said, pulling her close and embracing her. "I know this must be so hard, but keep the faith, okay? We can do this. We can bring Silas home to you."

"I hope so," Kendrick said, squeezing her eyes shut.

After Paige let go of Kendrick, she embraced Rebekah, too. "Good to see you."

"You too," Rebekah said, warmly hugging her friend.

"You know what's strange?" Kendrick said. "I've always been sensitive to the paranormal, so when I'm near Avery or Jesse, or even you, Jackey, I get this kinda ghost vibe."

"Ain't that somethin'?" Jackey remarked.

"Yeah, it's like I can tell when a ghost is near, and I guess I can tell when a former ghost is near. Weird thing is, the sensation is less strong with Rebekah. It's there, just kinda faint. Weird."

"Oh, that's probably because she's—" Silas began, then stopped short.

"She's what?" Jackey asked.

Silas mouthed *I'm sorry* in Rebekah's direction.

Gregory laughed. "It's all right." He glanced at his wife and she nodded.

"We're past the first trimester now, so ..." Rebekah said.

"You're pregnant?" Paige exclaimed.

Rebekah blushed and nodded.

"Oh, I'm so happy for you both," Paige said, hugging her again and grabbing Gregory next.

"Congratulations, honey," Jackey said with a warm smile. "What a wonderful mama you're gonna be."

"Thank you," Rebekah said softly. "That means a lot to me."

After everyone congratulated the parents-to-be, Remy clapped her hands.

"Okay, people. I think we've got everybody here and accounted for. Are we ready?" Remy asked.

Avery chuckled. "My goodness, I'm gettin' flashbacks from your tour guide days."

Remy laughed too. Kendrick had told Silas all about Remy's life in Gettysburg. She used to do both daytime history and nighttime ghost tours. In fact, Avery used to join the ghost tours while he was still a ghost. Remy even had a college degree in tourism. Yes, she knew how to handle a group.

"Okay, Silas," Remy said. "You lead the way."

Silas and Kendrick walked side by side as they led the group toward the area where he had died.

"I can't believe we got so many people to come today," Kendrick said.

"I know," he agreed. "I'm overwhelmed. In a really good way. Means so much to have so many people on our side. And they'll all be there for you in case ..."

"P—please. I can't even talk about that," she said, her voice quivering. He could see that she was barely hanging on emotionally, and it was unbearable. As always, he couldn't hold her or comfort her. He could only pray that would change today. They walked the rest of the way in silence. Silas didn't want to say anything else that might upset her.

Once they reached the spot where he had met with the soldiers last week, Silas gestured toward the trees.

"There's where I died."

"Okay," Sean said, charging forward like the sergeant he was. "First and foremost, we need to be very careful with Kendrick. I know you want to be near him, but unfortunately, that's not safe. You don't want to feel the bullet or whatever killed him."

Despite all the soul-bearing he'd done with the men, Silas never did get around to telling them the truth about how he died. He gazed down at the ground.

"It's nothing to be ashamed of," Kendrick said quietly.

"What do you mean, she might feel the bullet?" Jackey asked.

"Well, Kendrick is very sensitive to paranormal things," Sean said. With a brief, sympathetic glance over at Jesse, he said, "We found out the hard way that such sensitivity comes at a price. If someone like Kendrick has the bad luck of standing on the exact spot where someone died, and at the same time of day they died, she will actually feel the physical pain of what happened to that person. As you might imagine, it can be quite dangerous to have somebody like that wandering around a battlefield where people died."

"Oh, my goodness," Jackey said. "That's frightening."

"Believe me, it is. I felt a soldier's death here once," Kendrick said. "It really feels like you've been shot."

"Though it's not physically dangerous," Avery said. "It can be painful and traumatic."

Sean nodded. He scanned the group for a moment, and then he walked over to Deanna and Marie.

"Are either of you sensitive like that? Can you feel when ghosts are around?" he asked.

Silas had to stifle a laugh as he watched Deanna and Marie eye Sean up and down. The man was ridiculously handsome, and he was certainly built like a soldier. A modern day, well-fed, bulked up soldier. And even Silas had to admire the guy's dreamy hazel eyes.

"Ah—um—ah ... no," Marie managed to stammer. Silas heard Kendrick giggle softly next to him.

After looking Sean in the eye a second or two longer than necessary, Deanna responded, "No. Me neither."

Sean's wife, Theresa, muttered, "Hands off, ladies. He's mine."

Theresa looked more amused than annoyed, though. She actually resembled Kendrick a bit, with her strawberry-blond hair and blue eyes. Sean had said she was a therapist specializing in soldiers with PTSD, which Silas thought was incredibly important work. He'd known a lot of traumatized soldiers in his day who could have greatly benefited from such therapy.

Sean turned around, surveying the rest of the group. "Is anyone else here sensitive like that?"

"My Anthony is," Jackey said, gazing at her husband with concern. Anthony was a tall, handsome man with dark skin and warm, brown eyes. "He could always sense the spirits around him."

"Okay," Sean said, nodding at Anthony. "Good to know. Anyone else?"

Everyone else shook their head.

"Fortunately, this battlefield saw only a few hundred deaths during battle, unlike Gettysburg where thousands died," Sean said. "Still, we need to look out for each other here. Anthony and Kendrick, in particular. At the first sign of trouble, you give a holler. If you experience any pain, anything unusual, speak up right away and we'll get you off the battlefield, all right?"

Everyone nodded. Silas was touched by the love and concern he saw on each person's face. It felt like they were all in this together, and they would look out for one another. Truly, it reminded him of the brotherhood of battle.

"Kendrick, you in particular need to be careful," Sean continued. "From what we can tell, having a personal connection to the one who died can put you at greater risk. Don't get too close to where he died, okay?"

Wearily, she nodded. As if they didn't have enough physical distance between them already.

"You should know," Silas began. "I did die here, but I wasn't killed in battle. I just got sick."

Even after all this time, he still felt humiliated at that admission. He joined the battle for the stupid reason of trying to prove how strong and brave he was only to waste away from illness.

"Okay," Sean said, nodding and not missing a beat. "Do you know what killed you?"

"Yellow fever."

"Got it. I don't know if Kendrick would feel sick if she got too close or not. Do you know what time of day you died?"

"Not exactly. But it was in the afternoon sometime."

"I died of illness, too," Jackey said. "You were with me when I came back, Anthony. You felt all right, didn't you?"

"Yes. I don't remember feeling anything unusual."

"Good, good," Sean said. "Still, let's be careful."

"I agree, Kendrick," Silas said. "Be safe, all right?"

"I will," she said sadly, looking on the verge of tears.

Silas walked to the exact spot under the tree where he

had died so long ago. He heard Kendrick draw in a shuddery breath. Not being able to stand close to her was torture, but he would not put her in any kind of danger. He could still remember what it felt like to be deathly ill, and he was not about to let that happen to her.

"I feel like we should all hold hands," Kendrick said.

Silas watched as everyone joined hands. His heart filled with warmth and peace as he surveyed this sweet circle of love. A mix of old and new friends, all gathered here in love, support, and friendship.

"I want to say something profound here," Silas said. "But I don't think I have the words to express what it means to me that you're all here with us today. I'm a simple man, and I have only simple words. So all I can say, my dear friends, is *thank you*."

The loving smiles and nods he received in return let him know that his words were enough.

"Whenever you're ready," Remy said gently.

Kendrick nodded, holding hands with Deanna and Marie who were on either side of her. She drew in a deep breath and tried to speak, but only a sob came out.

"I'm s—sorry," she said, letting go of her friends' hands for a moment so she could wipe her eyes. Deanna and Marie both put their arms around her to steady her. Silently, they began to tear up as well. "I can do this," she whispered, mostly to herself. She joined hands with her friends again.

"I don't know who's in charge of things like life and death," she said, her voice stronger now. "I want to believe in God. I want to believe in God and the Universe and that there's a reason things happen the way they do. I know I'm just a simple woman, and I don't have any right to question the ways of the Universe. But I do know some things for sure. I know that Silas Murphy is a good man. He's made mistakes in life, as we all do. Whatever bad things he's done in life, or bad things he *thinks* he has done in life, he's paid for his mistakes and then some. We all know he is worthy of an existence far better than the one he's had to endure since his death. Please help him to know he is worthy too. I also know that nobody could ever, *ever,* love him as much as I do."

Silas heard a lot of sniffling. He could feel the empathy emanating from the circle. Every single person was pulling so hard for them to succeed in this quest.

"We are gathered here today to beg you, the Almighty, to allow ... to allow ... Wait a minute," Kendrick said, staring across the circle from where she stood. "Remy, are you in *labor?*"

Sure enough, Remy was grimacing in pain.

"I'm not sure. Maybe," she managed to say. After a few seconds, the pain in her expression eased as her contracting belly must have relaxed.

"*A chuisle!*" Avery exclaimed, eyes wide.

"I've just been having some contractions, off and on. It's no big deal."

"Of course it's a big deal," her frightened husband said, placing his hand on her stomach.

"It's a first baby," she said. "It's gonna take a long time. It will probably be hours, a day even."

"You don't know that, Remy," Kendrick said, walking over to her.

"I don't wanna leave you," Remy said, her bright blue eyes watering. "Not now."

"Everything's gonna be just fine," Kendrick said.

Unselfish as always, Silas knew there was no way

Kendrick would allow Remy and Avery to stay. And he agreed completely.

"You need to go," Kendrick said.

"I don't need to—"

"I'm not gonna have you stand out here in the heat when you're in labor," she insisted. "Go. Let Avery take good care of you. Go have your beautiful baby boy."

Avery nodded sternly, and Remy sighed, resigned that she wasn't going to win this battle. She flung her arms around Kendrick and squeezed her tight.

"I'm so sorry, Kendrick."

Kendrick laughed gently. "Don't be sorry, Remy. If your baby is born today, then today will always be remembered as a happy one, no matter what else happens."

Remy sighed wearily, then she reluctantly let go. Avery put a protective hand on her back and began to gently lead her away.

"Wait, wait! Before you go," Kendrick said. "Join hands again, everyone. Remy, stand in the middle."

Remy stood in the middle as the group closed ranks around her. Deanna gestured to Silas to come stand with them. He stood between Sean and Jesse, who joined hands behind his back. Kendrick placed a hand on Remy's shoulder while Marie held her other hand in the circle.

"Dear God in Heaven, please take good care of Remy and Avery, and their baby boy. Help him to be born healthy and strong to these wonderful parents who will love and cherish him forever. And Charlotte, dear girl, you look after your little brother you hear?"

After a brief moment of silence, Kendrick took her hand off Remy's shoulder and stepped back. They hugged again while the others expressed their well wishes for her.

Silas approached Avery and said, "Maybe the next time I

see you, I can shake your hand and congratulate you properly on the birth of your son."

"I hope so, my good man," he said. "I truly hope so."

Silas watched Kendrick's eyes as her gaze followed Avery and Remy on their way off the battlefield. He could see the fear and sadness in her eyes, and he was pretty sure he knew what she was thinking. It worried her to lose two participants of this critical prayer ceremony, and she was probably wondering if she would get the chance to start a family with Silas. At least, that's what he was thinking, anyway.

"You okay, hon?" Theresa asked Kendrick when she walked back toward the circle.

"I'm trying to be," she said in a quiet voice.

Theresa nodded. Then she silently wrapped her arm around Kendrick and squeezed her. Watching them together, you would never have guessed they had just met a short while ago. Such intense circumstances bonded people quickly, he mused.

Just like in wartime.

Trembling, Kendrick found her way back to her spot in the circle.

"Take your time, Kendrick," Rebekah said. "The rest of us aren't going anywhere. Take all the time you need."

"We knew for sure when my time was coming," Jesse said, walking over to her. "I had just enough time to tell my Lucy that I had to go back to Devil's Den where I died." He took Kendrick's hands in both of his. "She had the same terrified look on her face as you do right now. I know how hard this is, darlin'. But I can tell you from my experience, this was the worst part. The waitin', the not knowin'. But it wasn't long after the worst part that we got to the best part. Was only a matter of minutes after I got to Devil's Den ... then before I knew it, I was carryin' Lucy in my arms."

Kendrick's eyes spilled over. "I would give anything to be able to touch him."

"I know it darlin'," Jesse said, his blue-gray eyes filled with deep empathy. "Best thing to do now is gather your strength and get to it, okay?"

Silas felt the same way. This awful stress was too much for Kendrick. One way or another, it needed to end. He took his place near the tree and everyone else rejoined hands.

"I'm not even sure what to say anymore," Kendrick said wearily. "Like Silas said, sometimes you just don't have the words. But maybe we don't need words. Let's just take a moment here. We all know why we're here. We all know what we want to happen. We hope and pray for Silas to return to life. So that he can have a second chance, and so that he and I can be together. Maybe we can all just take a moment and focus on what we are asking. Focus not with words, but with our hearts."

Kendrick closed her eyes, and Silas watched as everyone else did the same.

There was such beauty in the silence. In the quiet, Silas could feel a tremendous sense of peace and power and love.

Though it saddened him to be standing away from the group, he was touched at the presence of all these people. These friends and these strangers, who indeed were no longer strangers, who had come from far and near for him. Then he had a thought that was incredibly simple and deeply profound at the same time.

All these people are here because they care about me. Kendrick Banner is in love with me. Maybe I'm not such a bad guy after all.

And with that, a blinding light appeared in front of him.

Deep within Silas bloomed the knowledge, the certainty,

that everyone he had loved and lost in life was on the other side of that lighted portal.

The temptation to go into that loving, eternal light was overwhelming.

Silas stepped inside the portal, toward everlasting love and light.

27

K endrick wasn't sure how long they all stood in silence, but when she opened her eyes, she knew immediately that something was happening.

Silas stood under the tree, his eyes staring straight ahead. If he hadn't been standing up, he would have looked like a dead body. Arms hanging limp at his sides, his face was expressionless. It was horrifying, as if his life and spirit had been snuffed out of him.

Kendrick gasped loudly and dropped her friends' hands.

"*Silas!*" she screamed. She ran toward him, only to have two pairs of strong hands grab her. Jesse and Sean gripped her tightly, holding her back.

"Kendrick, you can't go near him," Jesse said, eyes wide.

"I don't care if I get sick. I don't care!" she screamed. "Let go of me."

They held her as firmly as they could while trying not to hurt her. She was no match for the two men. Sean alone could have restrained her with one arm.

"What's going on with him?" Kendrick asked, watching

in horror as Silas's seemingly unseeing eyes stared straight ahead.

"I'm not sure, darlin'," Jesse said.

"Is this supposed to happen? What's going on? What's happening to him?"

"Kendrick, sweetheart, I wish I knew," Jesse said. "But crossing over ... or coming back ... It seems to happen different each time. What happened to me was different than what happened to Avery."

Jackey, along with everyone else, rushed over to where Kendrick stood. Nobody tried to approach Silas while he stood in this bizarre, frozen state.

"Kendrick, honey, when I came back, I was greeted by my loved ones," Jackey told her. "My parents and a dear friend."

"Right," Anthony said. "I was with her. I saw them."

"You saw them? Then why can't I see what he's seeing?" Kendrick asked, thoroughly panicked. "What is he looking at?"

"I was supposed to meet Jackey's friend, John." Anthony said. "I played him as a reenactor. Jackey knew him in life. Maybe that's why I could see him and Jackey's parents when they came for her."

Panting heavily and quaking all over, Kendrick was seized with terror at the thought that she might be seeing Silas for the last time. She couldn't understand what the hell was going on.

"Silas! Silas! Silas!" All she could do was sob and shriek his name over and over again. She kept struggling with Jesse and Sean, but it was no use. "Let go of me. I don't care what happens. I want to go to him. I want to go *with* him!"

Kendrick was dimly aware of Deanna and Marie

weeping just behind her. She also felt hands as several people attempted to rub her back and calm her.

And then, just like that, Silas snapped out of his trance and his eyes began to focus. He staggered forward a bit.

"Hold her back," Sean ordered Jesse, who nodded.

Jesse tightened his grip on Kendrick while Sean raced over to Silas.

"It's all right, darlin'. You stay here with me. Sean will figure out what's going on."

Kendrick's heart hammered wildly in her chest as she watched Silas turn and look at Sean. Thank God, Silas appeared normal again.

Then she watched as Sean reached out and *grabbed* Silas's hand.

He's touching him. He's touching him.

Her mind struggled to grasp what she was seeing. It all felt like a dream.

"Is he … is he …" Kendrick said.

Sean placed his hand over Silas's chest. Then he grinned. "We have a heartbeat!"

Kendrick let out a loud cry and her knees buckled. Jesse caught her and held her close.

"It's all right, sweetheart. It's all right. I know it's tough, but hang with me just a li'l while longer. Sean's got medical trainin' from the military. Let him check Silas out."

She nodded numbly, still scared to believe this might really be happening.

Sean eased Silas into a sitting position on the ground. He took Silas's wrist and held it. "Damn, your pulse is *strong*, my friend!"

Kendrick let out another choked cry.

"Things are lookin' good, Kendrick," Jesse said with a

huge smile. "Lookin' real good. Almost there. I promise, once I let you loose, you don't ever have to let him go."

"How you feeling?" Sean asked him.

"Weak," Silas said. "Very ... weak."

"Silas!" Kendrick cried. He turned to face her and found the strength to smile.

"My sweet," he said, gazing at her.

"He's gonna be just fine," Jesse assured her. "It can be quite a shock to suddenly be in a body again. And if he's like I was as a soldier, he's on the brink of starvation."

"Yes," Kendrick said. "He was starving during the war."

"That's probably why he's so weak. That, and he was real sick when he died," Jesse said. "But he'll likely get his strength back mighty quick. I was shot twice and stabbed, and I recovered quite nicely myself."

Kendrick laughed and cried at the same time.

Gregory and Orlando walked over to Silas and Sean. Anthony tried to join them, but Jackey pulled him back protectively.

The three men helped Silas to his feet.

They're all touching him.

Kendrick watched them help Silas to stand up; there was simply no doubt about it.

Silas Murphy had come back to life.

"Please, please," Kendrick begged.

"Stay there," Sean ordered. "We'll bring him to you."

Propping him up a bit, they helped Silas walk toward Kendrick. At last, Jesse released his grip on her, and she ran to him.

Lovingly but carefully, she pulled Silas away from the men and into her arms.

Sobbing, she relished the physical, solid feel of the man she loved. Silas threw his arms around her neck.

"Kendrick, Kendrick," he said over and over in her ear. She could feel his wet, warm tears on her face.

Loving applause and happy laughter erupted from all around them.

Silas pulled back slightly so he could look at her. Tenderly, he touched her face the way he had so many times before.

"You're warm, you're so *warm*," Kendrick said through her tears.

"My God, I can't believe it actually happened," he said, still exploring her face with his hands.

"I thought I lost you. I didn't understand what was happening," she told him. "You looked so strange. You were just frozen, staring, and I didn't know ..."

"It's all right. I'm here now. There's nothing to fear anymore," he assured her.

Kendrick slipped her arm around his waist, and they both turned to look at their dear friends. There were tears and smiles and nothing but joy and happiness all around them.

"Thank you, thank you, thank you," she said.

"You feelin' okay, my good man?" Jesse asked. "Are you feeling sick?"

"No, not at all. Still very weak, but not sick."

"Thank God," Kendrick said, renewed relief flooding through her.

"Good deal," Sean said. "Okay, let's get the hell off the battlefield now. No need to press our luck."

Jesse and Sean watched carefully as Kendrick helped Silas to walk. They were ready to step in and help if needed.

When they arrived at the parking lot, Kendrick gingerly helped him into the passenger seat of the car. She reclined the seat a little for his comfort. It was frightening to see him so weak, but Kendrick trusted Jesse's words; most likely, he would get his strength back soon. She left the door open for the moment.

As much as she ached to be beside Silas, Kendrick made sure to hug each and every person who had made the journey to help them. Everyone was incredibly gracious, mostly shooing her off and assuring her they would catch up with her later. Kendrick promised to keep them updated on how they were doing once they got settled.

Finally, Marie and Deanna walked toward Kendrick and she opened her arms. Laughing and crying together, they held tight for a moment.

When she let them go, she said softly, "I can't believe it really happened."

"Me neither," Marie said, her eyes filled with wonder.

"Once Silas is feeling better, we can all go out on a double date with me and Brody," Deanna said happily. "Or even a triple date, if Marie finally makes some headway with that guy at her work who may or may not be gay."

The three women laughed.

"That's sounds wonderful," Kendrick said. "Thank you so much. For everything. I can't begin to tell you how much comfort it brought me knowing you would be there for me, no matter what."

Kendrick gave them each one more hug and Marie and Deanna headed back to their cars.

"Gimme a sec," Jesse said. "Don't leave yet."

He took a large cloth bag out of the trunk of his car and brought it over to them.

"I was real optimistic 'bout what would happen today," Jesse said with a grin, "so I brought you some clothes and some other stuff. I do b'lieve you're 'bout the size I was when I came back."

"Oh, that's so thoughtful of you," Kendrick said, gratefully accepting the bag.

"No need to return nothin'. I used to be real thin, but I'm 'fraid I put on a few," he said, slapping his stomach, though the man was hardly fat. "That stuff don't fit no more anyway."

"Thank you so much, man," Silas said. "For everything."

"My pleasure. Kendrick, you got all our phone numbers and such. You need anything, you just let us know."

"I will."

"Now go take care of your man," Jesse said with a wink. He headed off to his car, and Kendrick shut Silas's door. Then she slid behind the wheel.

Turning to Silas, who was safely buckled into his seat, she asked, "Are you all right?"

"I'm weak and tired and completely overwhelmed ... and I have never been better in all my hundreds of years," he said with a smile. Taking off his hat, he said, "Ugh, this thing is so sweaty and disgusting."

"How are you feeling?" she said as she reached over and tenderly ran her fingers through his hair to show she didn't care if he was sweaty and dirty. He moaned softly.

"Mmmm that feels so nice. I'm doing okay. Worst part is I'm so damned thirsty."

"Oh, you know what? I've got some bottles of water in the trunk for emergencies."

She jumped out of the car and quickly retrieved three of them. Once back in the car, she twisted the cap off a bottle and handed it to him. He drank it down so fast he started choking.

"Easy, easy my love," she told him.

"Sorry," he said, slowing his gulping a bit. She tossed the empty bottle in the back seat and opened another for him.

After drinking some of that one, he sat back in his seat with a sigh. "Good, that's good. Thanks, my sweet."

"Do you want some food?"

Silas cocked his head and looked at her.

"What?"

"I always want food."

"I know that. I just mean, are you up to it yet? You can barely hold down water."

"I'll be good and eat like a rational human being, I swear. But please, yes. I want food."

"I can't begin to imagine how hungry you must be," she said. "All those years at war, and you never had enough food. I promise I won't ever let you go hungry again, Silas."

"I know you won't," he said with a smile.

Poor sweet Silas looked so weak, and Kendrick could hardly believe that she was able to take care of him now. No more thinking of him being out there alone in the dark. He was hers now, forever and always.

She grabbed her cell phone. "I can order some food online right now. Should be ready by the time we go pick it up, so you won't have to wait."

Silas laughed. "That's a dangerous thing with me around. The idea that you can just pick up a phone and call or order online and get food sent to you. That's always been one of the wonders of the modern world. To me anyway."

Kendrick pulled up the online menu for one of the modern restaurants in Merchants Square and ordered food for Silas. Once she was done, she turned to him and said, "I hope this is what you wanted."

"I'm sure whatever you ordered for me will be fine."

"No, I mean ... *this*. Being with me. I hope this is what you wanted. Staying here instead of moving on."

"Kendrick, how can you even ask that?" Silas sat up in

his seat and reached over to take her hand and kiss it gently. "Of course this is what I want."

"I just hope I wasn't being selfish. Wanting you to stay with me instead of moving on to eternal rest. You've earned the right to be at peace after all this time. I know you love me, but I worry that I pressured you into staying. I really did want what was best for you, but my God, Silas. When you froze like that on the battlefield and I thought you might leave me ... I totally lost it. I can only hope my screaming your name over and over like that didn't make you feel like you had no choice but to stay."

"To tell you the truth, Kendrick, I didn't hear you screaming until I'd already made my choice." Silas looked deeply into her eyes. "I have no regrets. Not about this anyway. Still have regrets about my first life, but that's in the past. I get a fresh start now, and I'm so damn excited, I can't hardly stand it."

Silas was still physically weak and weary, but his eyes danced with joy. He was happy, and that was all that mattered to her. Once he got his strength back, there would be no stopping him from making his new life a great one.

"I'm sure about this, Kendrick. Like *really* sure. So quit worryin' about me."

"I'll never quit worrying about you."

He laughed. "I do know that."

"Now let's get you fed." She put on her seatbelt and drove off the lot.

Silas drew in several deep breaths.

"You okay?"

"It is so weird to breathe again." He lifted up his arm and sniffed. "God, I *stink.*"

"No, you don't," she said kindly.

"Girl, I am *rank.*"

Kendrick laughed. "Don't worry. We'll get you all cleaned up when we get home."

"Home," he said with wonder in his voice.

"Yeah," she said, smiling.

"I made it. *We* made it," he said. "Can you believe it?"

"No. Sometimes I can't believe a single thing that's happened since the day I first met you."

A short while ago he had teetered on the edge of the other side of the veil between life and death. And now he was here with her.

"Silas, how did it happen? Were you actually given a choice to go or to stay?"

"Yes," he said.

"What did you see? Did you see, I don't know, *God*?"

"My sweet, I have so much to tell you," Silas said, reaching over to stroke her hair as she drove. "So much. Just lemme get some of my strength back, and I'll tell you every-thing. After all, we have time."

"Yes. Yes, we do," she said. No more quick lunch breaks when time was always running short. No more hurried meetings and agonized goodbyes. "I can't believe it's over."

"It's not over. Today isn't the end. It's the beginning. Say, what's today's date?"

"June 23rd."

"June 23rd," he repeated. "This will be an anniversary of sorts for us, won't it?"

"You're right. Oh, and maybe Remy's baby will be born today. Wouldn't that be so lovely?"

"It sure would."

Silas picked up the bag Jesse had given him.

"That was so cool of him. To bring me stuff." Silas said. "Got some nice clothes in here. Little bottle of mouthwash, some dental floss; he thought of everything."

He laughed and added, "He really did think of *everything*."

Kendrick glanced over in time to see Silas pull out a string of condoms. She giggled.

"Oh, my gosh that is too funny. I never even thought about stuff like that," she said, shaking her head. "I didn't prepare anything for you."

"Because you were afraid this wouldn't happen."

"Exactly. Most of the time, I wouldn't even let myself think about being able to bring you home with me. Kinda felt like decorating a nursery before you're even pregnant, you know? Like you're just asking to jinx it."

"I understand what you mean," he said. Glancing at the passenger side window, he asked, "Can we open this?"

"Of course." She pressed the button to roll the window down, making a mental note to show Silas the button on his side later so he could do it himself.

Silas breathed in the summer air, and what a joy it was to watch.

"That smells so good," he said.

"Yep. Nothing like the smell of fresh-cut grass."

Silas's smile widened and he nodded.

After a few minutes, Kendrick pulled into the parking lot near Merchants Square.

"Be right back with your food."

"Thanks."

She raced off to pick up her online order, hating to be away from Silas for even a moment. A part of her still feared that today had all been a dream. That she might wake up alone in her bed again.

Silas had his eyes closed when she came back to the car. He was so still, it frightened her, but he opened his eyes when he heard her door open.

"You all right?" she asked.

"I'm fine. Just resting."

"You don't feel sick, do you?"

"No, not at all. I feel every bit as tired and weak as I did on the day I died, but not exactly sick." His eyes opened wide. "Oh dear God, that smells like Heaven."

"You told me once if you could have anything you wanted to eat, it would be a steak."

Kendrick pulled out the takeout box and handed it to him. "I just hope you can eat it with a plastic knife and fork. There's also some potatoes in there. And a salad if you want."

She watched his eyes grow bigger as he opened up the box and stared at the thick, juicy steak.

"Should I wait 'til we get home to eat?"

"No! I'm not gonna torture you like that. Dig in, baby."

"You didn't get anything for you?"

Kendrick shook her head. "This morning I was too upset to eat, and now I'm just too excited. I'll be hungry later for sure. Besides, it's more fun for me to watch you eat."

"Now you know how I felt all this time during your lunch breaks."

She nodded, eagerly watching him take the first bite.

"Oh my dear lord," Silas said after swallowing his first piece of steak. "Forget what I saw earlier today. This right here is Heaven."

He nearly inhaled the steak and then made quick work of the potatoes, saving the salad for last. Kendrick worried he might get sick after eating so much after not having had food for so long, but so far so good. She marveled at how bright his eyes were now and the way he sat up straighter.

"Thank you, Kendrick. Feel so much better already."

"I love the idea of feeding you for the rest of your life,"

she said. "Problem is, I don't really know how to cook. But for you, I'll learn."

"We can learn together."

"I would love that."

"I love you, Kendrick."

"I love you too."

"No, you don't understand." Silas gazed intensely into her eyes. "I love you more than *food*."

Kendrick laughed and traced her hand across his warm, stubbled cheek.

"High praise indeed."

28

Having a good meal seemed to do wonders for Silas. Kendrick was impressed with how quickly he was able to walk up the two flights of steps with her to her apartment.

Well, *their* apartment.

She'd been worried that he might be weak and exhausted for days before he started feeling better, but that didn't appear to be the case. In fact, if he weren't still dressed like a Revolutionary soldier, a stranger would never have known there was anything different about him.

Kendrick unlocked the door to her place and let Silas inside. When she'd left this morning, she'd been so upset that she'd nearly thrown up, despite the fact that she hadn't eaten anything. Her greatest fear had been coming back later, utterly bereft and alone.

And now Silas was standing in the kitchen with her.

"Ah, feels so cool in here," Silas marveled. In fact, he had marveled at pretty much everything since they'd left the battlefield. Everything seemed new and exciting to him, and it made Kendrick see the whole world in a new light.

"The wonders of air conditioning," she said with a smile. "There's not much to the place, I'm afraid. Never did much decorating since I moved in."

"Well, we won't be here forever anyway," Silas said. "Someday we're gonna get a new house together."

"You're right," she said, her mind suddenly flooded with possibilities of the future. All those hopes and dreams they'd talked about. Her writing thrillers. His being a shop owner. Starting a family. It was all possible now. Even if all those things didn't happen, everything would be okay as long as they were together.

The first thing she showed him was the bathroom.

"I don't want to treat you like you're stupid or anything, but do you know how indoor plumbing works?" she asked.

Laughing, he said, "In theory, yeah. I've seen enough TV commercials for cleaners to know how to flush a toilet and all that." He spied her toothbrush, and his eyes flashed with interest. "Wow, I can actually brush my teeth now!"

Kendrick smiled. "You wanna try it?"

"Sure!" he said with so much enthusiasm it made her laugh.

She opened the cabinet under the sink to find a pack of toothbrushes. Fortunately, there was still one left.

"Hope you don't mind pink," she said.

"Not at all."

She handed him the toothpaste and watched as he squeezed out way too much.

"Sorry!"

"Not bad at all for a first try." She grabbed a tissue and wiped a little of the toothpaste off his brush. "Don't brush too hard and try not to swallow any of the paste. You can use this to rinse your mouth." With that, she handed him the top from the mouthwash bottle.

Silas grinned at her as he brushed his teeth, and it was the most charming thing she'd ever seen.

Laughing, she said, "Good job," after he finished.

"Ahh, that feels so much better."

"I bet it does."

Silas wandered around, taking in the place. It was so small, she hardly needed to give him a grand tour, so she simply let him explore.

"Come sit with me," he said, making his way into the living room after he'd seen the rest of the place. Sinking down into the fluffy couch, he said, "Ohhh, this is comfy."

Kendrick smiled and sat down next to him, feeling the softness of the cushions. It *was* comfortable. Funny how it took a soldier who'd spent years of his life sleeping on the cold ground to make her appreciate it.

"I need to talk to you about what I saw today," he said softly.

"Okay." His tone was so serious that it concerned her.

"Before I do, my sweet, I want to reassure you that I have absolutely no regrets about staying with you, all right?"

Kendrick nodded.

"I saw Levi," Silas said, his eyes dancing with joy. "He was the first to come greet me."

"Oh, Silas," she said, her eyes wide. He met her gaze and smiled warmly. There was no need to tell her how much seeing his friend had meant to him. With their deep and loving connection, she already knew.

"Yeah. I couldn't believe it. Was amazing to see him just as I remembered him. Last time I saw him ... was so gruesome, the way he died. It was healing to see him again. That goofy smile ... that laugh of his." Silas made a fist and placed it over his heart. "To see—to know—that he was in a perfect place of peace and love. I'm just so happy and relieved."

"That's beautiful, Silas," she said, relishing the happiness on his face.

"He told me I was stupid to hang around on Earth so dang long."

"He did?" Kendrick asked.

Silas laughed. "Yeah. That's how we always were together. Bustin' on each other.

"Then I saw my parents, my mother," he said, tearing up. "My sisters, my brother, they were all there. They're all at peace and they're happy and they love me still."

"Of course they do," Kendrick said, her heart full of joy as she listened. She had never seen Silas look so content, and it was the greatest gift she could have asked for. "I was told—not with words, but more with a kind of understanding—that I had done what I was supposed to do. In life and then in death, my work was done. And it was okay to come home. That's what they call it, Kendrick. It's not called Heaven or paradise; they just call it coming home. And that's what it is. The most beautiful, loving, peaceful, warm place you can possibly imagine, and everybody I ever loved is there. Well, except you."

"That's incredible."

"Kendrick," Silas said gently. "I saw Kurt."

She gasped.

"He's all right, Kendrick. More than all right. He's not a ghost floatin' somewhere all alone. Kurt is in that place of perfect peace and love and comfort. He's *home*."

Though Kendrick wanted to believe Silas with everything in her heart and soul, she couldn't allow herself to believe it.

"You really saw him," she said doubtfully.

"Yes, I surely did. He looks so much like you," Silas said fondly. "Same hair, same eyes."

"Well, we're twins. It's a pretty safe bet we look alike. Besides, I've got pictures of him in here."

Silas had explored the whole apartment, and she knew he had seen those photos.

"Are you saying you don't believe me?" Silas asked, sounding hurt. "I told you I would never lie to you, and I never did. Not after that first time."

Kendrick sighed. "It's not that I don't believe you. It's just that ... I know how much you love me, and I think you would do anything, say anything, to make me feel better about Kurt's death."

Silas laughed gently. "Kurt warned me you would need solid proof. He's got a scar right here," he said, pointing to the exact spot under his eye where her brother had gotten stitches.

"I told you about the scar," she said, feeling heartbroken. She loved Silas for trying to help, but she simply didn't believe he'd really seen Kurt.

With a sly grin, Silas said, "Pretty sneaky, sis."

Kendrick gasped and she covered her mouth. "Oh ... oh my God ..." Tears sprang to her eyes and her body began to shake.

"Yeah, I thought that one would do it," Silas said. He gently caressed her face with the back of his hand.

Pretty sneaky, sis.

Silas had said the words in the exact tone of voice that Kurt always used. Kendrick was sure she had never told Silas about that inside joke. She hadn't even thought of it in years. She and her brother had always laughed about the corny sitcom kids on television who called their siblings "sis" and "bro." It sounded so cheesy, and they'd never heard anybody do that in real life. So naturally, they started calling each other sis and bro. It always made their mother laugh, and she'd said it reminded her of a TV commercial when she was a kid. The commercial had a brother and sister playing some board game, and when the girl made a trick move and won, the brother said, "Pretty sneaky, sis." They'd even managed to find a clip of the commercial online. So the phrase had become a running joke in their family.

Kendrick began to sob, and Silas pulled her into his arms.

"It's all right. Everything's all right. *He's* all right, I swear to you. And the best part is, when the time comes, you *will* be with him again."

Silas held her for quite some time as she wept with relief. Eventually, she calmed down.

"Thank you, Silas. Thank you."

"Believe me, it makes me really happy to be able to deliver a message like that. And there's more to the message from him."

"There is?"

"Yup." Silas grinned. "It was no accident that we met, Kendrick."

"You mean, he ..."

He nodded. "Kurt knew we needed each other, so he made it happen."

"Wow," Kendrick said, trying to process this information.

"And there was one more thing."

Kendrick leaned in to listen, hanging on Silas's every word.

"A hatchet. In your book, Kurt wants to be hacked to death with a hatchet, like in some horror movie."

She laughed as she wiped her tears. "The bloodier the better. What did I tell you?"

Silas laughed, too. "He's cool, Kendrick. I like him. He would have been a kickass brother-in-law. And someday, we're gonna make sure our kids know all about their Uncle Kurt."

"I would love that. And I love you."

He wrapped his arms around her, holding her close again.

"Kendrick?"

"Yeah?"

"I know you're too nice to say anything, but I really do stink. *Bad.*"

29

───────

Silas sighed with relief when Kendrick took his hand saying, "Okay, let's get you cleaned up so you're more comfortable. I'll have to show you how to use the shower."

Kendrick led him down the hallway. He felt so much better already, stronger and healthier. But he couldn't help feeling embarrassed about being so filthy. Soldiers rarely got the opportunity to bathe. After a while, you got used to being around a bunch of smelly men, but Kendrick deserved so much better than that. Bless Jesse's dear heart for having the foresight to send along some fresh clothes.

Kendrick stopped in front of the hallway closet and grabbed a towel for him. Then she paused for a moment.

"What's the matter?" he asked.

She turned to look at him. "You know … we could always shower together."

Silas's eyes flew open wide. "Yes, please!"

Kendrick's lips slid into a sensual smile. Without taking her eyes off Silas, she reached into the closet and grabbed another towel.

"Follow me."

Silas went with her into the bathroom. They stood, facing each other in front of the sink. Between being near starving and utterly overwhelmed at returning to life, he hadn't had time to feel nervous around Kendrick. Until now.

"Don't be nervous," Kendrick said as if reading his mind. "As much as we love each other, all of this—this physically being together—will take some getting used to. And that's okay. There's no hurry to do, you know, anything."

"You're right," Silas said.

Then she took off her blouse.

"Wow," he said, staring at Kendrick in her bra. And just like that, his long-suppressed libido came roaring back.

She reached behind her and unclasped her bra.

Glancing down at her body and then back at him, she said, "You can take the rest off if you want. Only if you want to."

"I want to. I want to," he said eagerly, making her laugh softly.

He reached over and carefully pulled her bra off. Staring unabashedly at her breasts, he said, "Oh my sweet lord."

"Come on, soldier. You act like you haven't seen a naked woman in years," she teased.

Silas reached for her pants, and she helped him get them off. It wasn't long before he had her completely naked.

"This is all yours," Kendrick told him. "Only for your eyes."

"I'll never know how I got so lucky," he said, his raging erection straining the limits of his centuries-old breeches.

"My turn," she said seductively.

First, she removed his heavy, long blue jacket. The thing was gross and slick with sweat, and he hated that she had to touch it.

"That thing is way too hot for summer," he explained.

"Well, you'll never have to wear it again," she assured him.

When she reached for his shirt, Silas placed his hand over hers to stop her.

"Kendrick, you should know ... You should be prepared for ..."

"What?" she asked in a voice filled with sweet understanding and encouragement.

"I'm just ... I'm very thin right now. Not manly at all," he said, lowering his head and feeling ashamed. He couldn't help thinking of Sergeant Sean Stone, and how utterly ripped with muscles he was. Theresa was a lucky woman, being able to go to bed with that kind of man every night.

"Of course you're thin. You nearly starved before you died. Not to mention you were gravely ill. Please, my love. I want to see you."

Lovingly, she unbuttoned his shirt and took it off and then gently removed his breeches. It wasn't exactly sexy, the way undressing her had been. It felt more like she was a wife helping her sick husband out of his clothes.

Once he was completely naked, Kendrick took a step back and looked at him. Her eyes filled with tears, and she covered her mouth.

"You're just ..." she said, her voice nearly a whisper. "Perfect. Silas, you're perfect."

"How can you say that?" he said, looking down at his thin, nude body.

Pulling him close, she said, "You're beautiful and you're perfect and you're mine. I'm an emotional wreck because I'm struggling to allow myself to believe that you're actually *here*."

They stood, bodies and souls and hearts naked and bare,

holding each other for a moment. Kendrick let out a soft moan when he pressed his hardness between her legs, against her most intimate spot.

"You are *perfect* exactly the way you are, my sweet," she said. "As long as you're happy and healthy and well fed, I don't care if you never gain an ounce."

Silas closed his eyes, melting into the warmth of her all-consuming love.

"Now," she said in a husky voice. "Let's take a shower."

Kendrick turned the water on and let it run until it warmed up. She stepped in first, then held out her hand for him to join her.

Silas let out a moan as the warm water washed over him. "That feels so good."

His whole body relaxed as the water soothed his muscles.

"Easy for me to take things like a nice hot shower for granted," she said. "You make me appreciate every little thing. Every moment."

She reached for the shampoo and squeezed a little onto her hand. Then she began to gently massage his scalp as she washed his hair. The shampoo smelled fresh and so *clean*, and it was such a relief to feel all the dirt and grime wash away.

Silas closed his eyes and moaned, enjoying the feel of her fingers in his hair. Once she had worked up a good lather, she picked up the shower head and rinsed his hair until all the soap was gone. His scalp tingled pleasantly; he truly had forgotten what it felt like to be clean.

Kendrick gazed at him, a look of fiery lust in her eyes.

"My sweet," he said, pushing her gently against the shower wall. "I hope you know I've been wanting to kiss you all day, but I was waiting for the right moment."

He leaned in and pressed his lips to hers as the water cascaded all around them. She eagerly kissed him back. The kiss was hot and sweet and romantic, and it felt like they were kissing in the rain. He began kissing down her neck as she moaned softly.

"Kendrick, I can hardly wait to make love to you," he said, feeling his sex drive go into *overdrive*. "But I gotta warn you. Not only are you the most beautiful, sexy, and desirable woman in the universe, but I really *haven't* seen a naked woman in a long time. Seriously, I'll be lucky if I last ten seconds the first time we have sex."

"I understand," she said in a voice so sensual, he was in danger of having an orgasm just listening to her. "You haven't had the luxury of pleasuring yourself like I have while I'm thinking of you."

Silas groaned, still fighting for control.

"So, I think a little pregaming is in order," Kendrick said. Then she reached down between his legs and began to stroke his cock.

Moaning in ecstasy, Silas rolled his head back against the shower wall. Her delicate fingers, slick with soap, slid easily up and down his cock.

"Kendrick, Kendrick, oh my God," Silas cried out. The pleasurable sensation was so sharp, it almost hurt. Within seconds, he knew he was going to come. He pulled her naked body toward him, crushing her against his stomach just as the warmth of his seed spilled out. His climax was more powerful than he had expected, and with it came such a feeling of intense *relief*. Indeed, it was his first orgasm in several centuries.

"Does that feel better?" Kendrick teased, knowing the answer.

"Yes, God yes," he said.

Wrapping her arms around him, she murmured in his ear, "I used to get so turned on when I met with you. Especially when you told me all the things you wanted to do to me. I had lots of tension to relieve too."

Silas lifted his head and kissed her again. She reached for the soap and washed him all over, and then he did the same for her. There was no greater feeling in the world than being able to take care of the one he loved, especially after all this time of feeling so helpless.

They finished their shower and headed to the bedroom, where they toweled each other off. Kendrick sat naked on the bed, her nipples rock hard despite the warmth of the bedroom. After taking such a sensual shower, he knew she had sexual needs that needed to be attended to. And it would be his pleasure to take good care of her.

"It's all right if you're, you know, not ready to go again ... yet," Kendrick said.

Silas whipped off his towel to reveal a fresh new erection.

"Does this look like I'm not ready to go?"

The hunger Silas saw in her eyes made him feel like a man for the first time in a long time. She didn't look at him like he was a skinny, half-starved man. She stared at him like he was an exotic male dancer.

"My appetite for food isn't the only thing that's come back with a vengeance," he said.

"I can't tell you how happy I am to hear you say that," Kendrick said. Then she lay down on the bed and opened her legs slightly. Silas needed no further invitation. He quickly rifled through Jesse's bag for a condom and paused for a moment.

"I can help you," she said.

"Please," he said gratefully. He was pretty sure he could

have figured it out, but it would be more fun having Kendrick do it anyway. She tore open the foil package and then carefully stretched the condom over his erect penis. He groaned at the delightful feel of her touch.

He climbed on top of her and kissed her mouth and her neck.

"Yes, Silas," she panted. "Yes. I need you. I need you *now*."

Though he'd always pictured making love to Kendrick slowly and sensually for their first time, that clearly wasn't what she wanted. What she wanted, *needed,* was for him to take her hard and fast.

Silas plunged into her as hard as he could, making her cry out.

"Yes, oh God, Silas, yes!" she screamed as he pounded her as hard as he could. Her bright blue eyes opened wide. "Oh, this is just like my fantasy."

He grunted hard as he thrust in and out of her, her screams driving him wild. Silas was grateful that she had stroked him in the shower first because it helped him last much longer when he was inside her. Arching her back, Kendrick kept crying out his name. He had never seen her look so desperate, so out of control.

"Silas, please. I need you to ... touch me ..." Her eyes pleaded with him to satisfy her. At first, he wasn't sure what she needed. "Touch me ... there ..."

Now he understood. She couldn't reach orgasm through missionary sex. She needed more. Though he would have been more than happy to stroke her with his tongue, she seemed to love having his cock inside her. He slipped his fingers between her legs while he continued to glide in and out of her.

Kendrick threw her head back and cried out. He'd hit the right spot.

"Yes, yes," she panted. "Just like that. Don't stop. Oh God, Silas, I'm gonna come. I'm gonna ..." Her eyes rolled back in her head and her whole body shook as her orgasm took hold. As her climax consumed her, she let out the most erotic *ohhhhh*.

Watching her come was the most exciting thing Silas had ever seen. He grunted out loud as he came, surprised and delighted that his second orgasm of the night was as pleasurable as the first.

Catching his breath, he rolled off her, peeled off the condom and disposed of it in the trash and then quickly rolled back to her. He found her gazing at him adoringly, her pretty blue eyes delightfully relaxed with sexual relief.

"Was that really like your fantasy?"

"Better. Even better," she said. "What you do to me is way better than anything I could ever do to myself."

Chuckling, he pressed his lips to hers.

"You were so amazing, Silas. And don't take this the wrong way, but I never expected our first time to be this mind-blowing. First times can be awkward, and you just came back to life, but dear God, you're good in bed."

"Well, I'm not surprised we're so compatible between the sheets."

"Good point. We're a perfect fit in every other possible way," she said. "And speaking of possible ways ..."

"What?"

"I recall you saying you wanted to have your way with me by bending me over a table, taking me up against the wall, and on the floor."

"I did say that," he said thoughtfully.

"I want all of that and then some," she said. "But not all in one night. I don't want you to kill me."

"Right. After all, we've got time."

"Yes. We do."

Silas snuggled up against her. "This is the softest, most comfortable bed I've ever been in. And you are the best pillow I could imagine."

She laughed, tenderly stroking his hair. They lay together, dozing off for a while. It had been an exhilarating, emotional, and utterly exhausting day.

A while later, Silas jumped, startled awake by the sound of a loud *ding*!

"Sorry. Just my phone notification," Kendrick said. She picked up her cell phone and glanced at it briefly. Then she gasped.

"Everything okay?" he asked.

"More than okay," she said, turning the phone toward him to show him the picture of a tiny newborn baby. "Meet Conor O'Rorke. Eight pounds, one ounce."

"Born June 23rd," Silas said with a smile.

"Yeah. Oh, he's beautiful," Kendrick said, staring at the photo of the precious new baby.

"I'm gonna give you one of those someday," Silas said, reaching under the covers and rubbing her belly.

"I hope you do. Not yet, though. But still, I think it's a good idea to practice making a baby, don't you think?" she asked.

"Oh yes," he said, kissing her. "Lots of practice."

"I'm not quite ready for another romp, though. I'm starving."

"Oh, damn, I'm sorry. How could I forget? You haven't eaten all day," he said. "We gotta feed you."

"What about you? Are you hungry?"

"For future reference, my sweet, you never have to ask me that. It's always gonna be a yes."

"Good to know," she said. "How about we order a pizza?"

"To get sent here?" he asked, and she nodded. "Yeah, let's do that. That is so cool!"

Kendrick laughed. "I thought you'd like that. You are too funny. I hope you never lose that boyish enthusiasm of yours."

"Still got it after two hundred-plus years. Doubt it'll change now."

"I'm glad."

After the pizza came and Silas somehow devoured five slices after having already eaten a steak dinner, they made love again. This time, it was slower and sweeter, which suited him just fine. They enjoyed exploring each other's bodies and discovering new ways to please one another.

Silas fell asleep in blessed comfort that night, cuddled up in bed with his beloved, his belly and his heart full.

30

K endrick woke up in the middle of the night, frightened by a strange noise. She turned to find the source of the noise right next to her in bed.

Silas.

Yesterday's events came flooding back in a torrent of joyful memories. Crying, laughing, hugging, food, kissing, sex, more food, and more sex. And it was no dream. It was all real. Silas was alive and snoring right next to her. Kurt was in Heaven—or he was *home*, where he belonged. No doubt he was resting in eternity with their Grandpa Pete and their beloved Great Aunt Ted who had been like another grandmother to him.

Kendrick drifted back easily into a peaceful, comfortable sleep.

The next morning, she made pancakes for Silas. It was one of the few things she knew how to cook, and how she loved watching him eat. He was always happy and so grateful for food, for shelter, and for everything. And he made her feel grateful for every moment.

She was particularly grateful for the moments after

breakfast when he bent her over the breakfast table and had his way with her.

Gripping the table, she moaned and panted as he reached around, expertly rubbing her clit. Sex with Silas was so *exciting,* and he sure as hell knew how to please her.

"Ahh, ahh," she cried as he rubbed and pounded faster and harder.

Silas was no longer weak, that was for sure. She couldn't believe the man's *stamina.* Hundreds of years of pent-up sexual tension would do that, she supposed. And lucky her to be the recipient of all that sexual energy.

"Silas!" she cried after having yet another orgasm. Truly, she had lost count of how many he had given her. Perhaps it was a good thing they'd hadn't spent their first days together at O'Rorke's Bed and Breakfast. By now, Kendrick was pretty sure all her neighbors knew her lover's name.

He pulled out of her and she sank down, naked, on the kitchen floor and rolled onto her back.

"I can't move," she said.

Silas chuckled proudly. After dispensing with the condom, he lay next to her.

"You don't have to move," he said. "I'm fine right here on the floor with you."

Kendrick giggled. "I love you so damn much, Silas."

She stared at the ceiling for a moment.

"What are you thinking about?" he asked.

"I'm thinking about how scary it can be to love some-body as much as I love you."

"I get that," he said.

Of course he did. Silas always understood exactly what she was talking about.

"I feel that way about you, too. There are no guarantees.

Maybe we'll be married for fifty years and have a bunch of kids and grandkids," he said.

"And maybe we won't."

"Right. I'll never leave you, and you won't leave me. *That* much we know. The rest is up to fate."

"Yeah."

"So we shall talk and laugh and love for as long as we can," Silas said, making her smile. He'd said the same thing when he was still dead. And it was just as true now. "We'll enjoy every moment." He grinned at her. "And we're gonna have so much fun."

"Just lying on the floor with you is fun, Silas," she said with a smile. "You make everything fun."

"Death won't be the end, Kendrick. Whenever it happens. You know that."

"I do know that. I'll love you forever, Silas."

"And I love you, Kendrick. Forever and always."

SERIES ORDER

The Gettysburg Ghost Series

Somebody's Darling
Darling Soldiers
Forever, Darling

The Williamsburg Ghost Series

Eternal Love
Eternal Hope
Eternal Glory

www.ingramcontent.com/pod-product-compliance
Lightning Source LLC
Chambersburg PA
CBHW070602170726
48291CB00003B/660